SOME KIND OF GRACE

Robin Jenkins has been hailed as the 'greatest living fiction-writer in Scotland' (*The Scotsman*, 2000). Born in 1912, he studied at Glasgow University and has worked for the Forestry Commission and in the teaching profession. He has travelled widely and worked in Spain, Afghanistan and Borneo before finally settling in his beloved Argyll. His first novel, *So Gaily Sings the Lark*, was published in 1951 and its publication was followed by more than thirty works of fiction, including the acclaimed *The Cone gatherers* (1955), *Fergus Lamont* (1979) and *Childish Things* (2001). In 2002 he received the Saltire Society's prestigious Andrew Fletcher of Saltoun Award for his outstanding contribution to Scottish life.

ROBIN JENKINS

Some Kind
of Grace

Introduced by
James Meek

Polygon

This edition published in Great Britain in 2004
by Polygon, an imprint of
Birlinn Ltd
West Newington House
10 Newington Road
Edinburgh EH9 1QS

www.birlinn.co.uk

First published in 1960 by MacDonald & Co, London

ISBN 1 904598 19 6

British Library Cataloguing-in-Publication Data
A catalogue record is available on request from the British Library

Typeset by Hewer Text Ltd, Edinburgh
Printed and bound in Denmark by AIT Nørhaven A/S

Introduction

Among the foreigners drawn into Afghanistan in the late autumn of 2001 by the hijacked airliner attacks on America's eastern seaboard were many, like myself, who were seeing the country for the first time. As Robin Jenkins had more than four decades earlier, we saw beauty, desolation and ruin. His ruin had a different character to ours. Depending on the country we entered Afghanistan from, we saw how powerful empires had been unable to treat, with their rough medicine, this hard crust at the rim of their dominions. They had not been able to offer it their treatment, but nor had they been able to leave it alone, so they and their successors had scratched and poked at it instead, infecting it with warlords and weapons and broken industrial showpieces. If you came in from the south, the scab-pickers were Britain, the US and Pakistan. If you came from the north, it was Russia and Iran.

In 2001, we were walking among the ruins of the end of the Cold War; Osama Bin Laden as Islamist irregular general was a creation of the CIA, made to break the Soviets. The Afghanistan which Jenkins recreates lies in the Cold War's early years, when the US and the USSR competed not only through arms shipments, ideology and nuclear posturing but through gifts of roads, schools and clinics. The strategists in Moscow and Washington may have been cynical, but the engineers, teachers and doctors from the superpowers weren't, not always. The Russians and the Americans shared a belief in progress and human mastery over nature. Without realising it, both wanted to see a world of pretty nuclear families – their women unveiled – driving cars and having barbecues at the weekend. One of the things which strikes the later visitor to Afghanistan about

Jenkins' novel is that he shows how in this time of hope, the late 1950s, there were ruins already there. His is very far from a hopeless vision. But whatever our illusions about an idyll before the long, cruel Afghan war – which we tend to date from 1979, the year of the Soviet invasion – Jenkins removes them. He shows poverty, dirt, disease and despair generations old. He shows feudalism and backwardness, suspicion and bigotry, if tempered by generosity and piety. He portrays a local elite exposed to just enough of European and American ways to be attracted to them, without the ability to use them to change their country, and thus made more cynical themselves. In this book Afghan men are often said to look like Christ, but these Christs are not bringers of any good word; rather, harrowed peasants who wouldn't be surprised to be crucified, because crucifixion is the kind of thing that has been happening to men like them for thousands of years. When Jenkins describes the great stone Buddhas of Bamian, whose destruction by the Taliban was so mourned around the world, it is to mock the pomposity of the vanished conquerors who put them there before Britain, Russia or America existed. Looking at the Buddhas, the hero of Jenkins' novel, John McLeod, is reminded 'of the attempts by Renaissance artists to portray the infant Christ. Instead of divine innocence a crafty senility seemed to be achieved.'

How much is familiar in Jenkins' Afghanistan, and how much finds an echo now, down to the hero's decision at one point to pretend to be French in order to avoid death at the hands of British-hating locals whose religion and tribal pride have merged into one. The dust so fine that it is liquid, the ubiquity of weapons and the feudal levy of warriors by village, the isolation of women from outsiders, the ease with which well-paid, well-supplied foreigners make themselves comfortable at their compound dinner parties (although today they would be unlikely to wear black tie). Some things have changed. The everyday weaponry is more deadly. The poplars Jenkins writes of have largely disappeared into cooking fires; northern Afghanistan is bleakly deforested. Only the mulberry groves remain. And the outside world, for better and for worse, intrudes ever more deeply, usually to market rather than to teach. This is as true of global Islam – the Saudi brand, Wahhabism – as it is of satellite TV or Pepsi.

It takes a bad book to remind us how hard it is to write a good one. Because this is not a bad book, let me make the reminder of how narrow a space there is between avoiding sentimentality, on one side, and making your characters expressions of pure cynicism, on the other. Jenkins finds this space. He finds another rare spot, that place of honesty where multiple contradictory truths reside, where men and women can be both wicked and brave, vengeful and remorseful, bigoted and generous; where, when they go looking for absolute truths, they fail to find them.

> 'Tell me,' murmured McLeod, 'is it true, according to the Koran, that any faithful follower of Islam can make sure of his place in paradise by exterminating an infidel?'
>
> The Commandant chuckled, rather sourly. 'Yes, I believe you could find that somewhere in the Koran,' he said. 'It is like your own Bible. Everything is in it that suits you. If you wish to kill your enemy, search through the pages, and you will find sanction. If you wish to forgive him and love him like a brother you will find sanction for that, too. A man takes his choice of what God advises.'

McLeod and the man and the woman he is seeking in Afghanistan are from Scotland. In the hands of another writer this might be a barely relevant detail. They're all Brits, Europeans, westerners, abroad. Jenkins makes it otherwise. The hero's origins are expressed in the comparisons he makes and the language he uses. An Afghan headman is described through the eyes of McLeod – a senior British diplomat – as 'glaikit'. The hero is reminded at one point of Edinburgh Castle; he contrasts Afghan mountains with those of his native Wester Ross. Elsewhere the transference is more loaded, and points to a purpose. In the remotest, most serene Afghan valley McLeod visits, he hears someone call to him in Gaelic. McLeod recalls visiting the religious parents of the missing woman in Scotland who in the gentle voices of good churchgoers invoke eternal damnation for her partner in the bad fire. In his meetings with Afghans McLeod veers from contempt through an unpleasant disgust to admiration, almost an implied envy. They are the same emotions expressed by English and Lowland visitors to the remote glens and islands of Scotland hundreds of years ago, where English speakers were scarce. James Boswell, accompanying Samuel Johnson in Skye on a walk not much more than a generation after Culloden, talks of being accompanied by a local servant 'quite like a savage . . . the usual figure of a Skye-boy, is a lown with bare legs and feet, a dirty kilt, ragged coat and waistcoat, a bare head, and a stick in his hand, which, I suppose, is partly to help the lazy rogue to walk . . .' Later visitors saw the Gaels more romantically. Besides being an atheist among believers and a wealthy foreigner among the poor, McLeod, in the glens of Afghanistan, is a Highlander among highlanders, seeing the squalor and the dignity both as an outsider and, through history, from within. He understands the destructiveness of progress, destroying worldly innocence and worldly ignorance together, but he is aware, too, of the dark side of that apparent innocence. It is not just governments which can make trouble for these archaic, unmodernised clans, but individual adventurers from big cities overseas, concealing their selfishness under a banner of romantic ideals – Lawrence of Arabia, Osama bin Laden, in a smaller way, some of the characters in Jenkins' novel and, perhaps, in a sense, even Bonnie Prince Charlie – exploiting and provoking the unworldliness of the glens into actions whose terrible consequences they cannot foresee.

James Meek
June 2004

One

Tugging back the curtains, McLeod noticed that round the tawny hornet he'd killed the night before were swarming dozens of tiny black ants, devotedly dismembering it and carrying the fragments down a crack in the window ledge. For a minute he watched them, while from a wireless set in the bazaar across the street a love-song shrilled out, full of long, repetitive nasal passages, like a parody of bagpipes. It cheerfully told the story of a young man who after wooing a girl for years went off, just as she was about to admit his merits, and married another, for spite and peace of mind.

Into McLeod's contemplation another pair of unlucky lovers entered: Kemp and Margaret Duncan, as dead, so authority sadly but sharply insisted, as this hornet. Yet here to be seen, to be touched even, was the insect's corpse, though growing less minute by minute. Of Kemp's and Margaret's not so much as a red or yellow hair had been found. In their case who had been the scavengers? Wolves, the police had said; but did wolves, like domestic dogs, really carry bones off to bury them in the forest? And above all, in this land of public prayer, where the beggar in rags went down so punctiliously on his knees, would not a man so dynamic with the certainty of God, as Kemp latterly had been from all accounts, and so contemptuously destitute of the world's goods, be immune from the attacks of superstitious robbers?

Relaxing, turning from speculations that had troubled him for months, McLeod gazed out of the window. Already at eight in the morning the sky was blue, the sun hot, and the street busy. Last time he had seen this main street, five years ago, it had been made of earth like all the other roads in the country, but now, thanks to the astute benevolence of the Russians, it was tarmacadamed, though here and there the usual subsidences were marked off by large stones. One of the buses presented by the Russians to commemorate the recent visit of Krushchev came along, crammed to the doors; the postillion, in his brocaded skull-cap and cotton pantaloons, clung to the steps with toes and fingers, yet he would be, McLeod knew, grinning and marvellously good-tempered. Less carefree, with the burdens of their country's backwardness and neutrality to carry, came business men, government clerks, teachers and students, in lounge suits and woolly caps, cycling past with brief-cases fastened to the bars of their bicycles. Most of the private cars were tinny and Russian, with rancorous horns; but one, fitter for a Hollywood boulevard than for this mud-built, sun-lucky city on the roof of the world, glided by, long, gleaming, cream and crimson, with white-turbaned driver, and three women shrouded in silken shaddries as passengers.

Among the many pedestrians, walking by the open ditch, was a group of tough, black-bearded men newly down from the hills, carrying bundles wrapped in brightly striped rugs and looking at all these signs of modernity with reluctant amazement and limited admiration. Some had rifles slung round their shoulders, and all had killing knives at their belts. These would strike as instinctively as snakes. A gesture, not intended to be hostile, might well be interpreted by them or their like as such, with swift, snake-like suspiciousness. In their remote villages the gun and the knife and the bold hand were still law, as they had been for hundreds of years. If Kemp had angered the likes of these, as he could have in any one of a dozen characteristic ways, they would not have troubled to wait for darkness before despatching him, and with him the girl so unaccountably his companion.

In the middle of the street the traffic policeman stood on his circular dais of stone and made gestures that were more like vague threats than directions. Motorists regarded him as the chief of the many hazards. The drivers of ghoddies or horse-carriages were careful not to use their whips as they passed him;

these were forbidden in a country where it was not unusual for a prisoner to hobble shackled along the street, guarded by soldiers with bayonets, without anybody being shocked and with few being curious. Here, what would have caused gasps of horror in the West, was merrily laughed at. Dogs were handed lumps of poisoned liver and their agonies were found amusing. Yet fathers were publicly devoted to their children, and carried them about in their arms, with many caresses. Donald Kemp and Margaret Duncan might well have been murdered by such a father, who needed only to wash his hands before fondling his children again.

Raising his eyes, McLeod gazed over the many flat roofs at the far-off peaks, forever topped with snow. Among them, if his notion was right, Donald and Margaret might well be still surviving, in body at least; but from what he had already heard it could be that if he did succeed in finding them he and they would for the rest of their lives wish he had not.

Picking up his towel, McLeod went along to try his luck at the bathroom again. The corridor was wide and pillared; in a spacious alcove were basket chairs and settees. Magnificence had been diffidently attempted, shabbiness inevitably achieved; the effect was as everywhere in this country, a mixture of pathos and sinisterness. The pillars were sloughing; the coverings of the chairs were faded and stained; and dust lay everywhere as thick as pollen, obscuring the beauty of the native carpets.

McLeod knocked on the bathroom door, though all he needed to do to open it was to give it a push. There were a key and a lock, but the one didn't fit the other. The lavatory, which was meant to flush but didn't, stood in a corner and the door was out of reach of the longest, most anxious arm.

'Come in, if you got pants on,' drawled an American voice. 'Not that I could stop you, if I wanted to.'

McLeod hesitated, and then entered. Seated on the lavatory was a tall, thin man with grey hair, ascetic face, and gold-rimmed spectacles. Despite his posture he looked like a professor of semantics; such were numerous and prominent among America's contribution toward this country's progress. The trousers at his feet were of cream linen, dapper and freshly pressed. He stretched out his hand to indicate how, despite its gold amulet ring, it could not possibly reach to the door.

'Goddamn key's gone,' he said. 'Not, I grant you, that it was any use when it was here. Say, if it's ever found, d'you think it'd be a good idea using it to turn the lock on this shit-house of a country, giving me personally plenty time to get the hell out of it?'

McLeod did not smile. He knew that in return for his few esoteric duties the other would be getting a salary thirty times that of a Cabinet Minister; his long-tailed, two-toned Chevrolet would be waiting outside; his bank account in the States would be growing fat.

'Don't you like it here?' asked McLeod.

'Are you kidding? Nobody could like it here that's seen better. D'you know the height of the walls round the king's palace? Thirty feet. Now if you live in a place you love you just don't shut yourself up behind thirty-foot walls. No, sir. By the way, friend, if you want to shave, go right ahead. That tap's a liar, of course; there's no hot water. I got a bacha to fetch me some, in that blue mug there right under your eyes. Take a peek at it. I think I'm gonna keep it as a souvenir. There's a museum in my home town would sure give it pride of place. Genghis Khan passed this way; well, that was his true original shaving mug, water and all.'

The mug was handleless with chips round its rim. Inside was the grime, hardly of centuries, but certainly of weeks; about an inch of scummy water lay in it. McLeod could easily picture the sad, hopeless smile of the boy who had brought it; he would know it was dirty, he would wish it could be cleaner, but he would also feel that to make it clean to the point of acceptance by an American was beyond him.

The American was pulling the chain patiently but without hope.

'You English?' he asked.

'No.'

'Gee, if you'll pardon me saying it, friend, you sure look English, and you talk like it.'

'Scottish,' said McLeod.

The American laughed the distinction to foolishness. 'Same thing,' he said. 'Say, I feel like a bell-man doing this; no pealing cascades of water, though. Scotch, eh? Now there's the difference, see. Just before you came knocking at the door, there was a big Russian. When I hollered "Come in", he took one peek, saw me on the can, and vamoosed, shocked to hell. You never turned a hair. I guess we must be natural allies, after all.'

He turned at the door. 'Just arrived?' he asked.

'A couple of days ago.'

'Heartiest commiserations. Work at the Embassy?'

'No.'

'With the U.N.?'

McLeod shook his head.

'O.K. I pass. Mom says: "Wilbur, ask twice. If the man still says no, then he doesn't want to tell you. That's the time for you to shut your big mouth and go." Be seeing you, friend.'

He went. McLeod tried to shave; the cold water and the cracked mirror made it awkward. Outside the love song went on wailing. Twice he was interrupted, first by a German who clicked his heels in apology, and then by a Japanese, who bowed.

He was almost finished shaving when there came a solemn, rather peeved knocking at the door.

'Come in,' he called.

After a pause of about twenty seconds the door opened so slowly a child of two might have been pushing it. But it was a huge man who came in, recognisable as the Russian by his short neck and pout of embitterment. It was obvious he considered another barefaced imperialistic usurpation had taken place.

McLeod couldn't help smiling. 'Sorry if I've barged in before my turn,' he said.

The Russian was dressed in rather narrow blue-serge trousers, a blue shirt with white stripes, and broad braces all blue dots. In one hand he held his shaving equipment, and in the other a blue mug identical to the one the American had carried off as a souvenir. The water in the Russian's mug seemed hot,

for steam was rising from it. Was this a sign, wondered
McLeod, that the people here were better disposed to the
Russians than to the Americans?

'I'll not be a couple of minutes,' he said, in Persian.

The Russian had been gathering his English together. Now,
startled and unwillingly impressed, he considered using Persian too; but his complaint, he decided, would be more
effective in English.

'I was here the first time,' he said, with heavy dignity. 'There
was an American.' He tried not to look at the lavatory in the
corner, but his eyes betrayed him. McLeod noticed he had big
hands, like an engineer's.

'Please know,' he added, 'I have an appointment with the
Minister at nine and a half o'clock.'

It was now a quarter to nine, but surely he knew that
unpunctuality in that country was politer than being callously
on time.

McLeod withdrew from the wash-hand basin and dried
himself at the window. 'There you are,' he said. 'It's all yours.'

At once the Russian began to lather his face as if it wasn't his,
as if indeed it wasn't a face at all, but rather was a part of the
task he had been sent here to perform.

Before McLeod left he too tried to flush the toilet, but failed.

'Too bad,' he said. 'They have the equipment. Why the
damn doesn't it work?'

The Russian refused to smile, and as McLeod went out he
couldn't help thinking that true enough he and the Americans
were more natural allies, even if what united them wasn't
always as noble as they publicly proclaimed.

Two

When he went outside McLeod was relieved to find his Land-Rover where he had parked it, but a minute later he was alarmed to see that the policeman lounging near by was there for a special purpose. McLeod's entry visa had been grudgingly given, and might at any time be annulled. He wondered if he should hurry back into the hotel and telephone the Embassy.

However, when the policeman approached he slipped an envelope from his tunic pocket and handed it over, at the same time giving with his other hand a salute that was also an appeal for baksheesh. McLeod thought it prudent to be generous. The policeman was so pleased he took out the rag that was his handkerchief and began to wipe some of the dust off the Land-Rover.

McLeod sat in the car and read the letter. It was from someone he had known when he had been Oriental Secretary at the Embassy five years ago. Then Mohammed Hussein had been a brigadier in the Army, with the heaviest medals and the fanciest epaulets; now he was Commandant of the Secret Police. Small, grey-haired, fat, plaintive, garrulous, and pessimistic, he did not seem to McLeod suited to his new post; but one thing he would certainly do promptly and well, and that was obey any order whose execution meant his continuing in his high position.

'My good friend, John McLoud,' he had written, 'truely it greeves my hart to write this to you because of good times in the long ago, but it is for your good. If you have come to visit old friends we shall be pleased if you stay as long as you wish. But if you have come to look for Mr. Kemp, you must not, you see, you must instead go home. For Mr. Kemp and his lady are dead. This is very true. I have with my own ears heard the bad men who killed them. Be sure these and the other guilty ones have paid the price. Good friend, do not make trouble for everyone. Please give your promise to His Excellency, and we shall all be happy together again, as in the past.'

McLeod pondered that warning or threat. If Donald really had been murdered by bandits, why should officialdom object so earnestly to his going to investigate for himself? Was it afraid the same thing might happen to him? After all, the British Press had made a loud fuss over the disappearances, and the government had let it be known it urbanely disapproved. The authorities here were no doubt sincere in wanting no repetitions. It could be, too, they were afraid of displeasing the Russians who had been given certain prospecting rights in the north. It was far from impossible that Donald and Margaret had been mistaken for spies and shot; to admit that was more than any government could be expected to do. And all the time there was that other probable theory that Donald and Margaret had crossed the border into Russia itself. McLeod had already met several people who believed that; they thought either Donald had been killed outright or was now in training to be some kind of commissar. The government here, cherishing the neutrality that laid so many golden eggs, would not want it known abroad that its country was a way by which to steal behind the Iron Curtain.

McLeod started the car, returned the policeman's wave, and set off for the Christian church. In the earth street where it was situated he passed a string of donkeys laden with great lumps of snow from the cache in the bowels of the hill that like a camel's hump dominated that side of the city. Outside the church itself sat half-a-dozen camels, chewing, and casting, in Kemp's phrase, 'lofty blinks at so puerile an idea of God'.

The church was an ordinary house, with an extra-large lounge, where worshippers gathered. Its existence was a concession. No religion but Islam was legally permissible, but with so many Americans in the capital nowadays, and with so much American money pouring in, it had been decided, again in

Kemp's words, 'to let in a ration of their God, too. And what a God, Johnny. Picture an old gaffer with pink cheeks and snowy beard, so far beyond suspicion he could creep about a public park handing out sweets to little girls, without being jailed or assaulted. The pastor stands by, beaming, with hands clasped.'

The pastor's name was Goodwood Pinkerton Purdie, but he was known throughout the city as Goodwood P. McLeod had been so much prejudiced against him by Donald's report that he could not help feeling a little embarrassed as, with cries of welcome as spontaneous as bird-chirps, Purdie welcomed him into the house.

Though hardly any older than McLeod himself, Purdie seemed somehow to handle people as if he expected their souls to be as tender as an elbow with a boil on it. His eyes were as delicate as a doctor's hands, but they were as busy, too, and as imperious; so much so that within two minutes McLeod began to feel the itch that Kemp in his letter had mentioned, with such savage humour. 'Even in the way he keeps hitching up his white pants with the thin black stripes is meant to be an evangelistic tactic. He offers you a cup of coffee as if it was the blood of Christ. When he snatches off his spectacles, as he does every half minute or so, it's intended to be symbolic: he's hinting at the many layers that need to be stripped off your vision before you see, God help you, as he sees. Out of loyalty his wife tries to be infected by his energetic cheerfulness, but she's too honest-minded to be, though, mind you, she's so far had five children by him, representing God knows how many performances of the two-backed beast, for you and I, Johnny, know how these chums of Jesus fairly relish their houghmagandy.'

Mrs. Purdie came in. She was small, prematurely grey, with restless hands, and eyes in which smiles kept dying. Her husband greeted her rapturously, as if she'd just returned, not from the kitchen a few yards away, but from across an ocean.

'Oh, Thelma dear,' he cried, 'come and meet Mr. McLeod, who's just arrived from England. He is a diplomat at the British Embassy in Rio.'

'Was,' said McLeod. 'I'm between posts.'

'I really hope,' said Purdie, after a smiling, sly pause, 'I sincerely do hope, Mr. McLeod, you haven't sacrificed your leave just to come here and look for your friend, poor Donald Kemp?'

'Yes.'

'I can understand that, Goodwood,' murmured his wife, sadly.

'Do you mind if I smoke?' asked McLeod.

She didn't, but he did, with a great beam of apology.

'You see, Mr. McLeod,' he said, 'this isn't just our house where we live, it's our church, too. Somehow we get to feeling every corner has its own sanctity. I'm sure you'll understand.'

McLeod did, but he wondered if an exception was made for the tashnub, or lavatory.

'I'd be obliged, Mr. Purdie,' he said, 'if you could tell me anything that might clear my mind about Donald.'

'I'll sure do my best, Mr. McLeod, and Thelma will be pleased to help out, won't you, dear? But————' And he began to shake his head in twinkling-eyed sorrow.

Before he could say any more, into the living-room rushed, noisy as heathens, five small children, the oldest about seven, the youngest a grim fat-kneed toddler of two. They all took after their father in looks, so much so they seemed to McLeod to give the show away, for on their small faces, so like his, ordinary emotions raged, particularly vindictiveness and thwarted pride. They had been squabbling out in the garden over a cloth spaniel with one ear missing and a button for one eye, and now the tug-of-war continued fiercely on the sacred hearth, despite their father's cajolements, in which he mentioned Jesus, and their mother's timid, conscience-stricken threats. The second youngest, a dour little fellow called Aaron, was the most truculent; weeping, he aimed a kick at one of his sisters. Though he missed, largely because his father at the right moment lovingly pushed him so that he fell on the carpet, she howled louder than if he'd broken her leg.

'Please, Thelma,' whispered Purdie, and he called on the servant.

To get them out methods had to be used that their father winced at but pretended not to see.

'Come back as soon as you're through, Thelma dear,' he called after her, and immediately added, without blush or wink, 'To watch them grow up into grace is the most wonderful experience in the world. Children. Ah, no wonder the good Lord gave them leave to go to Him at all times; no need for them to arrange appointments.'

For a moment he listened, with benign stupefaction, to the howls from the garden. McLeod tried not to grin.

'Are you married, Mr. McLeod?'

'No.'

'Ah, but you soon will be, I trust. Mr. Kemp,' he added, with sudden sharpness, 'was not married either.'

'Not as far as I know.'

'I offered to marry them.'

Purdie paused then, and though he tried hard to mix behind his spectacles sadness and goodwill, what emerged was frank revulsion.

'I cannot say simply that he refused,' he said. 'Rather must I say he spurned my offer, like a wild beast caged against its will. Yes, Mr. McLeod, he carried his own cage about with him, poor unhappy young man.'

McLeod remembered what Kemp had written about the parson's pity. 'He pities, as a child soils its napkin, incontinently; but in some matters I fancy he could be gey costive.'

Evidently one of those matters was sex outside wedlock.

'He spent four days with you, Mr. Purdie, didn't he?'

'Well, Mr. McLeod, I hesitate to claim I gave him hospitality. He would not sleep in the house; he would scarcely consent to eat in it.'

'Where did he sleep then?'

'In the outhouse where we store our wood. Of course it's not heated, and it was cold then, with snow still lying in corners where the sun couldn't reach. I just didn't understand him, Mr. McLeod.'

Neither could McLeod, but he offered what seemed to him the extraordinary explanation. 'Wasn't it usual in the old days for holy men to cultivate hardships?' he asked. 'They still do, here, and in India.'

Purdie shuddered. 'I wouldn't call them holy men, Mr. McLeod. Jesus doesn't want us to torment our poor flesh and do mortifying stunts on His behalf. He really doesn't. That kind of thing horrifies Him really.'

'But Miss Duncan didn't stay here in your house, Mr. Purdie?'

'No. A good friend of the church gave her hospitality, which, poor girl, she accepted most gratefully.'

'Why do you say poor, Mr. Purdie?'

'Because, poor, unhappy, beautiful girl that she was, she wanted nothing more than to live a decent, normal Christian life among ordinary, decent folks. She came to me with tears in her eyes, and begged me to help her convince Donald they ought to get married. Well, in a way it was my business, Mr. McLeod. It was Christ's business, and here I try, humbly but sincerely, to be His deputy. But as I said, Donald snarled my offer away; indeed he did. Oh, he was sick, mentally and spiritually sick. Many of us prayed for him, Mr. McLeod.'

For the third time McLeod took out his cigarettes and furtively put them back. 'You were at the official enquiry, Mr. Purdie?'

'Yes. It was thought some Christian representative should be present.'

'Wasn't the British Consul there?'

'Yes, I travelled north with him in the same plane. A charming man, Mr. Gillie.'

'And the verdict then simply was that they had disappeared, and there was no evidence to indicate where?'

'Yes, indeed. The Governor was most upset. He must have interrogated a hundred persons, but it was no use, nobody could tell us anything definite. Privately I thought at the time – and many others shared my belief – that they had crossed the border into Russia. If you'll pardon my saying such a thing about your friend, Mr. McLeod, he did have an attitude towards ordinary people that would have recommended him to the Communists. You know those in the past condemned millions to die of hunger in order to make their social experiment succeed. I really do believe' – here his voice grew hushed – 'Donald Kemp would have approved of that hideous sacrifice.'

'I never knew him to be much interested in politics.'

'Well, I reckon he had changed a lot since you knew him, Mr. McLeod. Why would he not marry that poor girl? Remember she had already travelled over a thousand miles with him, sleeping beside him in caves, in wayside huts, or just under the stars. You see, Mr. McLeod,' and now the minister was whispering so quietly McLeod had to lean forward to hear, 'Our Lord Himself went chaste to the Cross. Yes, what I am saying is that Donald thought he was emulating Christ. What a blasphemy, really! I know I run the risk of sharing it if I dare to compare them, but Christ loved us all, whereas Donald Kemp was only too proud to tell us why he despised us.'

'But I understand the official view now is that they were murdered,' murmured McLeod.

'Yes, that is so. A whole village was involved. I believe they were all punished. The actual culprits themselves were removed to prison. They may still be there, but I am afraid they will by this time have been barbarously put to death. I asked to be allowed to see them, but my request was courteously refused.'

'So was Mr. Gillie's.'

'Yes. Of course the reason was obvious. I'm afraid there would be marks of violence on them. In this country, Mr. McLeod, they still have the awful custom of handing over the murderer to the murdered man's family, who stretch him out on the ground and cut his throat, in public, under police protection. Those two, however, who killed poor Donald and Margaret could hardly be handed over; so the authorities themselves exacted the penalty.'

'As is done in all civilised countries.'

Purdie noticed no irony. 'Yes, quite so,' he said. 'The motive was robbery – or so we are given to believe.'

'But you don't believe it, Mr. Purdie?'

'Not altogether. Oh, yes, I know the police have recovered a bracelet that belonged to poor Margaret, and a photograph of Donald's poor mother.'

'What do you think the motive was?'

Again the parson's voice became hushed. 'I simply think, Mr. McLeod, these simple villagers were outraged by their living together as man and wife when they were not married. In some parts, you know, adultery is still punished by death; by stoning.'

'But how would they know they weren't married?'

'He would tell them, Mr. McLeod; in some way he would let them know.'

McLeod saw that it was useless to argue. What he wanted was information; afterwards he could sort it out. After all, wasn't the most incredible thing about the whole business Donald's conversion? If that could happen, anything could.

'She was a very lovely girl, Mr. McLeod,' said Purdie, with a sigh, 'truly dedicated to the Lord. Did you ever meet her?'

'No.'

'Her hair, it must have distracted those men, Mr. McLeod. I have heard it described as – exciting!'

'So you think it roused their lust?'

As McLeod had expected, the minister didn't like the word; he seemed to hope that if he didn't say it he didn't have to acknowledge what it stood for, in other men and in himself.

'I've thought of that,' added McLeod drily. 'They didn't have much to steal.'

Purdie became quite agitated. 'Between them, you know, Mr. McLeod,' he said, 'between them, between Donald and Margaret, I mean, there was a very disturbing atmosphere. Everyone felt it, even my servants; they still talk about it in their quarters. By himself Donald was far from being a restful companion; on the contrary without uttering a word he could disturb one to one's bottom-most soul; but when she was present, in the same room, or even in the same garden, the air between them became charged with what – may Christ Jesus forgive me! – in my opinion was evil. Yet she, poor girl, was innocent. Please do not smile, Mr. McLeod. It is a word I seldom use, because the thing itself I seldom meet. Evil. But poor Donald Kemp's soul was so pitifully corrupted.'

'You mean, by his love for her?'

With his eyes closed, Purdie shook his head. 'Love?' he whispered. 'He did not love her. Whatever he felt for her could not have been love.' He opened his eyes. 'Because you see, Mr. McLeod, if that was love, then it is true that in the end we must all surely destroy one another.'

Mrs. Bryson lived under the great fort on the outskirts of the city. She wasn't the kind of woman McLeod had expected from the minister's description of her as a good friend of the church. Dressed in a pink bikini, she had been sunning herself on the terrace in front of her house.

'You're sure welcome, Mr. McLeod,' she said, in an American voice as rough as the minister's had been smooth. 'Goodwood P. told me on the phone you were coming. I guess it was a kind of warning. He wouldn't want me to shock you. You don't look so shocked, Mr. McLeod.' She pointed with her sunglasses towards the fort where McLeod could make out a group of soldiers. 'They got only the one pair of binoculars, so they got to take turns.' She paused to shout to numerous children 'raising hell' at the far end of the big compound, behind some trees. 'Just so long as nobody's killed,' she said. 'It's kinda awkward having to phone momma to tell her come and fetch junior who's got a tomahawk through his crew-cut. I guess like all the other Britishers here, Mr. McLeod, you think we're kinda barbarians?'

'Why should I, Mrs. Bryson?'

'Well, for one damn good reason, I'm talking like one. Sorry Sam's not here. He's my husband; he's in the south somewheres on some project. Just park yourself, Mr. McLeod, and we'll have a cup of coffee.' She yelled for a servant. 'Watch this,' she said. 'They pretend they hate like hell to see me like this.'

The servant was a handsome young fellow, in a silky uniform of white turban, red tunic, and wide pale blue bloomers. He appeared with his neck twisted so that he wasn't looking at her; it was like a deformity.

'Coffee, Nabi,' she said. 'For two.'

He hurried off, still wry-necked with modesty.

'The joke is,' she said, laughing, 'they spend half their time in there peeking out at me. And so, Mr. McLeod, you were a friend of Donald Kemp's?'

'Was?'

'Well, he's dead, ain't he?'

'So I've heard.'

'But you're not convinced, and you've come to see for yourself? If they'll let you.'

'You think they might not?'

'I don't think, I'm sure.'

They were silent while the servant set the table on the terrace.

'I've got a date with the Minister this afternoon,' said McLeod.

'He's the guy they call his li'l Excellency?'

'Well, he's certainly small. I knew him fairly well when I was here before. He wasn't a Minister then, of course.'

'It makes a difference,' she said. 'Anywhere it makes a difference; here, a very big difference. So you've been talking to Goodwood P.?'

'Yes.'

She grinned. 'Now don't get him wrong. There's not a nicer guy for a thousand miles round, or a more genuine Christian. Just ask at any of the villages around here. Who takes them medicines? Who's interested in all their boils and scabs? Yeah, only Goodwood P. But I grant you he sees things simple; he's just gotta see things simple. For him, faith's a thing you mustn't get tangled up; that's what Sam says; and his own is pretty well tangled. Love Jesus, and He'll love you: that's Goodwood P.'s faith, and he gets along fine with it. Now I'll tell you someone who wasn't simple, who'd got faith worse tangled than a kid with a ball of string. Your friend Kemp. He sure shocked old Goodwood straight to hell.'

'What was your opinion, Mrs. Bryson?'

'Of Kemp? I think he had the most magnificent face I've ever seen on a man; and that's saying something in this country, where half of them look like Christ, and the other half like Genghis Khan. Kemp's beat them all. He had red hair and a red beard, a nose like a hawk's, and eyes – God, what eyes! Blue as the lakes at Faizabad. You'll have seen 'em? So blue you see them afterwards in dreams, with great fish swimming twenty feet down. You could see things stranger than fish, and deeper than twenty feet, swimming in Kemp's eyes. Especially, especially when they were on her.'

'Margaret Duncan, you mean?'

'Sure. You know, the looks those two exchanged sure frightened poor Goodwood P. He thought they were both in a torment of guilt, because they'd slept together and weren't married. Now my thought was different. Sure they'd slept side by side, in caves, in ditches, behind walls, all the way from India to here; but, if my hunch is right, they hadn't slept together in the way Goodwood P. thought; no, not once. It was all on the one side, too, the abstinence I mean; sure, his. She wanted him bad. I don't wanna take the poetry out of it, as Sam says, but plain talking's sometimes best. Don't think, either, she was a poor li'l woman he liked to kick around. The man has never been born could kick Margaret Duncan around. For one thing, she wore her faith just about as brazenly as I'm wearing this bikini. I guess, too, she was as beautiful a girl as I've ever seen. My gals, Beatrice and Clover, were in ecstasies helping her to comb her hair. This is a sunny land, Mr. McLeod; her hair made it sunnier. They were a pair, they sure were.'

She paused to sugar her coffee and puff her cigarette. McLeod said nothing.

'Now why didn't he give her what she wanted, and what he

wanted, too, I guess? Don't tell me he couldn't, that he hadn't got what it takes? Here, in the public street, every day, you'll see a couple of them, holding each other's hand, and gazing into each other's eyes. This is a good a place as any to recognise that sort. Kemp was as like them as a wolf's like a rabbit. Say, you knew him years ago you said. Was he always chaste like that, bitter and fierce and chaste?'

'No.' Kemp in those days had been as gay a fornicator as most; particular perhaps, but gay and enterprising. Few undergraduates had known so many verses of 'The Ball of Kirriemuir', and few had been able to sing them so amusingly.

Mrs. Bryson read his thoughts accurately. 'I'm not surprised,' she said. 'So it was religion done it. Goodwood P. it makes as helpful as a milking cow; Kemp it turned into a wolf in the desert. O.K. it made him a kind of wolf, wanting to be alone and snarling over his beliefs as if they were bones. That's a picture I can accept. As Sam said, holy men in the old days must have been a bit like that. But none of them, I guess, had a lovely girl with hair like sunlight trailing after him. She complicated things for him pretty bad. Maybe she got him killed.'

'You think that was likely?'

'My God, you should have seen the looks they gave her here, in the city, where they think they're civilised, and where cops are commoner than camels. I wonder how they looked at her out on the hills, where the gun and the knife's the law.'

'That seems to be Mr. Purdie's opinion, too.'

'Mr. Purdie? Who – oh, you mean Goodwood P.? Yeah, I guess it is. It's really most people's; though some still think they crossed into Russia and are lying in prison there. What do you think yourself, Mr. McLeod?'

'I think they're still alive.'

'It's just a hunch? I mean, you've got no information the rest of us ain't got?'

'No. Just a hunch. We used to write to each other when he was in India and I was here. I once mentioned a valley I'd visited in the mountains in the north. He was extraordinarily interested in it.'

'Not Shangri-la, for God's sake?'

'Not quite. But I've never seen anywhere else people living such simple, happy lives.'

'Huh.'

'When he was staying here he wrote to me, and he said he was going to visit the valley.'

'That's sure interesting, Mr. McLeod. And you think they're there all the time, sharing the happy, simple lives?'

'They may be.'

'Huh. I hate to remind you of this, Mr. McLeod: a couple of guys from a village in the north have confessed to the murders.'

'Yes, I know.'

'You think these confessions were fakes?'

'They could have been. Nobody was allowed to see these murderers.'

'Sure. So you have this feeling in your bones that Kemp's not dead?'

'Yes.'

'What about her, Mr. McLeod? To tell you the truth, I'm more concerned about her. She was the one who had my sympathy. Do you have the same feeling about her? Do you think she's still alive?'

He did not, and the reason may have been that in Donald's two letters, the one written from here and the other from Mazarat, Margaret had never been mentioned.

'I see you don't,' said Mrs. Bryson. 'You think she's dead. Well, I'll tell you something funny. I have exactly the same feeling, that she's dead, but he's still alive. And why? Well, she looked mortal, beautiful but mortal, in spite of her hymn-singing; whereas he looked indestructible. I just can't picture thieves creeping up to him in the dark and cutting his throat. Even if he was sleeping, I guess he'd have irradiated enough force, call it spiritual if you like, to have paralysed them. But you'll ask me why he didn't use that force to protect her. You'll ask me that, Mr. McLeod, and I'll have my answer ready. I've given it to myself a thousand times, but so far to nobody else, not even to Sam. And this is it: if she's dead, it's quite on the cards that he killed her himself. In my sober opinion, he was mad enough for that.'

Three

The Ministry of the Interior, like the rest of the public buildings, from the outside from a distance, looked surprisingly substantial and imposing: the bright sun on the cream distemper, and the simple lines of the architecture, gave that impression. Seen from near at hand, however, it looked drab and seedy; inside, where the walls were chocolate-coloured, and the floors of grey tiles, and the air faintly polluted by smells from the primitive sanitary arrangements, the effect was of an antiquated station lavatory in Britain about which letters of horrified protest appeared frequently in the press.

The entrance was guarded by two young soldiers, of Mongol appearance with slant eyes and high cheekbones. Armed with bayoneted rifles, they were dressed in mauve uniforms that looked as if they'd been slept in during a retreat of a thousand dusty miles. One of them strolled with McLeod to where another lounged and yawned; he in turn conducted him to the door of the Minister's secretary's room, where two other soldiers picked their noses.

An orderly in a brown woolly cap ducked from under the blanket that covered the doorway, and ushered him in. The secretary, a thin man with a melancholy black moustache, rose from his desk and held out his hand.

'How do you do, Mr. McLeod,' he said.

'How do you do,' murmured McLeod.

'That is almost all the English I know,' said the secretary in Persian. 'Please sit down, Mr. McLeod. His Excellency will see you in a few minutes. He asked me to apologise on his behalf. I hope you do not mind waiting. As a matter of fact, His Excellency is with the Prime Minister.'

He hurried round the desk to offer McLeod a cigarette. On the desk were two portraits, one of the king and one of the Prime Minister.

'Have you seen many changes since you were here five years ago, Mr. McLeod?' he asked eagerly. 'Have we improved? Do you think we are now worthy of being called progressive? I know,' he added, with his voice falling to a whisper, 'we still have the veil, but no one approves of it; it will soon be a thing of the foolish past. We now have schools for girls. My own two daughters learn mathematics and physics. Women sing on the radio. We have cinemas that show American films. These are surely advances, Mr. McLeod?'

McLeod smiled and nodded.

'They say, Mr. McLeod, that when you were here at your Embassy you liked us. His Excellency speaks very well of you. You were with us for four years, I believe?'

'Yes.'

'I myself was in Germany then. I speak good German, but very bad English. You speak Persian very well.'

'I'm afraid it's a bit rusty.'

'No, no, it is really excellent. No foreigner I know speaks it better, not even,' he added slyly, 'any Russian. Many foreigners laugh at us. Yesterday I saw one, an American, take photographs in the park. There were poor men sleeping under the trees, and there were workmen who had stopped working for a little while to pray. Why was he photographing them, Mr. McLeod? I think it was so that he could show the photographs to his friends in America and they would all laugh at us. That is not polite; it is also not helpful. His country gives us a thousand tons of grain. We are grateful. Then he takes pictures of women in shaddries to laugh at us, and our gratitude is gone. Have you ever seen a Russian taking pictures of women in shaddries or of poor men praying?'

Then the telephone on his desk rang. He picked it up and listened with tittering subservience.

'Very good, Excellency,' he said. 'I shall bring Mr. McLeod in at once.'

He led the way over to an inner door. With his hand on the handle he turned and whispered: 'Please, Mr. McLeod, do not put us all to shame. Sometimes, if you wish to help us, you must believe us, even if you think we are speaking lies. We must speak them to preserve our pride as a nation. You, who represent Great Britain, will understand what I mean.'

Before McLeod could decide whether there was any irony in that remark about Britain, he had opened the door and announced: 'Excellency, Mr. McLeod of the British Embassy.'

The Minister was on his feet, with his chubby hand held out. He was a very small man with a large head and almost no neck. He wore a suit of light-grey flannel, with a cream rose in his button-hole. There were other roses on his desk. The air was fragrant with them.

'No need to introduce us,' he said in English. 'Mr. McLeod and I are old friends. Welcome back, Mr. McLeod.'

'Thank you, Excellency.'

'Sit down, sit down. Siddiq, before you go, break off a rose and give it to Mr. McLeod.' That was spoken in Persian to the secretary. To McLeod he explained in English: 'Hold it near your nose. For three days they have been trying to clean one little drain. So you see we are still far from efficient.'

McLeod accepted the rose from the secretary, who withdrew.

'Well, Mr. McLeod,' said the Minister, 'I have just come from the Prime Minister. Among the matters we discussed was your visit to us. He sends you his best regards.'

On the wall behind the Minister was a large portrait of the Prime Minister, bald and saturnine. On another wall was a smaller one of the king in general's uniform.

'You will please thank him for me, Excellency,' murmured McLeod.

'No, you will if you wish thank him yourself. He has expressed a wish to see you.'

'I should be honoured.'

'It will certainly be arranged. We know who our true friends are.'

The Minister pushed over a cigarette box of green marble. He took a cigarette himself.

'I think it is best for us to be frank, like friends,' he said, smiling. 'You have applied for permission to travel to a certain province in the north. Now, in normal circumstances, we should be delighted to grant you that permission; but I am sorry to say the circumstances are far from normal.'

McLeod said nothing but went on smoking and gently waving his rose.

'I am not referring to the sensitiveness of a certain neighbour in the north,' went on the Minister, 'though it is true that neighbour does not like foreigners from the West wandering about in that area. What I am really referring to is of course the tragic death of your friend Mr. Kemp. When Mr. Kemp applied months ago for leave to travel home to Europe through our country we did not, I must confess, investigate him very closely. It was enough for us that your Embassy vouched for him. It was, of course, made clear that he must keep to the usual route. As you know, he departed from it. As you know also, communications are bad or non-existent in many parts even today, and lawlessness prevails. We lack the resources necessary. To our horror and shame Mr. Kemp, and the woman who was with him, were killed, murdered. I have since heard much about him, how several years ago he gave up a brilliant career as a diplomat to work as a missionary among the poor of India. I confess I do not understand any man's motive in doing such a strange thing, but that does not alter the fact that his murder in our country was a disgrace to us.'

'Was it ever proved conclusively he was murdered?' asked McLeod.

The Minister's manner seemed sincere. 'Look, Mr. McLeod,' he said softly, and opening a drawer he took out a small photograph at which he looked with a queer, sad fondness as if he'd already looked at it so often the person depicted had become his friend.

That person was Donald Kemp's mother: white-haired, bright-eyed, erect, and smiling, just as McLeod had so often seen her in her Edinburgh home.

'You know the dear lady of course, Mr. McLeod?'

McLeod nodded.

'Prepare yourself for a shock. Turn it over.'

McLeod did so, and saw what might have been smears of dried blood.

'This was found upon one of the two thieves who confessed to the murders.'

In spite of himself McLeod's hand shook as he stared at those smears; these surely were more definite and convincing than a vague notion. When he turned it over and gazed again at Mrs. Kemp she seemed, too, like the Minister, to be shaking her head sadly.

As McLeod kept looking he remembered Mrs. Bryson, agitated fag on crimson lip, muttering: 'It's quite on the cards he killed her himself.' Better surely, if such a discovery was possible, to stop seeking now and accept these anonymous men as the murderers.

'This, too, Mr. McLeod.'

From the drawer the Minister now produced a gold bangle, oval rather than round, as if it had been violently squeezed. McLeod had never seen it before, but several people had told him Margaret Duncan had worn one like it. He took it and looked at it carefully. On the inside were the initals M. D.

'It was recovered from the other murderer,' murmured the Minister.

'Is it not strange,' said McLeod, 'that a murderer should keep this?' He held up the photograph. 'You'd think this would be the very thing he'd destroy.'

'Murder itself is strange and terrible,' said the Minister.

'What you have said would be the attitude of a sane man; but sane men do not murder innocent travellers.'

'These men,' said McLeod, after a long pause during which he felt the scent of the roses become almost unbearable, 'have they been executed?'

'You are convinced then that these objects are proof enough to justify condemnation and execution?'

'Were the bodies ever found?'

'We have wolves, bears, and vultures in our country.'

'So they weren't found?'

'Murderers are more cunning than wolves or bears at disposing of bones, Mr. McLeod.'

'They weren't found?'

'No. And now I shall answer your other question. These men have not yet been put to death.'

McLeod was startled.

'I suppose,' he said, 'it would not be possible for me to see them?'

'To question them, you mean?'

'Yes.'

The Minister was silent. One plump, beringed hand lay on the desk, the other held his cigarette.

'I can appreciate that our word is not enough, Mr. McLeod,' he said at length. 'You realise, of course, that what you are asking is most irregular?'

McLeod said nothing.

'Your Consul Mr. Gillie has made the same request, but his was firmly refused. We may be poor and still very backward, but we have our rights as a sovereign, independent nation. Mr. Gillie's request being official had to be officially rejected. But yours is not official; it is personal and private. Only there is one thing. If we allowed you to see them and speak to them, you would have to give your word of honour that you were dropping this so understandable but also so futile quest for your friend. Would you give it, Mr. McLeod?'

'If I was satisfied, Excellency.'

The hand on the table gave a little jump; much restrained arrogance was in the gesture.

'Of course, Mr. McLeod. But you are a reasonable man. You will not demand that the bodies be produced at your feet.'

'Have you seen these men yourself, Excellency?'

'Yes.'

But McLeod thought that the sudden stroking of the rose in the lapel indicated some kind of nervousness.

'Were you convinced?'

'Sufficiently to sign their death warrants. Please remember, we are all of us bitterly ashamed of this thing. We try to creep forward, with great difficulty; this pushes us back again into barbarity. Now for the arrangement of your visit. You are living at the hotel? Well, this evening about seven o'clock a car will call for you. It will take you to the prison. You will be allowed to ask whatever questions you please, but you will not, of course, be alone with the prisoners; this is for your own protection. Afterwards you will be taken back to the hotel, or to your Embassy if you so prefer. You may wish to make a report. Agreed, Mr. McLeod?'

McLeod rose, nodding. 'Thank you, Excellency,' he said.

The Minister rose, too. 'Do not thank me, Mr. McLeod. The decision was made by the Prime Minister himself. Good afternoon.'

'Good afternoon, Excellency.'

As McLeod went out he turned quickly to try and surprise some look on that big brown face behind the yellow roses that might tell more truthfully than the calm, plausible voice what the Minister really was thinking; but what he saw was a smile of correctly compounded friendliness, sympathy, and regret.

Outside, in the sunshine McLeod stood on the steps, smoking, reflecting, and casually glancing at the people on the street. It suddenly occurred to him that he might from now on be under police surveillance, and he gazed at the crowd with sharper interest. Here, though, everybody in sight could have been an agent in disguise: that ghoddy driver, pretending to be asleep while his bony horse drank from the ditch; the public letter-writer squatting at the corner, or his garrulous customer; the motionless coolie with the coil of rope and the jacket in tatters; the few women shuffling along under their faded shaddries; the chauffeur reading a newspaper in the red Buick on the other side of the street. But there was one not in disguise, rather in what might well have been the uniform issued to shadowers. This was a tall, thin man in a brown suit and a grey hat with an exceptionally wide brim; he was pretending to be intent upon the electric refrigerators and cookers in Siemens' shop across the street, not far from the Buick. It was likely he could see McLeod reflected in the window, but that didn't content him, for several times he peeped quickly round.

McLeod decided to find out. Crossing the street, he made to pass the shop window when he suddenly stopped and, with his hand outstretched, jovially approached the man in the brown suit, who was so embarrassed he seized the brim of his hat with both hands as if minded to pull it down over his face.

'Sadruddin, of the Ministry of Education,' cried McLeod, in Persian.

The other, in a kind of drill, pulled his tie straight, sheepishly tittered, knocked his knees together, and twitched both elbows.

'I am not Sadruddin,' he replied.

McLeod was incredulous. 'You must be his brother surely.'

'I have a brother who is said to be like me, but he does not work at the Ministry of Education. He is employed by the Ministry of Public Works; he edits a magazine.'

'But you are very like Sadruddin.'

'I am very like many men in this city.'

That was said rather sadly, but proudly, too; and it was true. The long, doleful nose, the brown, pock-marked cheeks, the mild eyes, and the frayed shirt collar, were all very common. The hat though was about as uncommon as a busby.

'I am sorry,' said McLeod, and walked away fast.

Footsteps pattered anxiously behind. He stopped so suddenly the other bumped into him.

'Did I drop something?' asked McLeod.

'No, no. Yes, yes, you have forgotten your car.' Even as he was saying it and pointing to the Land-Rover across the street he was almost in tears of dismay at his own foolishness.

'My car?' asked McLeod.

'Yes, I think it is yours, sir. It is an English car, you see, and you are English.'

It was then that McLeod noticed the chauffeur in the red Buick was no longer reading the newspaper, but was gripping the wheel in a frenzy of indecision as to what he should do. Pursuit of the Land-Rover had been planned; by walking McLeod was breaking the rules.

He continued to walk, while behind him the detective and the driver quarrelled passionately in gestures, before the former, with a last despairing tug at his hat, came scampering after.

About a hundred yards ahead was a cinema, its radio wailing an Indian love-song, though the posters advertised an American film, with an actress whose breasts were much more conspicuous than her face. In that country of strict purdah, where the only females a man could see were his relatives, such a film was as water in a desert. The street outside was thronged with turbaned men gulping at those posters, as they waited for admission to the oasis. The small vestibule, too, was packed.

It said a lot for their native courtesy towards foreigners that no one protested when the man in the ticket office sold McLeod a ticket. He was too polite to mention as he handed it over that no seat was at present available. Hurrying into the cinema, McLeod was struck by the contrast between the strong smell of grease from fat-tailed sheep and the scene on the screen, which showed, in a bedroom of sophisticated, perfumed luxury, the poster woman exercising her bosom in front of a mirror; she seemed to be trying to portray the anger of love scorned. As McLeod hurried down the aisle he had to ignore attendants who wanted to instal him in a seat even if its present occupant had no wish to vacate it.

There was another exit, at the side of the screen. Going out by it McLeod found himself in a corridor that boomed with the snarled indignation of the giantess on the screen, whose scornful lover had evidently joined her: 'Get out of here, and get out quick.' Good advice, McLeod thought, turning a corner and coming upon a patron relieving himself. The latter, though a little startled, pressed his hand against his breast in friendly greeting, which McLeod felt bound to return.

Coming to a door he immediately opened it and entered. Within sat two men, one smoking a blue hubble-bubble pipe, the other counting a heap of the most dilapidated money McLeod had ever seen. "Salaam,' he murmured to them, and made to go out by another door, but found it locked. Controlling his astonishment, the cashier jumped up, produced a key from somewhere in his baggy pink breeks, unlocked the door, and bowed McLeod out.

He knew where he was, in a side-street near the rear of the national bank. Into the courtyard of the bank he hurried, to find a squad of soldiers being drilled, with as many turkeys strutting about in what looked like deliberate derisive mimicry. Passing the open fire where the bank clerks' pilau was cooked, and their bicycles stacked in dozens, he went into the bank by a side-door, with a smile to the soldier there, strolled along the corridor, and left by the main entrance. There was no sign either of the man in the wide hat or of the red Buick.

It was as good a time as any to pay another visit. Leaving his Land-Rover outside the Ministry of the Interior, where he thought there would be enough soldiers to look after it, he hired a ghoddy, in it crossed the bridge below which the river trickled, lurched down a side street of cloth-sellers where every bazaar was brilliant with red, green, blue, and purple drapes, and reached the main thoroughfare, called after a supposed victory over the British in the old wars. A monument, at present hidden behind scaffolding, commemorated the victory. At its foot were two field guns, claimed to be captured from the British Army; they had their wheels chained together, because there was always a chance that some enterprising chief from the hills might creep down and steal them.

Behind that broad street, in which could be bought such wares of civilisation as lavatory bowls and radiograms, was a section of the city unchanged for hundreds of years. There the smells were varied and pungent. Squatted among their weird and miscellaneous goods, shopkeepers drank tea, slept, or shouted banter at rivals. There was kebab to be bought, on long skewers of iron; sweetmeats virulently green in colour, or dark purple and gluey; guns of ancient design, with eagles and lions chased on the butts; moccasins like parrots, with the upturned toes their crests; skull caps beaded in many colours, to be worn in conjunction with snowy white cloth wound round the head; and even chamber-pots, copied, it would appear, from Genghis Khan helmets.

McLeod remembered that narrow, hot, smelly, cheerful street with fondness. He walked slowly down it, delighting the merchants by understanding their chaff and returning it. Several called to him to come and join them at their tea. At the entrance of the serai he was making for he hesitated, not sure yet that he really wanted to go in; and as he stood there, with one merchant trying to sell him a British sabre and another a sheepskin tunic, he remembered the girl he had come to enquire about. He did not see her against that background, but rather against a background of a green field by a river, with glades of thin poplars and mountains beyond. He saw her racing in that field, with a white rose in her glossy black hair, and her teeth whiter still in her face whose shade of duskiness and whose capacity for vivid joy he could never have described though thousands of times, as now, he had remembered it poignantly.

He went through into the serai. An old man with a shy, wispy beard dozed at the foot of some stairs. McLeod recognised him, and when he awoke seconds later he recognised McLeod, with a child-like giggling glee. Yes, yes, he cried, Abdul Rasaq Khan was upstairs in his office. Still giggling, and turning at every step to touch McLeod, he led the way up.

Abdul Rasaq Khan, the karakul merchant, was seated cross-legged on a rich red rug, with a silver teapot beside a silver tray with small cakes on it, and a cup and saucer as fragile as his own thin fingers. He wore native dress, loose, white silken trousers, black tunic embroidered in gold, and pale blue blouse with long sleeves. He was a man of about seventy, curiously sweet in that place of strong sheep smells, with his feet bare, and his beard as snowy as the turban on his head.

He welcomed McLeod with suave cordiality and invited him to sit beside him on the rug.

'So you have come back, John McLeod,' he said.

'I said I would.'

'Many words are said; much snow melts on the hills.'

McLeod remembered the high hills behind the house in the north, where the snow never melted.

'You are looking very well,' he said.

'Thanks be to Allah. You also are well; a little fatter perhaps.'

'And all the others of your family, are they well, too? Your brother especially?'

'They are all well,' replied Rasaq, with a smile. 'Karima is married of course. She already has a son.'

For almost a minute McLeod sat, trying to smile; and the old man was silent, too.

'Whom did she marry?' asked McLeod at last.

'A man with a hundred thousand sheep,' said Rasaq. 'Like them he is fat. He cannot run in the field.' He paused. 'It was not possible, John McLeod; you knew yourself at the time it was not possible.'

'Because I didn't have a hundred thousand sheep?'

'That was one reason, of course. My brother would never have allowed his daughter to marry a man who could not pay a large sum for her; not because he is mercenary, but because he felt his honour as a chief was involved.'

'If you had been her father?'

The old man smiled. 'You alter all destiny,' he murmured. 'In any case, she will long ago have forgotten me.'

Rasaq shook his head. 'She will never do that,' he said.

'I thought,' said McLeod, 'that I might be passing that way, on my way home. I thought I might call in. Now it is out of the question.'

The old man nodded. 'I have heard you have another purpose in returning to our country,' he said.

'Yes.'

'To enquire after the Englishman who disappeared some months ago, with a woman. It appears they were both murdered by thieves.'

'You hear most things that are said, Abdul Rasaq. You have many contacts. Is it true they were murdered?'

The old man raised a frail hand in protest at that reputation of omniscience. 'I am a quiet old merchant, who minds my own business,' he said. 'What I know about this matter everyone in the bazaar knows. The village where the crime took place was punished, and the two men accused were brought here to the city. They have not been tried; but then men are frequently put to death here in private without trial. And why not, if they have confessed?'

'Perhaps their confessions were false.'

'It is strange to confess falsely to murder.'

'I meant perhaps the authorities are pretending they have men in prison who have confessed.'

'It is not impossible. To be convinced one would have to see these men for oneself and hear their confessions.'

'I am to see them this evening, but perhaps even then I won't be convinced.'

The old man gently rubbed his beard. 'You always had influential friends here,' he said. 'You speak our language so well, too. You could have become one of us. Many are lighter in skin than you are; in some northern valleys there are eyes blue as your own. Yes, you could have become one of us. Our faith is easy to accept and carry.'

'It's too late now,' said McLeod. 'Is she happy?'

'She has her son.'

'But is she happy?'

'Her husband, though he is fat, in body and wits, is fond of her, and dotes on the child.'

'But she's not happy?'

'No, John McLeod, she is not happy; and if she hears that you have come back she will be more unhappy still. So she must not hear. Please go away again quietly. Return if you like after many years, when both you and she are too old for regret, and I am dead. Will you promise that?'

'If these men convince me they did kill my friend.'

'I think they will convince you. The women in your country are beautiful, too. The one who was killed with your friend is still spoken about in the bazaars. It seems she was most memorably beautiful. So you will soon find one to bear your sons. I give you that advice,' he added, with a little chuckle, 'though I sought for more than fifty years and found none. Now tell me what you have been doing since we last met.'

Four

McLeod was brushing his hair in the hotel bedroom when the door suddenly burst open and one of the servants came in gasping. He was the little squint-eyed man who looked upon McLeod as his special responsibility. Now he tried to stammer some warning, but fear had driven a nail through his tongue. Next minute in marched, or rather imperiously waddled, General Mohammed Hussein, Commandant of the Secret Police, in an ostentatious green uniform with facings of scarlet and large epaulets of orange. His topboots were black and shiny. In his fat right hand he carried a cane with gold bands with which he began to strike the little servant across the face, at the same time yelling to him to get out.

Two brawny policemen, with thug-like faces, rushed in, seized the servant, and hauled him out.

'Here, wait a minute,' shouted McLeod in protest.

Hussein stopped him with a flabby, fond paw. 'It is all right, McLeod, my friend,' he said, laughing wheezily. 'The little dog thought we had come to arrest you.'

'I know he did,' McLeod pushed past and went out into the corridor. Only the two big policemen were there. In glee they explained they had merely kicked the servant's backside and sent him about his business.

Hussein took McLeod's hand and led him back into the room. One of the policemen shut the door behind them.

'You see, McLeod, my friend,' said the Commandant, 'I did not strike him because I am a cruel man. I am really a soft-hearted man, with five children. That is why I struck him. No one must know I am soft-hearted, or I should surely lose my job.'

He found that so amusing he had to collapse on the bed to manage his laughter. But all the time a gleam of cool cunning remained steady in his brown eyes.

'So, McLeod,' he said, 'you are still a very clever man. You must be, to have caused His Excellency to change his mind. I understand the Prime Minister himself was consulted. So they decided to disregard my advice. You got my note?'

McLeod nodded.

'I still think I was right, McLeod, my friend. I do not think it is good for you to see these men.'

'Why?'

The fat shoulders hunched, the thick lips pouted. 'They murdered your friend. They are crawling reptiles. They should have been wiped off the earth long ago. Seeing them must make you sick. But,' here he tapped McLeod's hand with the cane, 'I must do what you want. It would be foolish to offend a man with such important friends.' And again, with that slyness always in his eyes, he laughed till the bed creaked.

'I see you are dressed for a party,' he said, for McLeod wore a black dinner-jacket.

'Yes.'

'Is it at the Embassy?'

'Yes.'

'Perhaps His Excellency is giving a party in your own honour?'

'No, it's at Mr. Minn's house, and it's not for me.'

The Commandant's face bulged with melancholy. 'Ah, those parties at the British Embassy,' he said, with a great sigh. 'No one invites me any more. But I remember them. Sometimes in the beautiful houses, sometimes on the lawns. The ladies with their gracious smiles and beautiful dresses. The food, so strange but so good and so much of it; and the Scotch, the wonderful golden Scotch.'

McLeod remembered how the brigadier and his friends had loved to sip whisky out of disguising tea-cups.

'Well,' said the Commandant, 'shall we go?'

'I'm ready.'

'You are making a mistake, McLeod. It is still time to change your mind.'

'No.'

'Perhaps you want to spit in the faces of the men who killed your friend? That is only natural. Be sure myself and my friend the Governor of the prison will turn our backs whatever you wish to do. I think if you were to kill them, in revenge, nothing at all would be said.'

They were walking along the corridor. The Commandant kept smacking his thigh with his cane. Behind tramped the two tough policemen.

At the foot of the stairs the little servant, with tears in his cross eyes, raced forward and took McLeod's hand.

'He still thinks,' roared the Commandant, 'we are taking you away to beat you up.' And he gave the servant a swipe on the bottom with the cane.

The Italian manager of the hotel was in the vestibule, very nervous but brave. In French he asked McLeod if he should telephone the British Embassy on his behalf. McLeod said it wasn't necessary.

'What did he say?' asked the Commandant, when they were outside

McLeod explained.

'Foreigners don't trust us, McLeod. Why? Don't they know that our souls are ripe like fruit to be plucked by the first person who trusts us?'

It seemed to McLeod pointless to remind him of his country's history of treachery, not just because that was the past but also because it could be said of any country.

'However, McLeod,' said the Commandant more cheerfully, 'we have as you see a luxurious American car. Why not? Are we not entitled to a little comfort? The road is bad. Life itself is a road full of holes.'

As McLeod entered the car, with the Commandant's hand on his back, it occurred to him that in these modern times many men had thus been luxuriously conducted to their necessary if regrettable liquidation. To encourage the thought, a beefy guard sat in front beside the driver, and a jeep of Russian design got ready to follow with the two brutal-looking policemen.

'Tell me,' murmured McLeod, 'is it true, according to the Koran, that any faithful follower of Islam can make sure of his place in paradise by exterminating an infidel?'

The Commandant chuckled, rather sourly. 'Yes, I believe you could find that somewhere in the Koran,' he said. 'It is like your own Bible. Everything is in it that suits you. If you wish to kill your enemy, search through the pages, and you will find sanction. If you wish to forgive him and love him like a brother you will find sanction for that, too. A man takes his choice of what God advises.

'Were you, McLeod, my friend,' he added softly, 'reading in your Bible before I came for you tonight?'

'No.'

The Commandant sighed. 'I have not read the Holy Koran for years,' he said. 'But I have to listen every night to my children practising their recitations.'

He gave a great sigh, and was silent.

Soon the tarmac and electric lights of the city were left behind. In the headlamps the dusty road shone like snow.

McLeod wondered if true enough he was making a mistake in going to see these men. Obviously they had been brutally handled, first to get the confessions out of them, and then because they had confessed. He would not be able to avoid the feeling that any cruelty which had been inflicted on them had been in some way inflicted by him.

'I saw a girl once at a party at your house, McLeod,' murmured the Commandant. 'She was Swedish, and very beautiful, with hair like wood ash in colour, and like silk to touch. I could not sleep for many nights afterwards, thinking of her. Sometimes I still lie sleepless and remember her, though my own wife is lying beside me, and my five children are in the next room. Is that foolish? Foolish or not, it is true; and often there are tears in my eyes as I remember.'

And those tears of regret, McLeod realised, would be as

genuine as the snarl of disgust with which the Commandant would look on the condemned men. No wonder the Koran and the Bible, advising human beings, had to give such contradictory advice.

The Commandant gazed out to where the stars shone as bright as anywhere on earth.

'Perhaps she is married, too, now,' he said, sighing, 'and has children.'

Remembering Karima, McLeod wondered if he would see her in the cell beside the two men, her countrymen, with their faces the same colour as hers, and their eyes as brown?

'But here is the strange thing, McLeod, my friend,' said the Commandant. 'She does not know of my existence. I might live in one of those stars for all she knows. At the party she passed very close to me once, and I smiled, but someone else spoke to her just then, and so when she smiled perhaps it wasn't at me at all, but at this other person.'

Suddenly he shouted to the driver to stop.

They had passed a shrine tended by a holy man. The car backed until it was alongside the heap of stones with the stick decorated with rags. The guardian had come creeping hopefully out of the hole where he lived. He was all dust, hair, bones, and rags.

The Commandant gave the driver some money to thrust into the skinny claw. Blessings were muttered.

'Do you know, McLeod,' said the Commandant, as they drove on again, 'some people say – Moslem people – that these holy men ought to ask some blessings for themselves. Look how poor and dirty he was. If you have the lamp of Aladdin in your hand, why not give it a rub for yourself. But you and I know how difficult it is to foresee what will please God. Your friend was killed by people less valuable than rats, and I lie at night, unable to sleep for love of a woman I never even spoke to.'

Then they were at the fort in which the prison was situated. Towering above in the moonlight, it reminded McLeod of Edinburgh Castle. The road spiralled up to it, and the Com-

mandant grunted to the driver several times to be careful.
There was a drop, he muttered, of at least a hundred metres,
and the road often broke away at the edge. A lorry had gone
over about a month ago; ten men had been killed, and thirty
injured; luckily most of them had been criminals.

At the gate they were scrutinised by an officer who, recog-
nising the Commandant, saluted three times and then went
screaming to his men to open the gate.

'This is a place very bad for the nerves,' muttered the
Commandant. 'It stinks, too. Look, I have brought a handkerchief soaked in my wife's perfume. I should have warned
you to bring something; one of His Excellency's roses, perhaps.'

He was still jealous and suspicious of McLeod's standing
with the Minister.

They got out at a long white building that glimmered
sinisterly in the starlight; it looked as if it might contain
torture-house and gallows. Appropriate therefore was the
stench of human excrement that the brilliance of the stars
intensified. The Commandant kept dabbing peevishly at his
nose with his handkerchief.

The Governor of the prison, dressed in military uniform,
was expecting them in his office. On its walls were at least two
dozen portraits of the king and Prime Minister, while on the
desk was a picture of a young man with a flat nose so like the
Governor's he must have been his son. The Governor also had
pointed ears, and an amiableness and anxiety to oblige so
continuous and excessive that they soon began to fret
McLeod's nerves more than the smell and the dreariness. With
quick glances at the huffy Commandant, the Governor kept
uttering his silly pleasantries in a shrill voice that would all at
once become shriller, like a bird's whose song is apprehensive.

'It is for you to say, gentlemen,' he cried. 'I am at your
service. Do you wish to see them here or in their cell? You will
find it more comfortable here.'

'I'd rather have them here,' said the Commandant, 'but it's
for Mr. McLeod to say. This is his party. As you can see, he's

dressed for it. I hope, wherever we see them, they're in a fit state to be seen?'

'Certainly. Though I would like to say I was given very short notice.'

'We don't expect to find them in the best of health. As long as they can speak.'

'Yes, they can speak. I mean, they still have their tongues. But you know how it is with men in their position: they seem to withdraw from the world.'

'There are means,' sneered the Commandant, 'of bringing them back to the world.'

'I assure you,' said the Governor, laughing, 'what is necessary to know is known.'

'Well, McLeod?' asked the Commandant. 'Where is it to be? Here, in comfort? Or in their cell?'

McLeod for the past two or three minutes had been on the point of deciding to give up the whole thing, and going away tomorrow; but now, angered by the Commandant's sneer, he said. 'I'd rather go to their cell.'

'I knew it,' muttered the Commandant, displeased. 'All right, let's go.'

The way led through a labyrinth of narrow passages between walls the colour of faeces. Out of the cells came chanting, laughter, angry cries, moans, or most often silence. Men in uniform with rifles stood in coffin-shaped nooks in the walls. The Commandant, with his handkerchief constantly at his nose, was furious when he brushed against anything.

The cell was in a passage where the light was particularly dim and where the other cells seemed to be empty. Two guards, ugly as wrestlers, lounged outside. One, at the Governor's command, unlocked the door, while the other pointed his revolver as if he expected some savage beast to come rushing out.

Yet even after the door was open the cell remained silent. The dim light could not penetrate into it. One of the guards offered his torch to the Governor who offered it to the Commandant who signed to McLeod to take it. He did so, and stood for a few seconds with his thumb on the button. Again, even there on the threshold, he was minded to turn and go. If what he had been told was true (and now he found himself wishing it was so that the whole sordid business could be considered at an end), then all he had to do was flick on the torch, and before him would be the men who had killed Donald Kemp. It was then he realised that Kemp had never really been his friend, not even in their undergraduate days; they had never understood or even liked each other very well. It could not have been for Donald's sake, therefore, that he was there; and as for Margaret Duncan, he had never set eyes on her. Why then had he come, perhaps endangering his career?

The Commandant, sure that the torch must be broken, cursed the guard and demanded he fetch another; but while the man was protesting that it had been working a minute before they arrived, McLeod switched it on.

He had not known what emotion he might feel, and now he did not know what emotion he was feeling. The cell was small and had no furniture, not even beds. Crouched against the wall, shackled to it with chains, were the two men, dressed in tunic and short trousers made of some kind of sacking. Their heads were shaved and glinted in the torchlight; their faces were bruised and swollen. One, the elder, had his hands resting on the brick floor in front of him; they seemed strangely tranquil, in spite of the heavy manacles, and of the raw places where his finger-nails had been. The other, instead of toes on one foot, had a contorted mass of flesh; but that might have been a deformity from birth.

Against his will McLeod was moved to a feeling of sorrow. These men had conquered resentment. God knew what mal-treatment they had suffered, and yet as they blinked out at him like blind men they smiled. The effect was of beauty, a terrifying, pathetic beauty. He could find no other word for it. Those gaunt, bruised, cut, forlorn faces were beautiful; not even the shaved heads could spoil it. Not only had resentment been conquered, but pain also, and the fear of pain, and the imminency of violent death, and above all the sorrow of never again seeing people they had loved. They had more peace of mind than any of the men staring in at them.

'Mad,' muttered the Commandant, through his handkerchief.

McLeod went into the cell. The man with the misshapen foot tried to cower back further against the wall, but he kept smiling, too. His companion sat very still.

McLeod realised they could not see him. For all they knew he was another strong-armed guard with a thick club.

'I haven't come to beat you,' he said. 'I am English.'

Behind him the Commandant laughed. 'I thought you never called yourself that, McLeod? British you always said, not English.'

'Do you understand?' asked McLeod.

The one with no finger-nails nodded. 'Yes, sahib.'

'What are your names?'

'I am Jamil, he is Sarwar. He is my nephew, sahib. All his life he has been like a little child in his mind.'

No child, thought McLeod, ill-treated as he had been, would have smiled like that.

'Where do you come from?'

'Haimir, sahib.' It was a village McLeod had never heard of.

'Heaps of mud and stones,' muttered the Commandant. 'Primitive. Hasn't changed in a thousand years. Dig the ground with their hands. Can't build proper houses. Some still live in caves in the cliff-side.'

McLeod asked Jamil if they were both married.

'I am, sahib. He is not.'

'Look at them,' said the Commandant. 'Would you think one is the headman's brother, and the other his son? I tell you, our country is to be pitied. The Indians say we are one hundred years behind them. They are too generous. We are three hundred years behind.'

'Have you any children?' McLeod asked Jamil.

It was the Commandant who answered. 'He has five,' he cried, 'as I have. You see, McLeod, why be surprised? We are all animals. But, my friend, you must come to the point. In the first place, it is very far from pleasant here; and in the second place, your friends at the Embassy will be waiting for you. So, please, come to the point.'

'They say,' said McLeod, 'you have confessed to killing an Englishman and an Englishwoman who were guests in your village about eight months ago.'

Jamil nodded wearily. 'Yes, we killed them, Sarwar and I.'

'Why did you?'

'Do you ask a wolf why it's a wolf?' muttered the Commandant peevishly.

'Why did you kill them?' repeated McLeod. He had minutes ago put out the torch, so that he could now scarcely see the two men huddled on the floor.

'We were cold and hungry because of the snow. We are always cold and hungry during the winter. We thought they would be rich because they were foreigners. So it was planned to kill them while they slept. Sarwar and I were chosen.'

'So there it is, McLeod,' said the Commandant. 'A plain case of murder, with robbery the motive. For God's sake, let us go now, before my head bursts.'

McLeod ignored him. He spoke to Jamil. 'What was the man like?'

The description was so accurate it was clear he must have seen Donald; indeed, he spoke with a kind of weary affection.

'And the woman?'

He described her as if she was standing before him in sunshine. Her hair he spoke of fondly as being in colour like a certain flower, one of the very few that in spring grew on the barren hills round his village. Not once did he sound to McLeod like a man with two murders on his conscience. But after a month of beatings in this dark cell even guilt itself could have become refined into this peaceful acceptance of pain and imminent death.

'You say they were sleeping,' said McLeod. 'Where were they sleeping?'

'In one of the caves.'

'I told you about them,' said the Commandant. 'They're in

the hill-side, just above the village. Do you know how long they've been there? Two thousand years. Don't forget to ask them about the bracelet and the photograph.'

'We took them from the bodies,' said Jamil. 'We took everything, even their clothes. There was a book.'

'They stripped her naked,' muttered the Commandant. 'I did not see her, but everyone tells me she was very beautiful. Think of her, McLeod, naked in the snow, with her blood staining it red.'

'What book?' asked McLeod.

For the first time the Governor spoke. 'He sometimes speaks about a book, but nobody knows anything about it.'

'It would be a Bible,' said the Commandant. 'Of course they would burn it.'

'She was sick,' said Jamil. In the dim light his chains rattled as he made some kind of gesture. 'Perhaps she would have died soon. Perhaps,' here his voice sank very low, 'he would have killed her himself.'

'Of course,' scoffed the Commandant, 'every murderer merely anticipates death.'

McLeod stooped and clutched Jamil by the shoulder. The man could not help wincing.

'What do you mean?' whispered McLeod.

'She was sick and weeping. He was angry.'

'But do men in your village kill their wives because they are sick and weep?'

'I don't see the point of your question, McLeod,' said the Commandant, 'but the answer is: of course they do. What's the good of a sick wife to a poor man? She eats but she doesn't work. She produces children but she can't feed them or look after them.'

The Governor whispered to the Commandant, explaining what the prisoner had said that had evoked McLeod's question. Crouched beside the prisoners, with his hand on a chain, McLeod listened, and felt his whole being sicken.

The Commandant came in and stooped beside him. 'I did not intend to tell you this, McLeod,' he whispered. 'It seemed unnecessary. But I must tell you now. Your friend Kemp did not want her to go with him. That seems strange, but it is true. In our investigations we discovered that time and again. At every village they visited it was the same story. He seemed to speak roughly to her most of the time. Perhaps he was sick, too.'

'What did you do with their bodies?' McLeod whispered to Jamil.

Again the answer though prompt was listless. 'We took them to a place where the wolves meet.'

'How far?'

'About three miles.'

'You and this man yourselves? He is a cripple.'

'You forget the whole village was in it, McLeod,' said the Commandant. 'They took it in turns to carry the bodies through the snow to hide them in the wood.'

'Wood?'

'Yes, quite a big one. There are wolves in it, and bears.'

'Have you seen it?'

'No, but I've spoken to others who have. It's about five hundred miles away, McLeod.'

McLeod thought, if it was five thousand he must go and see it.

He rose. 'Right. Let's go now,' he said.

The Commandant was pleased. He patted McLeod on the shoulder. 'No use making yourself any more unhappy than is necessary.'

The Governor led the way back to his office.

'Well, McLeod,' said the Commandant, as he walked behind him, 'are you going to tell His Excellency you are convinced?'

'Yes.'

'You think they were telling the truth?'

It was the Governor who answered. 'I have always found that men who are about to die tell the truth. You see, they are to die tomorrow morning; and they know it.'

The Commandant hadn't known it, and he was annoyed. 'When was this decided?' he demanded.

'This afternoon, about three o'clock. His Excellency telephoned.'

It must have been after McLeod's visit.

'You might have told us,' grumbled the Commandant. 'I wondered why the fellow seemed to have an advantage over us. That was why. How are you going to do it? Will it be a rope or a sword? If you ask me it's time we got back to the old way: shoot them out of a cannon; splatter the multitude with their blood and guts.'

'His Excellency wants it to be done in private,' said the Governor.

'Of course, McLeod,' said the Commandant, with a grin, 'if you wanted to be present, I'm sure it could be arranged.'

McLeod did not reply.

'What you need now,' said the Commandant cheerfully, 'is to go to your party and let the beautiful ladies and the golden whisky help you to forget. I wouldn't mind going myself. At whose house did you say it is?'

'Mr. Minn's.'

'Ah, the respected head of Chancery. Do you think, McLeod, he would object if I was to accompany you for an hour or so?'

Frequently officials who were invited turned up at parties with others who weren't. It was diplomatic to make them all seem equally welcome. Minn and his wife Hilda were both expert at making annoyance look like rapture.

'No, I don't think he would,' said McLeod.

The Commandant was delighted, and in a hurry to go. 'Ah, how nice it is,' he said, 'to see the ladies like flowers and the men gallant and wise as philosophers, because of the golden whisky, because of the golden whisky!'

Five

In his letter Kemp's description of an Embassy party had been different from the Commandant's. 'I suppose this is the kind of heaven our civilisation imagines and deserves,' he had written, 'and this Embassy's the perfect setting. Three miles away the dirty, smelly, dust-swept city, with its three hundred thousand souls, represents earth. Here then, behind the high white walls, with the gilded gates closed and guarded, a representative group of the chosen, from various races, both men and women, sit in crowded rooms, or stand rather, with glasses of whisky or gin, miraculously replenished, in their hands, and revolve in their minds, sometimes uttering them, inanities that they know to be infinitely dreary and trivial, but which none the less are the total substance of their eternal existence. This heaven is truly cosmopolitan: here a Chinese woman with gold dragons on her black dress slit to the silken thighs chats to an Indonesian diplomat in a black bow-tie; there a crew-cut Yank listens indulgently to a small, beaming Jap, neither of them forgetful of the "little yellow bastard" days; while in a corner a long, thin, sleepy-eyed Swede stands beside an eager turbaned Sikh and his plump horn-rimmed wife in a sari of gold and green.

'Outside, above the spacious, silent gardens, the moon shines on the white walls, balconies, and flowered terraces of the Residence. Here God lives. Tonight he mingles with them for an hour or two, with his wife who yearns for the tennis season; but soon in velvet jacket he will return to his omnipotent dreams, and for a few minutes the inanities will grow a little brisker and dancing will begin cheek-to-cheek thigh-to-thigh in the small room with the lights turned low. Now the Military

Attaché yearns to return to his toy soldiers, of which he claims to have one of the most complete sets in the world. The First Secretary chuckles as he reviews his scheme to reorganise Chancery, and so once again to discomfit his subordinates. Those subordinates, watching him, see the backside of an elephant, which is their symbol for his ego. The Doctor dances like a bear full of bromides, holding at arm's length a giggling, gin-soaked female anatomy.

'Christ, Johnny, how I long for the desert again; and those green valleys you wrote about, where they speak about the greenness and the work that achieves it and God who makes it possible.'

When McLeod and the Commandant arrived, the ambassador and his wife had just gone, and the party freed from restraint was almost lively. Loud laughter burst from one group, an excited female voice from another, and in the little library where Bhudda in green jade squatted on top of a bookcase two couples danced or rather posed amorously.

Roger Minn, tall, jolly, with the glaze in his eyes merely incipient, welcomed them at the door. To the Commandant he was particularly effusive; but as soon as he had handed him over to a group containing some compatriots, he came back to McLeod and whispered: 'For Christ's sake, McLeod old man, what made you bring him? I didn't know he was a pal of yours.'

'He thinks he is.'

'I suppose he might be useful, but they say he'd slit his grandmother's throat if she stood in his way.'

'They say that about a lot of us.'

Over his whisky-and-soda Minn blinked at McLeod, and decided not to challenge that remark. His own ambition was insatiable; and though both his grandmothers happened to be dead there were other expressions that might be applied; indeed, his staff, he knew, applied them daily.

'By the way, McLeod,' he said, 'this isn't really the place to discuss it, but I think I should warn you the Minister was on the telephone this afternoon to H.E. about you. He wants us to

restrain you from dashing off into the wilderness to look for
Kemp and the girl.'

'And what did H.E. reply?'

'Dammit, McLeod, what could he, except to say he would.
Oh, I know he can only advise you, but I think you'd be wise to
listen.'

'Yes. By the way, Minn, is that offer of hospitality still open?'

'Wider than ever, old man. If we have you up here, we can
keep a closer eye on you, you know. When d'you think you'll
move in?'

'Tonight, if it's suitable.'

'Had enough of the hotel, eh? Of course it's suitable.
Brought your stuff with you? No, you can't have, for you
came with Hussein, didn't you? Want me to send a car and an
orderly down for it?'

'No, thanks. I'd better go myself. Hussein's going to run me
down.'

'How in God's name did you happen to be in his company,
old man?'

'He took me to see the two men accused of—'

'The murders of Kemp and Miss Duncan! By Jove, did he
really? That's extraordinary. Gillie's been trying for weeks to
get permission to interview them. He'll want to talk to you
about it. So will H.E., I wouldn't be surprised. But I've got to
remember I'm host; can't leave it all to dear old Hilda. You
actually saw these fellows?'

'Yes.'

'You were allowed to speak to them?'

'Yes.'

'Well, were you convinced? I know Gillie's been doubtful. I
don't know why. Seemed to me a plausible enough explanation:
murder with robbery the motive. What did you think?'

'I think they did it.'

That wasn't of course true. McLeod was by no means sure.
But Minn had to be deceived.

'I'm glad to hear you say it, McLeod old man. It must have
been a hellish thing for Kemp and the girl, but it's over now,

and it's best we should be able to call it finished business. Strange chap, Kemp. De mortuis and all that, I know, but I must say I didn't care for him at all. Granted we're all damned, and likely to roast in hell for all eternity, but surely for God's sake, McLeod, that's no reason to grow a wild beard and have gloating in your eyes; not to mention turn up at a party wearing old flannels all mucked up with cow shite and a shirt that hadn't been washed for a month, and no tie, of course. I can't say I've ever taken to these leper-lovers.'

'Leper-lovers?'

'You know what I mean, old man. All we ordinary people, he just hated our healthy guts; but he'd have kissed a leper's sores all right. He'd his eye on the Almighty all the time; reminded me of a sneak at school. And then his treatment of that poor girl! He had her under a spell; it made me think of Rasputin. I'm not joking, McLeod. Hilda agreed with me; you just ask her. What are you to think of a man who'd let a woman lick the dirt off his feet, but wouldn't sleep with her? You've heard of women who like to rouse men and then refuse at the last second: cock-teasers, they're called. Well, Kemp kept her at the last second all the time. Hilda says *she'd* have clubbed him with a hockey stick. Now if it had been a case of religious scruple or a desire for priestly celibacy, then one might have understood and even sympathised. But it wasn't that. How could it have been? As I've said, he hated all our guts. You should have seen how he went out of his way deliberately to insult H.E. The most charitable thing to think is that he was mad. We all did our best, you know, to dissuade her from going with him.'

'She must have loved him, surely.'

Minn looked shocked and disgusted. 'I suppose she must have,' he said, 'but God knows why. She was a stunner, you know. She borrowed a dress, and she was really beautiful. Glorious hair. At home if she'd given him a second look it would have been of astonishment and disgust; but India and then this country turned her head. Of course she was a bit God-demented herself. But I'll really have to go about my hostly

duties, old man. I see lots of empty glasses. We'll continue this
chat later. I'm fearfully interested.'

He hurried away, and McLeod stood on the edge of a group
of Americans, among whom was Mrs. Bryson.

'Yeah, hardship post number one,' a woman was drawling,
'that's what they call this in Washington. They say the place
sure has them worried. A hundred healthy people are sent out,
and a hundred and ten sick people return.'

They all laughed. Few of them were sick, but it was true
that the Americans there were remarkably prolific. Kemp had
commented on it. 'Is it a sign of confidence in the Dollar or
in God? Is it an attempt to outnumber the Russians here? Or
is it simply there are no rubber-goods shops round the
corner?'

Mrs. Bryson caught sight of McLeod, and pushed out of the
crowd to take him aside.

'Well, Mr. McLeod,' she said, 'I see you're still with us.'

'Where did you think I'd be, Mrs. Bryson?'

'See that fat creep over there in the fancy uniform, drinking
whisky out of the tea-cup. Know who that is?'

McLeod laughed and nodded.

'I wouldn't laugh, Mr. McLeod. That guy's dangerous.'

'Mrs. Bryson, I brought him to the party.'

'For God's sake, don't tell me you're a friend of his!'

'He thinks so.'

'Maybe I oughtn't to be associating with you, Mr. McLeod.
They say dungeons are full of folk that guy and his buddies
didn't like. Did you see his li'l Excellency?'

'Yes.'

'Did you get permission? To go off and look for Kemp, I
mean?'

'No, but he gave me permission to go and see the two men
who say they killed Kemp.'

'You don't say! Say, you must be a real buddy. Did you go?'

'Yes. Your fat creep took me.'

'And did you see them?'

'Yes.'

'Gee, Mr. McLeod, this is sure exciting. Were you allowed to speak to them? Did you get the whole story out of them?'

'Yes.'

'And that was how it was after all? They killed them for robbery?'

He nodded. 'In the snow,' he whispered.

She repeated it, with a shudder. 'In the snow. If you're ever going to murder me, Mr. McLeod, for God's sake do it in the sunshine, when it's warm. I wouldn't want my blood cold to start with. And so the search is off?'

McLeod had noticed Mohammed Hussein approaching them. It was the General who, breathing into her neck, answered her question.

'Yes, dear lady,' he murmured, 'the search is off. I hear from our charming host that Mr. McLeod is going to live with him here in the Embassy and attend all the jolly parties. That is much better than to travel for hundreds of miles over our bad dusty roads, visiting our uncivilised villages.'

Though she was smiling, her lips were forming the words: Fat creep, go away. Then they opened in dismay when Gillie the Consul tugged McLeod by the sleeve and took him away.

'I'd like a word with you for a minute, McLeod.'

They found a quiet corner in the flower-room. Gillie, a big, brusque, red faced, spluttering dandy, at once demanded: 'What's this Minn's been whispering into my ear?'

'What about?'

'About you visiting these fellows in jail, by special leave of his pompous little nibs.'

'What about it?'

'Don't be so bloody Scotch, McLeod. You know what I mean. I want to hear all about it.'

'Now? Here?'

'Maybe this isn't the best place. I understand you're moving in with Minn. What about my office, tomorrow at ten? I'd better get your story before H.E. starts asking. You've no idea what a headache this business has been to me. H.E. has considered it a personal affront, and I've had to carry the can. Kemp was about the most inconsiderate bugger possible.'

'He's dead, Gillie.'

'So you're convinced they did it?'

McLeod nodded. Then they were sought out by General Hussein, still carrying his tea-cup.

'Ah, Mr. Gillie,' he said, 'I know what you and McLeod must be talking about. It is good. He will tell you this unhappy affair is now ended. Or rather that it will end tomorrow at dawn.'

'What happens then?' asked Gillie.

'You tell him, McLeod,' said the Commandant.

McLeod could hardly keep his voice or his glass steady. 'They are to be hanged then,' he muttered.

'Hanged or beheaded, what does it matter?' asked the Commandant.

'So I'm not to get to seeing them?' asked Gillie.

The Commandant shrugged his fat shoulders. 'It is not necessary. They will be put to death.' He paused to sip his whisky. 'It will not bring back your compatriots, but –' he paused again, to take another delicious sip – 'justice will have been done, and good men, like you and me and McLeod here, will be able to sleep in peace. Does it not say in your Bible: A life for a life? Two lives therefore for two lives. You may say you have got the worst of the bargain, since the two to be killed tomorrow morning are poor, murdering scum, but I should like to remind you of something your own Mr. Purdie once said to me. He said that in God's eyes all men are of equal value. But please bear in mind that the entire village from which these men came has been punished. We did not put everyone to death, men, women, and children; but then, I do not think you would have wanted that.'

Gillie had listened with a grin of admiration growing wider all the time. 'No,' he said, 'we wouldn't have wanted that.'

Staring at their two faces, each smug and pleased in its own national way, McLeod remembered the faces of the accused men, so resigned and beautiful.

The Commandant was looking closely at him.

'I think, McLeod,' he said, 'it was a very unpleasant experience for you this evening. You are lucky to have the whisky to help you to recover. I am lucky, too; but I do not always have whisky. Mr. Gillie, I am about to take my leave. Before I go, I would be honoured if you would present me to your charming wife.'

'Delighted. Now where's she got to? Let's go find her.'

'If you're going soon, Hussein,' said McLeod, 'will you give me a lift to the hotel. I want to fetch my stuff.'

'I shall even lend you some policemen to carry it down to your car.'

'Thanks,' said McLeod.

There could be no better way of deceiving them all than by getting policemen to start him off on his flight.

He stood quietly smoking among the plants and flowers, while Gillie and Hussein went off to look for the former's wife. By the time this party was finished, he thought, he would be a hundred miles nearer that village.

Six

As he drove out of the Embassy gates in the Commandant's car, McLeod noticed, shimmering in the moonlight on the lawn in front of the Residence, the ambassador's pet crane, lost in a one-legged meditation. An hour later in his own Land-Rover, with his luggage on board, he was out upon the road miles from the city and the Embassy, in a countryside fit for dreaming cranes.

He drove as fast as the badness of the road let him. In the light of the headlamps dust swirled up like genii taking shape. On all sides swelled great tumours of dry, barren earth, now pale as salt. Far away, above the intervening hills and plains, gleamed the clouds and snowy peaks of his destination. Villages slept behind their high compound walls, and on the ground round about them melons shone like skulls. Sometimes dogs howled, and once a donkey brayed.

Soon he was in the grip of the feeling that that countryside had always inspired in him, by day and night: all was hallucination; the landscape and his presence in it, the hordes of humanity behind in the city, the bored revellers at the Embassy party, the crane, the men in prison, the fat Commandant, the detective with pock-marked face so like many other faces, and the small Minister with his deodorant roses, all these were phantoms in a vaguely remembered dream; and the future, to which he had been looking forward so anxiously and for which he had been planning for weeks, seemed also an illusion at the heart of which Donald Kemp and Margaret Duncan kept fading.

He had decided to keep travelling until next day about noon, by which time it would be too hot. From then till dusk he could rest in some shady corner among the hills; thereafter he would drive all night, and again next day would rest and hide. He calculated that he would arrive in Mazarat in the middle of the night, when its inhabitants and garrison would be asleep. There was an excellent chance that the Commandant and the Minister would not find out for a day or so that he had fled. Indeed, if Minn and the others at the Embassy had any gumption and loyalty, with luck the discovery wouldn't be made for a week, by which time he would have visited the village, and either would be returning to the capital, or would be going on into the mountains.

When dawn came, bright and sudden, he was about two hundred miles away. There were no spouts of dust behind, raised by pursuers. Nor did he expect any, for even if by accident his flight had been discovered pursuit would hardly be immediate. Recriminations would be shrieked within police headquarters for hours, and a scapegoat sought. Then would begin frantically the consultations to decide whether he was to be pursued, where, by whom, and with what intention. Before anything else at all could be done, the Commandant would have to make sure that whoever else was blamed and degraded he mustn't be. To that end every Minister in the Cabinet would have to be waylaid and entreated. The Prime Minister himself, and even the king, might be involved.

But though there was little danger of pursuit or ambush, the journey called for determination and endurance. He became two cramped hands on the wheel, a numbed backside, a sharp pain between the shoulder blades, a mouth gritty and dry with dust, and eyes smarting with it. Though he had tried beforehand to make the Land-Rover as dustproof as possible, very soon he had to tie his handkerchief round his nose and mouth. Except for a few scattered green patches around villages, everywhere was the flat tawny desert. It was a land being ground down by the hot, patient hand of God into this fine dust. Rarely a flower would be seen, spiky and fast-withering. Stones of all sizes lay on the desert as if they had just fallen from the sky.

Occasionally a lorry would pass, crowded with hitch-hikers who endured the heat, thirst, dust, and bumps with incredible composure. The engines were American, but the bodywork was native, painted with gaudy designs, roses, and lions, and domed mosques. The driver, crushed by the half-dozen or so in the cabin with him, could hardly be seen at the wheel. When glimpsed he never seemed to be concentrating on driving, but rather on the stories his passengers were telling. No doubt they had all prayed together at some roadside shrine for a safe passage. It was therefore in God's hands; why should they worry?

Once he passed a long caravan of more than a hundred camels, pacing with wonderful patience along a ridge, so that they seemed to be walking across the blue sky itself. And once an aeroplane droned overhead, bound for Mazarat. McLeod wondered if Mohammed Hussein himself, or some subordinate with miraculous enterprise, was aboard, and was now gazing down past the silvery wing at the puff of dust that would represent the Land-Rover. If so, he would be waited for at Mazarat; but he did not think it likely.

Apart from the aeroplane, the only other means of swift communication between the capital and Mazarat were with him most of the time, pathetically at his mercy. These were the telegraph wires, sustained by small poles at crooked angles, no larger or more substantial than those tossed as cabers at Highland games. A few snips of pliers, and there could be no excited gabbling between the two towns.

He stopped for breakfast at a green place where there was a spring of unpolluted water and shade under some trees. He hoped he wouldn't be disturbed there and moved about cautiously, but while he was eating he caught sight of a woman hurrying through the fields, almost running, apparently towards him. She was enveloped in a loose robe of blue cotton, and under it carried tightly what seemed to be a child. Close behind her, his very gait showing his irritation at her haste, came a young man, almost a boy. After him flocked other men and children.

McLeod quickened his chewing. If he was right in his surmise as to their purpose, appetite, weak enough already, would never survive once they reached him.

He was right. When she came near the woman, or young girl rather for she couldn't have been more than fifteen, removed tenderly the dirty cloth from the baby's face, which, so wizened and contorted, was the face of death. The young man, obviously her husband, wanted in a fit of anger to restrain her, because she ought not to speak to a male foreigner, but he also wanted to encourage her because in spite of himself he shared her hope that the white sahib might be able to cure their child.

At first she didn't speak, but peeped out from under the robe, as shy about revealing her own face as she was eager about displaying her baby's. Then she asked McLeod if he was a doctor. When he replied he was sorry he wasn't, she didn't heed: hope was too strong in her then to be so easily uprooted.

In his first-aid box he had aspirins, some penicillin lozenges, anti-malaria pills, bandages and Elastoplast. To produce any of those would have been to fertilise her hope cruelly; not to produce them would be to trample upon it. Now that the girl had exposed her face, he could not help seeing her as Karima's countrywoman; both of them were much lighter-skinned than was usual.

While he hesitated, wondering whether he should at least make a show of trying to revive the baby, the others arrived. Though several of these had come with sores and ailments for attention, all were hilarious. The reason was an old man with a wrinkled, merry face; he kept croaking witty remarks, mostly at his own expense. He tried bravely to laugh, too, but a painful hoarseness made it difficult for him.

Probably he had cancer in his throat. Round his neck was wound a bulky, grubby bandage. This, to the accompaniment of shrieks of laughter and even some clowning assistance, he began to unwind delicately, as if it was a mummy-cloth. It was so long and he was so careful that it took him almost a minute to get it off. Still his neck couldn't be seen. Wrapped round it was a silken scarf, at which McLeod gazed in astonishment. It was an Edinburgh University scarf.

Noticing McLeod's excited interest, the old man, giggling and coughing, drew back; his skinny, blotched claws protected his prize. For him it had magical properties. That it hadn't yet cured or alleviated the agony in his throat was merely because God, who could not be hurried, had not yet consented. Then suddenly it occurred to him that if a second sahib touched it, God, whose whims were as unpredictable as a child's, would give consent all the sooner. So he slowly unwound the scarf, too. When it was off he held it out for McLeod to touch, but not to take; with his other hand he guarded his ravaged throat. Eagerness had filled his mouth with slaver, some of which dribbled down his chin and some he swallowed with winces of pain. Yet all the time he tried to smile as he gazed at the scarf.

Surely, thought McLeod, the only possible possessor of such a scarf to pass that way recently must have been Kemp. Turning it, with his hand involuntarily flinching from the contact, he saw the tab, soiled, but with Donald's name and the Edinburgh address where less than a month ago McLeod had visited his parents.

The old man nodded and brought his hand down from his throat to point to the tab. Yes, he croaked, that was the sign of the sahib who had given it to him; it had been given, he protested, not stolen. The sahib had been very kind.

Immediately the others broke shrilly into praise of Donald, whom they evidently remembered with interest and affection. He had spent eight days with them. They had lent him rugs and quilts because the weather had been cold. Every evening many of them had visited him, and though he hadn't been able to speak their language nearly as well as McLeod could they had enjoyed his company. Just to sit and watch him had been for them pleasure and comfort. He had been brave, wise, and happy.

McLeod thought they were deliberately omitting Margaret, or perhaps by that time Donald and she had parted company, which might account for his happiness and assurance. But no, when he asked he found they remembered her, too, just as affectionately. Being men, though, they couldn't be expected to praise a mere woman too highly. Yet, casual though their remarks about her were, it was clear she had impressed them memorably. She had nursed sick babies and old women; she had bandaged sores (one youth of about fifteen showed a bandage round his leg; from the colour of it it might well have been the one she'd put on months ago). It was the old man, now tenderly rewinding the scarf round his throat, who spoke, with jovial hoarseness, about her beauty. The rest joined in gleefully, comparing her to the stream, the flowers, the blue sky, and the trees that gave shade.

What was most movingly evident from those happy recollections was that Donald and Margaret themselves must have been very happy during that visit.

Forgotten in the excitement, the girl with the baby cried out: 'She was old and she had no children.'

The men turned to frown at her in disapproval for having raised her voice so brazenly in their presence. Her husband beside her made an angry gesture to her to hold her tongue, or rather he tried to, for as he stared at her face against the face of their dying child, his raised hand came down softly upon her head in an anguish of love. Then, though the men had begun to chatter to McLeod again about Kemp, he thrust a way through them for his wife. She followed timorously but resolutely, and offered the baby to McLeod.

As he gazed at it, shaking his head, he was sure it was already dead. Again he explained that he wasn't a doctor and had no medicines that would help.

The old humorous man, inspecting the infant, told her it was dead, but cheerfully assured her there would be other children, better than this. He himself had seen eight of his die in infancy; those that had survived were the best.

Her husband grinned mournfully at that prospect, and threw his shoulders back to assert his manhood; but she went on quietly weeping.

All McLeod could think of was to offer money; if it couldn't restore the dying, at least it could help the living. She refused it, with a sad, quick look of reproach that had him grinning in shame; but her husband, confident that the child could be replaced, took the notes, worth about thirty shillings, enough to keep him and her for several weeks.

The rest were shocked by what they considered McLeod's ingratitude. *They* had been entertaining him and answering all his questions about his friends; *these* on the other hand, to whom he had given the money, had been pestering him and making him sad. So they clamoured, holding out their hands, and even trying to snatch some of the young husband's money, so that, holding it under his clothes next to his heart, he crept to where his wife huddled by the burn, with her own face and the baby's hidden.

McLeod had to buy his escape. Some of them weren't pleased with what he gave them, and kept plaguing him during his preparations to leave; but what troubled him most was the sight of the young woman crouched by the burn, heedless of her husband's eager whispers and of the notes which he kept trying to make her look at. As he drove away McLeod found himself wishing he had the assurance of Kemp, or even the naïveté of Purdie, so that he could pray for her and expect his prayers to do her good even though the baby had to die. That wasn't cynicism, for he knew that Purdie often came into these lonely villages with a supply of the latest drugs. No doubt a fasting spittle or a squashed spider would be as efficacious upon these virulent syphilitic sores as the ointments with which he smeared them; but that smearing itself was heroic and surely not altogether useless.

Yet in spite of his pity for the young mother he felt much lighter in heart. Donald and Margaret had come along that road too, months ago, on foot or in a bus or on borrowed donkeys. He knew that they had been happy together. Whatever had happened before or afterwards they had looked on those red hills and this glade of poplars with joy. For him, then, hills and trees were transfigured.

Seven

He arrived at Mazarat with the moonlight gleaming upon the four hundred domes of its blue mosque. After the long drive across the desert he was too tired and benumbed to take the precautions he knew were necessary. He did not try to keep to shadowy side-streets, but drove along the main street, rousing the pariah dogs sleeping there and so having the accompaniment of their querulous barking.

So he wasn't unprepared when in front he saw a white pole across the road, with policemen in front of it, and all around. For a moment he was minded to go crashing through. Then he realised this might be a Customs check-point, with officials only too pleased to let a foreigner through. Knowing the language well was often better even than having the right permits.

As soon as he stopped, a police officer ran out of the shadows to him.

'Salaam,' said McLeod, as pleasantly as he could.

The officer didn't return the greeting. 'I am Major Samad,' he snarled. 'Give me your passport.'

McLeod scowled. Exhausted and hungry, he felt like telling this boor to go to hell. In any case, it looked as if the authorities in the capital had after all got in touch with Mazarat, and his journey was at an end. If lucky, he would be escorted straight back; otherwise he might spend a week or two in some hideous jail first.

'Your passport,' shouted the Major, just as nastily; indeed, he dragged his revolver out of its holster. He was a beefy fellow, with a crass, conceited face.

'Usually in your country,' said McLeod, 'I am treated with courtesy and kindness.'

'We are too humble,' said the Major. 'We are better than foreigners, so why should we be humble towards them?'

'Nobody's asking you to be humble,' said McLeod, and handed over his passport.

The Major turned the pages with the barrel of his gun. 'British?' he asked.

'Yes.'

The Major spat three times. 'British!' he repeated, with disgust.

'I think I should warn you,' said McLeod, 'that I am a British diplomat, with some influential friends, among them His Excellency, the Minister of the Interior.'

The Major had been about to spit again; instead he swallowed it.

'I'm tired,' said McLeod. 'Either take me to your superiors, or let me pass.'

'When it suits me,' muttered the Major. He swung round suddenly, as if to catch his subordinates smiling. They had been, but stopped in time.

'I do not wish to have to report this,' said McLeod.

There seemed a likelihood then that the Major would fire his gun, perhaps at the sky, perhaps through the windscreen, perhaps through a policeman's head, perhaps through his own. The last was most likely.

Suddenly he rushed round and climbed in beside McLeod. 'Drive to the station,' he said. 'Follow that truck.'

The pole was removed, the truck set off, full of policemen, and McLeod followed it down the broad, moonlit street.

'You speak our language well,' muttered the Major.

McLeod grinned; the Major had meant 'too well'.

The Major's next question astonished him. 'Are you married?'

'No.'

'I am not married either. But in your country it is different. If you want a woman you can go out into the street and buy her. Here a man who cannot afford to marry just burns.'

So that's the trouble, thought McLeod, amused.

'Do not laugh,' muttered the Major. 'It is not good for a man, and it is not good for a country.'

They rattled past the mosque. Doves flew about its domes.

'Do you pray?' asked the Major.

McLeod didn't answer.

'I do not,' whispered the Major sulkily. He was like a small boy in a huff with his teacher. 'What I have I had to get for myself; and I have never enough. I have no car, no house, no land, no wife.'

'Whom shall I see at the station?' asked McLeod.

'The Colonel; he is expecting you.'

'Is he in charge of the police here?'

'Half an hour ago he was. Perhaps he is not now. Do you know why? Because he may be dead. He is sick, you see. He has been sick for weeks, in his mind as well as his body. Do you know why? I shall tell you. Three months ago he had a wife, two sons, and one daughter. Now he has no one, like me. They are all dead. He prays, every day he prays. For what? He does not know for what.'

'What happened to them?'

'Small-pox.'

'Was there an epidemic?'

The Major was amused at the note of alarm in the question. 'No,' he said. 'Only five people died. Just the Colonel's wife and children, and a beggar in the bazaar. The Colonel does not understand that. I understand it. That is why I do not bother to pray. There is the station, with the cannon in front. Do you recognise them? They are British; they were captured from your army long ago.'

Another officer met them in the corridor; sleep bleared his eyes.

'How is he?' asked the Major.

'In his office, lying down. He had to be carried in.'

'Did you send for the doctor?'

'He wouldn't have it. Is this the fellow?'

'I think so. He's British anyway.'

'I understand English a little. Let me see his passport. Yes, he's the man he wants. John McLeod.'

'And what does he want me for?' demanded McLeod. 'Why should I be brought here in the middle of the night like a thief?'

The officer shrugged his shoulders. 'We do not know. The Colonel will tell you. There was a telephone message from the capital. The Colonel took it himself. Perhaps it was from your Embassy. You see, he is ill and sometimes as a consequence behaves strangely.'

By this time they were outside the Colonel's office. A guard yawned there. The Major knocked softly, once, twice, three times; there was no reply of any kind.

'Wait here,' he said, and entered.

McLeod immediately followed. It was a dismal room, lit by a shadeless bulb hanging over a desk. Always melancholy, but more so there, the king's portrait hung tilted on the wall; in it he was a young man of about thirty, so it must have been taken soon after his father's assassination twenty years ago. Otherwise, there was no one in the room.

The Major crossed to where a blanket covered a doorway. He drew it back enough for McLeod to see a charpoy, a native bed consisting of four wooden legs and a plaiting of rough rope. On this, under a grubby pink quilt, lay the Colonel, his eyes closed.

The Major saluted. 'I have brought the Englishman, sir,' he said.

The Colonel moaned.

'I have brought the Englishman,' repeated the Major. 'If you do not wish to see him now, I shall take him away again, and bring him in the morning.'

The Colonel opened his eyes. 'What is his name?' he asked.

The Major couldn't pronounce it.

McLeod said it.

'Go,' muttered the Colonel to the Major.

'Perhaps I should stay, since you are not well.'

'Go,' shouted the Colonel.

'Very good, sir. Here is his passport. I shall leave it on your desk.'

The Major went out with a murderous pout.

'Excuse me, Mr. McLeod,' said the Colonel, staggering to his feet, and lurching over to his desk. 'I fell asleep. Please sit.' He fell into his own chair, and looked for about a minute as if he was going to fall asleep again.

He was a small, handsome, grey-haired man, as fair-skinned as McLeod himself, and with a moustache in need of trimming. He gave the impression of being naturally dapper and even vain, but now he was unshaven, with his eyes bloodshot, and his uniform crumpled.

He gave a great shiver. 'I beg your pardon, Mr. McLeod,' he said. 'As you see, I have a touch of malaria.'

'Should you not be in bed?'

'But I have just come from my bed.' He tried to smile.

'I meant, in your home.'

Still trying to smile, the Colonel with an effort that exhausted him opened a drawer. He had to rest before taking out what he wanted.

It had nothing to do with McLeod. It was a snapshot of a woman seated in a garden with a baby in her arms and two other young children beside her. She was not good-looking; her nose was too large and hooked, her eyes too close together. The children were all like her. Even the baby was gleeful, holding out its hand towards the person taking the picture. This, McLeod realised, must be the family wiped out by small-pox. The Colonel himself must have taken the photograph. Though he was not in it his presence, happily expostulating, could be easily imagined.

'I'm sorry,' said McLeod. 'The Major told me about it.'

Mention of the Major reminded the Colonel he was a police official. He picked up the passport.

'You are John McLeod?' he asked.

'Yes.'

'Today—' He looked at his watch so long he seemed to have forgotten; McLeod noticed it was half-past one. 'Yesterday I had a telephone call from His Excellency the Minister.'

He paused again.

'Well?' said McLeod.

'He warned me you might be passing through Mazarat. It appears you gave your word you would remain in the capital.'

'I did not.'

'His Excellency thinks so. He said you gave it to him personally.'

'No, I said I would if I was satisfied.'

'Satisfied? What about?'

McLeod noticed how his hands couldn't rest, how they kept picking up the snapshot, and how damp this was with sweat.

'I'll explain,' he said, 'as briefly as I can. About five months ago, two friends of mine, a man and a woman, both British, passed through Mazarat.'

'But, Mr. McLeod, I know all about them.'

'It is said they were murdered in a village about two hundred miles from here. I saw the two men who confessed to the murder. I thought I would like also to see the village where it happened.'

'You did not believe these confessions?'

'I wouldn't say that. I just felt I would like to see the place where it happened.'

'Mr. McLeod, I have seen the place; some huts of mud in a wilderness of stones, and some holes in the cliff. It was I who went to arrest those men and punish the others. They were punished. Even your friend would have been pleased with their punishment.'

'Why do you say that?' asked McLeod.

'Because I knew him. He was in this office. He did not sit, he rushed up and down, like a mad camel, striking the desk with his fists.' The Colonel brought his own fists down on the desk with an exaggerated gentleness that, vivider than violence, suggested Kemp's rage.

'Why?' asked McLeod. 'Was it because he was being refused permission to continue on his journey?'

The Colonel stared strangely at McLeod. 'He had permission. It was something else.'

'What else?'

'The woman sat in that chair; yes, the one you are sitting on yourself.'

McLeod could not help looking at it. One of the spars between the legs was missing. The leather covering the padding was torn. It was the kind of chair to be found in every office in that country.

'Weeping,' whispered the Colonel.

But why should she be weeping, wondered McLeod. So far as he knew they had been happy and reconciled. What had happened here? He began to think the Colonel was talking in a delirium.

'It is secret,' said the Colonel. 'No one in Mazarat knows but me.'

'Knows what?'

'The men who did it were put out of the way.'

'Did what?'

'The policemen, too, had to be transferred. That was unjust, but the secret had to be kept.'

'I'm afraid I don't know what you're talking about,' said McLeod. 'What happened? Did it concern my friends?'

'If my wife and children were alive, Mr. McLeod, and I was a man with hope, I would not tell you. I would consider my position and my career; I would be afraid for my family.'

'Tell me what, for God's sake?'

'Now there is no need for me to be afraid. So I shall tell you.'

But he was in no hurry to tell, and sat smiling insanely while McLeod waited, cold with horror.

'The woman was attacked, Mr. McLeod.'

'Attacked?'

'Yes. By two men maddened with hashish.'

'Christ!'

'I shall tell you about it. It was night when they arrived in Mazarat. I did not know they had come. They should have reported to me, but they did not. It was cold and wet, too. There is a hotel here; it is not good, by your standards, but it is safe at least. For some reason your friend did not choose to go to the hotel. It could not have been lack of money, because it is, again by your standards, very cheap. He did not go to it. Instead, he asked for hospitality at a chaikhana. It was in a bad part of the town, but he could not have known that, as he was a stranger and it was dark. The proprietor allowed them to sleep in a hut next to the shop.'

He paused, to recover strength and memory. He was sobbing with weakness.

McLeod waited.

'While they slept they were attacked.'

McLeod could picture it, in its sordid terror; but he was still not sure whether the Colonel was recounting a hallucination or actuality.

'There were two of them. You cannot question them, Mr. McLeod, not in this world.'

'You mean, they were put to death?'

'Yes. Your friend waited here for four days until with his own eyes he saw the sentence carried out.'

It must be hallucination or nightmare, thought McLeod. 'Two of them?' he whispered.

'Two. They were both equally guilty.'

'But death is a punishment for murder.'

'And in our country, for rape also; especially if the woman is a foreigner. We are poor, Mr. McLeod; we must seek friends; perhaps we seek too humbly.'

McLeod had his face covered with his hands.

'Your friend could not prevent them. They were too strong with the drug. But he fought hard; it was the marks of his blows that helped us to find them. But they over-powered him. The cloth that they wind round their heads as a turban can have various uses; it can fasten a man's hands and feet, it can muffle his mouth.'

And cover his eyes, thought McLeod. Rather foolishly he said: 'But why? They were poor, humble, with nothing to steal.' But even while he was speaking he was remembering the Major's bitter grumble about the plight of men unable to afford to marry.

'Are you asking me why men are evil?' asked the Colonel. 'Ask me also why God allows such evil men to live, and takes away the innocent and good. It is because I cannot understand these things that I have told you this.'

'Was she badly hurt?'

'In her body? It appears not. They left Mazarat again in five days. She was able to travel. I gave them a police car as far as Kalak, where the great Buddhas are.'

'But surely she needed medical attention?'

'I had the best doctor in Mazarat to attend her.'

'Can I see him?'

'No. He has gone away. Please understand, Mr. McLeod, this has been kept a secret. It is not in the official records. It never happened.'

Perhaps it hadn't.

'Why are you telling me?' asked McLeod.

'Because my wife and children are all dead. If one had been spared, only one, I would not have told you.'

But that surely was a delirious man's reason. The whole thing sounded more and more like an evil dream.

'But wasn't it possible she might have become pregnant as a result of this?' asked McLeod.

'We are not babies, Mr. McLeod. We know how children are conceived. The doctor said he did what he could. It was against his religion, but he did what he could.'

And God knew what that had been, thought McLeod. Even the best doctor in Mazarat wouldn't be up to much; and that doctor bothered with religious scruples would be worse than useless.

'And it was against your friend's religion, too, Mr. McLeod.'

'Did he object?'

'I understand he did. Of course he had a right to; she was his wife. But, you see, Mr. McLeod, it appears she was already pregnant.'

'How do you know that?'

'She said so herself, to the doctor. Every morning she had been sick; her breasts were tender to touch. Those are symptoms, Mr. McLeod.'

'It would seem,' burst out McLeod, bitterly savage, 'that the people who murdered my friends afterwards should have been rewarded, not punished.'

'Why do you say that, Mr. McLeod?'

McLeod could not tell; he made an angry baffled gesture.

'They were still alive,' murmured the Colonel, smiling. 'They still could sleep in each other's arms. Their child would be born. The world belonged to them. Their murderers took it from them, and so deserved punishment. I saw to it myself. I said to my men: "For the next hour they are yours, do what you want with them, except kill them." There were women, some of them young, though none so beautiful as your friend's wife. Justice was done, Mr. McLeod, in every way.'

McLeod was almost convinced the Colonel, in spite of his calm voice, was raving. His bloodshot eyes moist with tears, his face glistening with sweat, his distracted hands picking up and dropping the snapshot, were those of a man in a nightmare, who until he died would have this vision of his own wife being raped by death.

'I should like,' said McLeod, 'to see this village.'

'So you cannot believe your friends are dead? I do not blame you. You did not look upon their defiled bodies. You did not see their faces hideous with the kisses of death. You did not watch the hole dug. You think because she sat in that chair she must be still alive. If the chair exists, so must she. If the stars shine, so must her eyes. If a donkey brays in the night, why should she, too, not have a voice, to sing, and speak?'

'I should be obliged,' said McLeod, 'if you would put on my passport whatever stamp is necessary to allow me to go on my way.'

The Colonel, more than ever like a man in delirium, pulled the passport towards him, rummaged in the drawer, took out a rubber stamp hardly any more impressive than one in a child's post-office set, and stamped the passport.

'This will get you beyond Mazarat, Mr. McLeod,' he said.

'Not any farther?'

'For that you would need a permit signed by the Governor. I

advise you not to seek it. I think they will be looking for you in the morning; and perhaps for me, too.'

McLeod rose, holding his passport. 'Good-bye,' he said, 'and thanks.'

The Colonel bowed his head.

Outside there were two guards; one held McLeod there, while the other raced for the Major, who, in about five minutes, came buttoning his tunic and yawning.

He asked for the passport, examined it, and handed it back.

'Was it a message from your Embassy?' he asked.

'Yes. The Colonel is ill. He should be in hospital.'

'He refuses. If he dies,' went on the Major, with a sour smile, 'they will send someone else to take his place. My father was not a friend of the king, as his was. I was not given a vineyard for a wedding present.'

He stood on the top of the stairs watching McLeod climb into the Land-Rover.

'At least,' he called, 'please tell your friends in the capital that Major Samad, of Mazarat, was helpful to you.'

As McLeod drove away he glanced back and saw the moon still shining on the many domes of the mosque.

Eight

All next day he travelled up a narrow river valley, where the two thousand years since Christ were forgotten, or rather might never have been. On the strips of soil on either side of the white-bouldered river men still lived and worked as they had in His time. The corn was threshed by the feet of oxen going round and round, encouraged by a peasant who ran with them, bare to the thighs, sometimes singing. Men with sticks sent the chaff swirling about them like snow. Women, peeping round as the car passed, crouched in the small green fields, their fingers busy. Little canals in which water flowed as preciously as blood criss-crossed from the river into the fields. The road was of earth and stones, and the bridges of wood. Often the road twisted through narrow gorges or along thin ledges high above the river. So as not to take up any of the fertile land, the houses were built into the hillside, and often were screened by delicate trees.

Yet at one time there had been cities in this valley, not built trustfully on the low land but high up on the red hills, protected by walls on the brink of the precipices. Remnants of those walls still stood, and could be seen from the road. McLeod knew that if he was to cross the river and trudge up the steep path that led through the solid mountain he would be able to pick up pieces of pottery used by the inhabitants a thousand years ago, before Genghis Khan, marching in revengeful triumph out of Central Asia had slaughtered them all, to the last child. The cities had never been rebuilt, and though in time trust had timorously returned, enabling men to live again close to the river, ambition had been abandoned for good. Hope could not be kept away: it was present in the young trees, in the ripe corn, and in the children on the flat roofs laughing through the leaves; but nowhere was it urgent or impatient. It knew this valley was too accessible: there was no high, difficult mountain range to guard it, as there was guarding that other valley in which, if they were still alive, Donald Kemp and Margaret Duncan might be found.

If they were still alive . . . Now, whenever he thought of them, it was with a feeling of doom. Inimical forces, pursuing them, had been too powerful. Their love for each other, which ought above all to have sustained them in their flight, had itself often been treacherous. But if their journey had been a flight, from whom had they been fleeing, and whither?

That night he camped a mile or two outside Kalak, on the other side of the river from a hill on which could be seen, silhouetted against the moonlit sky, the ruins of what was called the Noisy City. Ever since its destruction by the Mongol hordes, it had been avoided, as if a curse was on it. Perhaps, in this land of Islam, the curse was that of Buddha. Legend had it that the city had been called Noisy because its citizens, every day at a certain hour, had congregated to watch, a mile away, the great arm of the carved god rising slowly in the sunshine, manipulated by the priests from their caves within the rock, but fancied by the people to be the Buddha's own miraculous daily gesture of benediction. They had therefore shouted all together, in a joyful pious acclamation. Now no place could have been quieter than their strange pyramidical hill, and the colossal idol, its face sliced away by time or human malice, was without arms.

When at last he fell asleep it was to have a weird violent dream peopled by Donald Kemp wearing a Mongol's helmet, the Colonel with his face terribly pocked, the Major naked with flames licking at his loins, Margaret Duncan impassive and gargantuan as the great idol, and McLeod himself climbing up her in a frenzy, past her knees and swollen waist and dripping breasts towards her head, on which Donald and the Colonel and the Major sat gambling, with snapshots of the Colonel's family as cards.

Next morning early, with the sun already brilliant, he set off for Kalak, where the Buddhas were. He had once described these to Kemp, who had replied that if he went home that way he would certainly stop to have a look at them, and to climb, by the tunnel through the cliff, to the head of the larger, one hundred and sixty feet high, whence a godlike view could be had of the wide, green valley. If ever there was a vantage-point to suit an attitude of religious arrogance, that was it. McLeod felt therefore that if he stood there himself, he must be able to feel Donald's presence, especially after that dream last night. Margaret would be there, too, for there was no doubt that, whatever injuries she had received at Mazarat, she would think her place was by his side, even on the giant idol's head.

There were two surviving Buddhas, about a quarter of a mile apart, hewn out of the red cliff. There were also niches where others had stood or reclined, before Genghis Khan had passed. In the cliff now were thousands of caves so that it looked like an enormous red maggoty cheese. Before the coming of Islam with a sword, this had been one of the most famous Buddhist shrines in Asia. The noses and lips of the images had been sliced away, but now the Government recognised the place as a tourist attraction; to prevent the smaller statue from collapsing a great buttress had been built, more conspicuous than the statue itself.

Those enormous carvings had never impressed McLeod favourably. What remained of the faces reminded him, for all the difference in size, of the attempts by Renaissance artists to portray the infant Christ. Instead of divine innocence a crafty senility seemed to be achieved. Those great idols might have been urchins in Brobdingnag, looking down upon the tiny Gullivers not with holy compassion but with vast, pudgy sadism.

Almost under the larger Buddha lay the school, with window spaces but no windows. The children, in a variety of dress like Hallowe'en guisers, were already gathered in the playground. They clutched their tattered books and called shrilly to one another, like birds. Most had their heads newly shaved, and were like novitiate priestlings of the monster that towered over them in its painted niche. For some reason they were greatly interested in McLeod and came rushing out to cheer him as he passed. He was surprised, for cars, though not numerous there, were far from unknown. From their shouts they seemed to take him for a teacher of some kind. He heard the word American. There were several Americans teaching English in the capital. Was it possible there was one here, too, in this outpost?

It would have been too conspicuous to leave his car by the toe of the great statue, so he parked it a short distance away, in the shadow of the cliff. Then he set off to climb up to the great head, but not by the hair-raising way in his dream.

The path was steep. He had to go slowly at that altitude of seven thousand feet, pausing to take quick breaths of the thin, bright air. Below stretched out the vivid greenness of the valley; nearer were the toy hovels, with the people moving about them, tiny as lice. Further away he could make out against the sky the gigantic two-headed dragon, said to have been slain by Ali, son-in-law of Mahomet, and thereafter turned to stone. Nearest of all, in the very hill he was now climbing, were the caves where the priests had lived more than a thousand years ago. Some at the foot were still inhabited, by people who evidently preferred them to a mud house; others at the top seemed to be inhabitable only by birds, but at one time a maze of sloping tunnels within the cliff had given access. These cliffs, like all the mountains in view, were of soft red rock rapidly crumbling. Geologically they were infants compared to the mountains of McLeod's own native Wester Ross in Scotland. Resting there, he remembered those hills of home rising from the salt sea-lochs. Once he had spent a holiday climbing them with Donald Kemp.

The entrance to the tunnel that led through the solid rock to the Buddha's head was guarded by an attendant. He might have been put there by the authorities, or it might have been his own idea. He said or did nothing, except hold out his hand for alms. He was a young man whose memory might be dependable. Perhaps he had been there earlier in the year when Donald and Margaret had paid their visit.

McLeod dropped a note into the ready palm.

'Many foreigners come here,' he said, smiling.

The young man waited wearily; his fingers had closed upon the note.

'About four or five months ago,' said McLeod, 'two friends of mine, British, came here. I think you will remember them. One was a man with a red beard, the other was a woman whose hair was like gold.'

The young man looked wise, but said nothing.

'I think you remember them,' said McLeod.

The other nodded eagerly.

McLeod, too, became eager. 'Tell me about them,' he cried.

But the guardian of the idol opened his mouth wide, stuck out his tongue, and pointed with unresentful finger into the cavern of his mouth. He had not spoken because he could not. He made harsh friendly noises of proof.

Dismayed, McLeod hurried on into the dark cool tunnel that would take him to the great stone god which too was dumb.

Less sure-footed than a louse, he stepped cautiously across the gap on to the enormous head. After the darkness of the tunnel the light dazzled him, so that he had to cover his eyes and for a few moments stand swaying, overcome by the giddiness of the height and by recollection of his hideous dream about this place.

He sat down and tried to let the splendour of the view reassure him. On the other side of the valley he saw the hotel shining in the sunshine, and remembered the cockroaches in its bath. One hundred and eighty-three there had been, according to the indignant American who first had counted and then had decimated them all with a buzz-bomb. There had been no shovel to lift out the upturned carcases. In any case, as the American had suddenly discovered, who could take a bath after that? Especially as there was no water, hot or cold, in the taps.

Craning, McLeod saw his Land-Rover still in the shadow, like a Dinky toy. Then he noticed three men beside it, with a curious air of dutifulness. One wore a long native robe, the others had sports jackets. They kept looking round. He thought at first it must be for a friend, until he saw the man in the robe shouting to a couple of policemen, who ran over to him. Was this an emissary from the Governor, come to ask, with the most adhesive politeness, to see McLeod's permit? If so, it was hardly likely McLeod would have the same luck with him as he had had with the Colonel.

Above and on either side the walls of the great niche in which the Buddha stood had at one time been covered with paintings, now either faded or disappeared. In one women musicians could be made out playing a kind of harp. Not only were their faces bare, but their breasts, plump as melons, were as casually covered as those of any modern sex queen. As he was gazing at these remarkably emancipated women and contrasting them with their unfortunate sisters of today whose very noses were shrouded, McLeod noticed the names of previous visitors, scribbled in Persian mostly, but there were one or two in English also. Though he thought the search was foolish, he began to look for any sign that Kemp might have left. He had little hope of finding any, for Kemp was hardly likely to be among those who feel mortality can be cheated by leaving their names or signatures for posterity to gape at.

Then among the Persian scribbles he saw some pencilled in tiny English. They were so exactly what he was looking for, but never expecting to find, that he could scarcely believe he was seeing them. They were the names Donald Kemp and Margaret Duncan, with the date below; but bracketed with Margaret Duncan, in the same handwriting but more agitatedly, was written Mrs. Donald Kemp.

For ten minutes McLeod sat there, staring at those inscriptions and wondering what to make of them. Had they really got married, according to the customs of this country, by some mullah between here and Mazarat? Or had it been a gesture anticipating the marriage to which both were looking forward? Or had Margaret added that third inscription, in a great hurry, after he had gone, so that he hadn't known she had done it?

McLeod did not know what to think, but his very doubt conjured up their presences vividly on this great stone head of the idol. They were deeply in love, but that doom which he had felt so strongly for them before was now much stronger; it made their urgent voices sad, and lit up their faces with a sinister dedication. It was as if they had been aware they were going forward to their deaths by sordid murder, and not only were reconciled to it, but wished it, as a kind of glory.

Hallucinations, thought McLeod, must be catching.

Nine

An hour later, when he went down, the three men and the two policemen still hung round his car. The robe of the tall official was purple with vertical gold stripes. As he gazed about with stretched neck or listened to his companions' shamefaced remarks, he looked like a Merlin contemplating a masterly transformation: perhaps the car into a camel, or the gigantic, faceless impiety behind him into a cockroach.

The two others were ordinary in their uneasiness. The smaller, whose sports jacket was checked like a grouse-shooter's, kept his thin shoulders hunched in a dejection that no amount of desperate puffing at his cigarette through his cupped hand could alleviate. Under his other arm was tucked tightly a large thin book which, McLeod thought, must either be a treatise on the Koran or an album of Indian dancing girls, so reverently did he keep nudging it.

The taller, who kept close to him, also smoked, in quick, frenzied puffs. He had a long, bent, lugubrious nose, which he kept trying to bend still more. As if to draw closer attention to the book under his colleague's arm, he held his own arms far out from his body, with chimpanzee wideness.

The two policemen stood yawning about twenty yards apart. Once one took off his cap, examined inside it fondly, scratched his shaven head, and then put on his cap again, with an air of re-assuming the burden of existence.

The longer he studied them, the more confident McLeod became that whatever their purpose in waiting there it wasn't to demand his permit and arrest him if he couldn't produce one. Besides, there was no official car or truck about; but, of course, if they did intend to carry him off to be interrogated by the Governor, they would insist that he drive them all there. However, the impatience of the long-robed, long-necked magician was not that of authority savage for its prey; nor were the despondency of the young man in the loud jacket, and the grief of his friend with the tender elbows.

McLeod decided to risk it.

Boldly and calmly, like any harmless tourist, he approached his car, pretending to be still over-awed by the huge statue in front of him. The moment they caught sight of him, it was obvious that whatever they took him for it certainly wasn't an intruder without permit. On the contrary, had General Mohammed Hussein in his most splendid uniform been by his side, with his arm about McLeod's shoulders, those five couldn't have welcomed him more gladly and respectfully. Indeed, the policemen with great grins retreated, backwards. The others, except the man in the purple robe, looked as if they, too, would have liked to bow themselves off out of sight, behind the Buddha.

McLeod was so relieved and amused that he couldn't help winking up at the enormous idol. It, too, was without the proper credentials. It was too big to be dragged off for interrogation. What was saving him?

It was the man with the big, gloomy nose who came forward, hand outstretched, lips parted in a smile only sycophancy could have achieved in so short a time.

'Mr. Shoopbaum?' he cried.

Shoopbaum? McLeod refrained from laughing. If that was the pass-word, let it be cherished.

The man with the book – it was now clasped rather more conspicuously to his breast – also held out his hand.

'I am Mohammed Farouk, teacher of English at Kalak school,' he murmured, with a peculiarly American accent.

McLeod thought it prudent to have an American accent, too.

'Pleased to make your acquaintance, Mr. Farouk,' he said.

Farouk smiled, as if begging McLeod to make that pleasure sincere. 'And here,' he went on, 'is my headmaster, Abdul Naim.'

Bowing, Mr. Naim insisted on again shaking hands.

'And this gentleman,' said Farouk, now introducing the man in the robe, 'is Nour Mohammed, secretary of His Honour the Governor. He has come to welcome you in the Governor's name, and to invite you to lunch, after you have visited the school and witnessed my demonstration of how to teach English according to the book.'

The effort of reciting that brought sweat to the brow of the teacher. 'You may well not be over-satisfied, Mr. Shoopbaum,' he added, 'but I have done to the best of my utmost endeavours.'

So that was it. Shoopbaum must be one of the American educationists engaged in teaching native teachers to teach English. A book, McLeod had heard, had been compiled; he had heard, too, from biased sources, that it had some peculiar features.

'I have,' said Farouk passionately, 'been guided by the book always, as you will see.' Those last words were added almost as a threat.

McLeod held his head as if upon it sat a baseball cap with scarlet peak, and moved his gums.

'Sorry I'm late, gentlemen,' he said. 'Had a flat a couple of miles along the road.'

'The book,' said Farouk desperately, 'has been a good, a very good, an excellent guide.'

'Sure it has, Mr. Farouk. A lotta hard thinking went into that book. I'm sure you've done a good job.'

'I have tried to do a good job, certainly.'

As he said that, Farouk turned and piteously scanned the caves at the very top of the cliff; in one of those he would humbly retreat for the next hour or two, if no one objected.

But someone did. His headmaster, with bundles of confidence under his arms now, suggested in Persian they would now go to the school, where the pupils might be growing impatient.

The teacher sadly translated. He added that the pupils if kept waiting too long might go off home. Then he smiled the suggestion that he personally was prepared to wait another three hours anyway.

The Governor's secretary, Nour Mohammed, meanwhile wasn't pleased at being neglected. He was a smooth, self-happy, vacuous man, frequently stunned by the weight of his own dignity. Now he insisted on saying, in Persian: 'Education is the key that opens the treasure chest of knowledge.'

Farouk, asked to translate, conveyed by the very droop of his eyelids that when McLeod, alias Shoopbaum, came to the school and opened the chest there, Lord, what jewels he would see.

'Shall we go?' asked McLeod, and led the way to his car.

The secretary wanted to know why Shoopbaum, an American, had a British car. The last time an American had come he had had an American jeep, with an emblem painted on it showing two clasped hands. That meant, said the secretary, friendship among nations; which was a beautiful thing.

The teacher translated the words but not the smug zest.

'Maybe I should tell you,' said McLeod, trying to retain the American accent, though he was now speaking Persian, 'that I understand a little Persian.'

'You speak it very well,' said the secretary.

'Very well,' repeated the headmaster, whose eyes rolled as he tried to remember if he had let drop anything that might have offended this American who might complain to the Minister of Education who might as a punishment reduce an already low salary to a level at which even a cigarette a day couldn't be afforded.

Stuck on one of the back windows of the Land-Rover was a small flag showing a lion rampant. McLeod had forgotten it was there, so he was at first puzzled when the secretary tapped him on the shoulder and asked him what the lion meant.

'Lion? Oh, yes, that is the emblem of my college,' he replied.

'It is a strange emblem for a college.'

'The lion, you see, is about to devour ignorance.'

The secretary was so delighted he made his jaws go like a lion devouring ignorance or an American chewing gum.

Abdul Naim, the headmaster, wasn't so pleased. In his school, he murmured, there was too much ignorance to be devoured; it could be the feeding-ground not of one lion but of a thousand.

Farouk, the English teacher, with a moan concurred.

The result was that as McLeod drove into the playground he saw all the tawny heaps of earth and boulders there as those thousand lions, and the small brown faces at every window as their cheerful victims. His companions were not surprised by his laughter. Perhaps the thousand lions had been there before in the person of some previous high priest of the book.

In one place the playground had been heroically cleared to make an attempt at a basket-ball pitch. There the corrugations were at least regular and the stones small. The posts for the nets were so crooked, like a camel's legs, and so obviously nailed together with more enthusiasm than skill, that again McLeod couldn't help laughing. This time his laughter was snapped up as a cat would fish.

In a country where the national bank was shabby, McLeod didn't expect to find refinements in a village school. What he found affected him as the basket-ball posts had done. Here was a corridor, high, with mud-brick floor, and mud walls full of sores out of which pieces of straw stuck like bones. Along it then was advancing towards them an old, bearded, ragged man spraying water from a skin-bag slung over his shoulder. Perhaps he was deaf, perhaps he liked to start at one end and reach the other in one go, perhaps he was accompanying the libations with a prayer whose efficacy would be destroyed if interrupted. Whatever the reason, he came crouching on despite the shouts of the headmaster and the gesticulations of the secretary. Everyone had to go to the wall to escape a drenching; even so, they were well splashed. Farouk would have dried McLeod's shoes with his handkerchief if he had let him; the old man, he said simply, was poor. The secretary, though, whose gold-striped robe was now bedraggled at the skirts, like an incontinent old woman's, was greatly huffed. How, he asked, with hisses between every two or three words, could their country ever advance when such things happened? The headmaster shouted reproof after the old servant, who must have thought it was praise, for he came scurrying back, leaking all the way, with his hand held out for baksheesh. Only McLeod gave him any.

Then the headmaster led the way to the classroom. It was, no doubt, the best in the school. Certainly there was glass in some of the windows, and the desks were solid lumps of wood fresh from the saw. And it was, surely, the brightest class. McLeod did not have to be told that only the smartest were allowed to study English, or at any rate to parade their knowledge of it before the inquisitor. As soon as he entered forty pairs of the keenest, brownest, slyest eyes he had ever seen glittered at him, as if he was about to be overwhelmed in a booby trap, or else his fly buttons were undone. With such mischievous hope might a puppy wait for a frog to hop. At a signal from the teacher they sprang up to greet the visitors, and yelled what at first McLeod thought must be a local salutation, but a moment later realised was: 'Hi!' Glancing towards Farouk, he learned that this form of address was not irrepressible youthful impertinence, quaint when uttered by urchins with shaven heads and spotted pyjamas, but rather well-rehearsed idiomatic English, according to the book. He half-expected Farouk then to tell them to sit by asking them to park their fannies.

A bench was reserved at the front for the headmaster and the secretary. Smirking with duplicity, McLeod stood by the teacher's desk near the blackboard; he took care not to lean on it, for it had only three legs. Book in hand, with his eyes closed oftener than open, Farouk faced the class. They would now, he told them in Persian, demonstrate the vowel sounds of the English language, as explained in the book.

Each pupil had a copy, covered with the outside of an old *Time* magazine. There on those desks that smelled like a sawmill were the faces of Dulles, Eisenhower, Chiang Kaishek, Adenauer, and other famous friends of America. The boys were all quiet, but when told to open their books and begin enunciating hounds in full cry after a fox couldn't have shown a noisier more competitive zest.

'Bee, bee, bee!' they yelled, with glee, as if they knew what the letter frequently stood for. Such an instinctive grasp of the language reflected much credit on the teacher, thought McLeod. A moment later they were shrieking, in onomato-poetic spurts: 'Pee, pee, pee!' Then it seemed to him they must have got out of control, or else were using some language he had never heard of: 'Boob, doob, pood; nem, meem, meed; nob, neen, deen; tot, toot, teet; gook, goom, geem; zoop, zop, zood; gosh, joosh, posh; fop, fooch, goof; yot, yoot, yooz.' And the climax, with the hounds racing one another for the kill, was: 'Box, fox, pox.' Then, exhausted, with their faces pink, sweat on their brows, and spit on their lips, they waited for the next pursuit.

When the teacher slowly turned and wistfully looked at McLeod, he could only smile and nod. Obviously it was all in the book; Farouk never could have invented it. The real Shoopbaum would have the key.

Encouraged a little, the teacher turned to another page, and called upon the class to turn to it, too. This they did, bouncing in their seats with anticipation; the next lesson was evidently one they had rehearsed well and thought they were good at. Like an orchestral conductor the teacher pointed to the boys in the row nearest the windows. At once they piped softly, three times: 'A teacher, a teacher, a teacher.' Then his finger pointed to the middle row; with rather bolder conviction these cried: 'A good teacher, a good teacher, a good teacher.' The last row was ready. 'He's a very good teacher,' they shrieked, three times. Finally, with a frantic sweep of his arm, he had the whole class on their feet, bawling: 'We think he's a very good teacher, we think he's a very good teacher. WE THINK HE'S A VERY GOOD TEACHER.'

McLeod was convinced, but the teacher was taking no chances. Six times he had the class go through the performance, and the sixth time was the loudest. Only then would he turn to see if Shoopbaum had approved. The real Shoopbaum would have certainly, and perhaps have shown it by taking off his cap with the scarlet peak; but the impostor had a hard job keeping his face straight, especially as the secretary had, in so well-bred a fashion, one finger permanently in one ear, and another finger of the other hand wandering near enough the rim of the other ear to run in and close it whenever necessary.

The headmaster kept bending his nose, and so producing grimaces which indicated that in his private opinion this was a lunatic method of teaching anything, but since it was the method of the book he would listen to it, and applaud it, even though half of those thousand lions were to come growling at the windows.

The teacher pressed on with the demonstration. For the next exercise the class was divided into groups; each group had its own particular sentence to shout out in its turn. Inspired irrelevance had selected those sentences: 'I feel fine. Fill the tank. He sells bikes. He was ill last week. The farmer sells his sheep. Let me see the list.' And so they continued, chanting, bleating, yelping, singing, hooting those absurdities, until the secretary's fingers were permanently in both ear-holes, and the headmaster's nose was bent so far he had to breath, or rather gasp, through his mouth.

At once followed a performance by individuals, the stars of the class. Up sprang the first, slant-eyed, red-pyjama'd, and shrieked: 'I hear with my ear.' Hardly was he seated than, in another part of the room, shot up another, hooknosed, Semitic, glossy-headed, hooting: 'He has a hat as old as his shirt.' Then a third, Orientally plump, softly chanting: 'This is his home.' The fourth, with the whites of his eyes immense, intoned the finishing touch: 'Harry hit it with a hammer.' Next time round each had a different sentence to say. No sooner was the fourth round finished than the whole class was shouting, crescendo: 'The beauty of the view. Cute twin mules. The puny dwarf was thwarted. I like humour and music and beauty.'

Then there was silence.

Soon the secretary's fingers crept out of his ears for a moment, were reassured sufficiently by the continuing silence, and so went dancing down the front of his robe on to the desk. The headmaster softly clapped his hands, and beamed at McLeod to be as charitable.

Farouk's mild eyes begged a verdict.

'Do you like teaching in that way?' asked McLeod.

'But, Mr. Shoopbaum, it is in the book.'

'Yes, I'm sure it is. Do you think it's a good book? Does it really help you?'

Eyes huge with necessary mendacity, Farouk said it was a wonderful book; he was grateful to the clever men who had written it to make his task of teaching English so much easier. If his pupils weren't as good at English as they ought to be, it was his fault as a teacher, because his own English wasn't good enough. It was also because most of them came from very poor homes, where they had no peace to study. It was because, moreover, education was new in his country, especially in that province so far from the capital. And it was, furthermore, because all winter the land and houses were under snow and ice, so that the intelligence of the pupils was frozen. Though by this time running out of excuses, he was prepared to find more of them for his pupils' shortcomings. Among those excuses, though, was certainly not going to be the fatuousness of the book.

McLeod suggested that excuse. Farouk jumped from it as a mouse might from a trap gone off prematurely. No, no, the book must be very good because it had been written according to the latest scientific principles. It was, everybody knew, the best possible book, no book could be better. How wise the Ministry of Education was in ordering copies for all the schools in the country, especially as, owing to American benevolence, it was being supplied free.

'Cute twin mules!' said McLeod. As an expression of incredulity it was as eloquent as any he had ever heard.

Farouk almost grinned; swift as a mouse, though, the grin vanished back into his face.

McLeod wished he could end the imposture and whisper that he wasn't Shoopbaum; but, inured to irrelevance as the teacher had to be, he would never have understood. No combination of words in English could ever surprise him, or indeed have any meaning for him. He could, with equanimity, have read hundreds of pages of Gertrude Stein at a sitting.

He came close to McLeod and whispered: 'The salary is not much, Mr. Shoopbaum, but I need it.'

A sentence, McLeod thought, so pregnant with sense and relevance, he ought to have had his whole class reciting it, and it only, with a hundred different intonations.

Then into the playground, to halt beside McLeod's Land-Rover, roared in a swirl of dust an American jeep, with that emblem of the clasped hands prominently painted on its side. Beside the native driver sat, indisputably, the real Shoopbaum. In one particular only had McLeod been wrong; this keenfaced educationist's cap did not have a scarlet peak, it had a sky-blue one, which went rather better with his blue-checked lumberman's shirt and blue jeans.

The quickest way out for McLeod was by way of the window nearest him.

'Here is a colleague of mine,' he said, and had clambered out before anyone could reply.

He ran across the playground. Shoopbaum, carrying a fat brief-case, stopped to gape at him. There was no point, McLeod decided, in waiting to explain. Already Mr. Shoopbaum looked dumbfounded; to tell him about the imposture would be worse than having his own cute twin mules kick him.

'Good morning,' called McLeod, as he climbed into the Land-Rover.

Shoopbaum took a step nearer. 'Hi!' he said, not too cordially.

'Sorry I can't wait,' cried McLeod. 'Mr. Farouk will tell you all about it.'

All the same, he thought, as he drove fast out of the playground, it would have been worth seeing and hearing Shoopbaum, not to mention teacher, headmaster, and secretary, when the explanations began. One thing at least was certain: as the book proclaimed, they would all hear with their ears.

Ten

McLeod felt much lighter in heart as he left Kalak and its giant Buddhas. Thanks to that whisper of the teacher's: 'The salary is not much, but I need it,' he was able to see life again, and especially his own present part in it, from a man's height. Even if he were to have it confirmed that Donald and Margaret had been treacherously murdered, there were still compensations. He remembered these with gratitude: the merry old man with the cancerous throat; the young wife and her dead baby; the Colonel at Mazarat; the old fellow who kept the dust down in the school; and even Shoopbaum, bewildered under his blue-peaked cap. All those were as much part of his search as would be the two bodies in the bloodstained snow.

Not far along the road too, after leaving Kalak, he was to meet another.

The road, now only a churned track in the thick dust, climbed by a very steep, spiralling pass up into a wide plateau at the far end of which were the snow-capped mountains, his destination. At the foot of the pass were a chai-khana or tea-shop and a wayside shrine: refreshment for both body and mind before tackling the long, dangerous ascent. Waiting by the tea-shop was a heavily laden lorry, leaning far to one side like a lame camel; it would need the help of God to get up. Its driver, a small, humorous man in a dirty turban and an old American army tunic, sat cross-legged, drinking cup after cup of sweet, weak tea. Over the rim of the cup he kept squinting in amusement at his young assistant who, with his large mallet-like implement beside him, was on his knees at the heap of holy stones and rags. In the tea-shop were the crews and passengers of two other lorries that had just safely descended;

these were loud and cheerful with relief, and laughed at the driver's sly remarks about his colleague's piety. The latter, a youth of about seventeen, must have heard the jokes and the laughter, but did not allow them to disturb or spoil his prayers. When he got up, lifted his club of office, and walked to get his own tea, he, too, was laughing, as if better than they he saw the joke. His round, happy face under its skull-cap was coated with dust, and his eyes were bloodshot. Although his job, that of leaping off the lorry to stop it from running backwards to destruction, required the nimbleness of a goat, he wore broken sandals with long, upturned toes. McLeod could not have shuffled in them, never mind leapt.

Sitting placidly on the ground, drinking tea, with his club beside him, the boy grinned at the jesters; and half an hour later, all the way up that dizzy hillside, he kept on grinning, although he had to run most of the way, and at each of the four hair-pin bends had to scurry about thrusting his mallet under the back wheels, just in time to save the lorry from slipping over the edge and bouncing to the foot hundreds of feet below. Driver and brakes shrieked, the driving-wheel was spun round like mad, the lorry lurched, disaster looked certain, but always that mallet was pushed in time behind the wheels. Now squatting, now kneeling, now flat on his stomach, now rushing to one side to direct the driver and now to the other, always in a smother of dust, he stuck to his task and ignored his own danger. McLeod kept as close behind as was safe, intending to offer help if it was needed and could be given in time. In the midst of his exertions the boy had time and spirit available, as he dashed in and out of the lorry's dust storm, to grin back at McLeod, as one motorist to another.

When the lorry reached the top, therefore, and the youth had clambered up on top of its bulky cargo, with his mallet flung up before him, it wasn't just the sudden nearness of the blue sky or the spaciousness that exhilarated McLeod with hope. No, it was also the sight of the boy crouching on the sacks, not even rubbing his bruises, with his head bobbing against the sky. Thus every day he earned his wage of less than ten shillings a week.

All day afterwards McLeod drove across the wide plain, seeing occasionally herds of fat-tailed sheep and goats attended by their lonely shepherds, and sometimes an encampment of nomads with their black, many-steepled tents, aggressive dogs, inquisitive children, and aloof camels. Villages were rare now, and were built far apart from the road on heights as mud-coloured as the houses. To see someone moving there was really to feel that mortality had been overcome; those movements were inscriptions written upon time itself.

Towards evening he had reached the foothills, and camped by a river whose clear water and smooth clean pebbles reminded him of the rivers of the Scottish Highlands. Here, though, instead of birches and rowans, were wild apricots and glades of poplars in which wolves and bears and even leopards might lurk. What caused him most apprehension, however, was the knowledge that the chief who held sway over that district, defying the authorities who were too distant and indolent to curb him and his wild hill-men, was an old ruffian famous throughout the country for his life-long hatred of the British. In the war against the latter, about forty years before, his father had been killed and he himself had lost his right hand. Years ago a friend of McLeod's, travelling with a party of Germans, had had to pretend he was a German, too, so ferocious and apparently genuine were the old chief's imprecations and one-fisted gestures against the British. If Donald Kemp and Margaret Duncan had fallen into his clutches, either they were still there as prisoners or had been ceremonially slaughtered. McLeod did not wish to have to investigate, and so as discreetly as possible he made his camp in a place by the river almost surrounded by trees.

He had just finished eating and was lying in his tent when he heard first a drumming of hooves and then splashes. Looking out, he saw coming across the river about a dozen horsemen, led by a huge man with a black beard. Their silence alarmed him as much as their guns and knives. If they had been calling in a friendly way some of them at least would have been yelling like cowboys at a rodeo; but all rode in silent ferocity. Their horses were small but powerful. Anxious though he was, McLeod couldn't help but admire their horsemanship. Few in the world were their superiors. The favourite sport of these wild horsemen of the north was a game called buz-kashi. He had seen it played several times; it was like American football played on horseback, with a dead goat for a ball.

He decided to call himself a Frenchman, on his way to join his compatriots at an archaeological site about fifty miles away. Therefore, as the two leaders, Blackbeard and a man with a moon-like, sadistic face, came crashing through the trees right up to the tent, McLeod was waiting to greet them in French. The fat man suddenly drew a long sword and held it high.

They came right up, pushing their horses' breasts against him. From that conquistadorial height they scowled down. The fat man, for practice it seemed, took a slash at the tent and made a great slit in it. The sight provoked him to an imbecilic joy, and he would have slashed the tent to pieces, and McLeod, too, if Blackbeard hadn't growled to him.

'Who are you?' asked Blackbeard, of McLeod.

'A Frenchman, on a journey,' he replied.

'What journey?' yelled the fat man, slavering with anger. 'Who gave you permission? Don't you know this is our country?'

McLeod explained he was going to join his colleagues who were digging up the ground looking for relics of the past.

All the riders frowned with contempt. Digging was women's work. But only the fat man laughed. It was peculiarly shrill laughter. McLeod had already noticed he was the only one without a beard; indeed, his great chubby cheeks and several chins were totally hairless. Nevertheless, he seemed to have more authority than Blackbeard. The latter would have no compunction about killing, but he would do it with a thrust of his dagger or a bullet. This fat madman, though, would take pleasure in first slicing off ears, nose, hands, and that other member which, it seemed, had been sliced off him.

'You must come with us,' said Blackbeard.

'Why? I am a simple traveller, doing no harm.'

'Our chief wishes to see you.'

'Who is your chief?'

'Abdul Raof Khan.'

As McLeod had feared, Raof was the hater of the British.

'And I am the son of Abdul Raof Khan,' cried the fat man shrilly. 'I shall be the next chief.'

McLeod noticed that Blackbeard scowled at that, and glanced round at the other horsemen.

'The chief is very sick,' he said.

'But I am not a doctor,' said McLeod. 'I have no medicines to cure a bad sickness.'

'No doctor, and no medicines can help him now. Tonight, tomorrow, he will be with God.'

Well, thought McLeod, why the hell look so glum about that? The old rogue had had a long enough innings of rape, pillage, and banditry. In any case, wasn't death for him an entry into paradise where brown-eyed houris would be so accommodating he'd never miss his right hand. It would be different, though, with the fat son: the orthodox paradise might well be hell for him.

McLeod took care not to let his thoughts show on his face. It was wiser to wear a bold but not provocative look. If he appeared frightened, they might slit his throat like a sheep's.

'Our chief wishes you to come and speak with him before he dies,' said Blackbeard.

'But he does not know me. I am sure he did not know I was coming.'

'We have been watching the road for days for an Englishman.'

'But I am not an Englishman.'

'No. So you say,' Blackbeard scowled. 'But you are a feringhee, a Christian foreigner. You will have to do. If we wait the chief will die.'

'His hand is white,' cried the fat man. 'It will do.'

McLeod couldn't resist glancing at his right hand; it wasn't white, but he knew what the fat man had meant.

'For many years,' said Blackbeard bitterly, 'the chief has had only one hand, though the meanest beggar in the city has had two. With one hand he has been a great warrior; no horseman in the land has been more skilful. But it is different now. He says a man of pride cannot go to God with one hand missing. What God gave must be returned in the same condition. So our chief says.'

McLeod couldn't be sure whether this was meant as a grim joke on Blackbeard's part or whether the chief really did want to take someone's hand with him when he died. It was only too likely that the old scoundrel, in pious, delirious shame at having to give back to God not only a soul steeped in bloody sin but also a maimed body, had conceived this notion of having a feringhee's hand buried with him. No doubt in the past, wielding his little tyranny, he had punished enemies by such amputations. Perhaps the friends of some such enemy had made his son a eunuch in revenge.

To remember that that very morning he had listened to the younger generation enthusiastically reciting 'Cute twin mules' was incredible enough, but hardly reassuring. This was still a country where the vague but sincere efforts to progress by a few were despised and so crippled by millions of traditionalists. Yet had not hospitality to strangers always been an important part of that tradition: McLeod had himself in remote poverty-stricken villages been given the best carpets to sit on and the choicest mutton to eat.

'How far is it to your chief's house?' he asked.

'An hour's ride.'

'Can I go in my car?'

'There is no road for a car. You must ride a horse.'

'Perhaps he cannot ride a horse,' shrieked the fat man.

McLeod ignored that. 'Who will look after my belongings while I am away?' he asked.

'I shall leave two men,' said Blackbeard.

'Maybe you will not come back,' cried the fat man, shrilly giggling.

McLeod glanced up at Blackbeard, but found no reassurance in his dark scowl.

'Here is a horse,' said Blackbeard, as one of the two men who were to wait led it up.

As nimbly as he could, McLeod mounted. The first thing he discovered in the saddle was how useful two hands were. Was driving, he wondered, easier than riding to a man with only one.

As the fat man rode past he reached out with his sword and struck McLeod on the hand. He used the blade, but even so the blow was hard enough to cause pain and bring blood. When McLeod looked round at the other men, he thought some of them gave him smiles, stern enough but sympathetic. One, indeed, tapped first his brow and then his loins with his middle finger. It might have been an unconscious gesture, but it also might have been a hint that the chief's son was out of his mind, and also that there was a reason for it.

As McLeod splashed across the river in the midst of that tatterdemalion but formidable cavalry, with his two hands conspicuous on the horse's black mane, he realised that he would never be allowed to return to the capital parading a bleeding stump. Safer and tidier, after the truncation, which would of course be performed by the fat sadist with the out-of-date sword, to put a bullet in his head and dump him into a hole that even warriors like Blackbeard might condescend to dig. Besides, they had still to discover he was British.

For over an hour he rode into the hills. Several villages were passed that could have been turned into fortresses, and held against an enemy a thousand times stronger. But the village where the chief lived turned out to be the most impregnable and also in the most beautiful setting. The armoured cars and tanks of the government forces would have been useless there. Bombs might have destroyed it, but the planes would have had their wings sliced off by the sharp pinnacles that like giant porcupines lay all around.

Children, dogs, cockerels, donkeys, and even women watched the horsemen and their prisoner pass in the gloaming. One very old woman, shouted for eagerly by her small grand-daughter, came tottering out of her house to look, and then to

snarl and spit in exasperated disappointment at seeing so little
to deserve her attention. Even more than Blackbeard and the
fat smirker she frightened McLeod. They might cut off a hand,
to punish an enemy; she was capable of tossing it to her dog to
eat. Perhaps in the same battle where the chief had lost his hand
her husband and sons had been killed.

Women were still working in the fields surrounding the
chief's house. They stood up and waved, so that McLeod could
hear their bangles jingle. Some of the escort waved back. He
did not know whether to be encouraged or further alarmed by
that exchange of greetings. In any society where lovers waited
for leisure and darkness to embrace, men could be treated
hospitably, or men could be murdered: love and cruelty were
each part of the pattern.

Inside the large compound of the chief's house, where they
dismounted, some scraggy hens ran about squawking, and a
donkey, whose pizzle almost touched the ground, stood mel-
ancholically with its nose against a wall. It wasn't a sight to
inspire a man balanced on the edge of the grave. Perhaps no
sight could. Certainly the hills didn't, mauve in the twilight, or
the tip of the moon gleaming above them.

They had to wait until Blackbeard and the fat son went in
to prepare the chief. It had turned chilly, and McLeod
couldn't keep from shivering. He thought his guards might
interpret it, not quite unjustly, as fear. None of them,
though, stood near him, so that McLeod was reminded of
the Englishman in Newbold's poem condemned to die at
dawn in sight of the Afghan snows. During the hours of
darkness, sitting alone, he had remembered scenes of home,
and so, sustained, had died in the morning like a gentleman.
No cute twin mules and lovelorn donkeys had wandered into
his memories.

At last Blackbeard came out. He gave orders for McLeod to
be searched; this hadn't been done before, apparently just to
show how little they feared him. It seemed the chief was more
cautious. But it wasn't McLeod's revolver they were looking
for; this they handed back to him still loaded; his passport, with

its gilt Britannic coat-of-arms, they took in ahead of him to their chief.

As he passed through an outer room where mutton was roasting on a charcoal fire, McLeod heard the weeping of women, and was so angered by it he nearly shouted to them wherever they were skulking to shut up for Christ's sake. To grieve for an old bloodstained rogue was bad enough, but to do it while he was still on his deathbed planning more cruelty and bloodshed was intolerable. Likely, too, somewhere a pet mullah or two were oiling the gates of paradise.

The room in which the chief was lying was opulently furnished with red carpets and the skins of leopards; they covered walls as well as floor. The chief lay on and under quilts, red in colour with birds like pheasants embroidered on them in gold. His head and shoulders were propped up by red pillows. His left hand, clenched and veiny, was visible; it lay upon McLeod's passport.

McLeod was taken aback. He had been expecting to see a crafty old cut-throat; instead he saw the patriarch of a tribe of harmless shepherds, with long white hair and beard, and a face refined by suffering and compassionate thought. Or so it seemed. Over his shoulders was a tunic with brass buttons; it was, McLeod realised, part of a British officer's uniform.

Round the walls about a dozen men squatted on the carpet. They looked not half so formidable off their horses; but concern, too, was making them less fierce. On one side of the bed sat the fat man, nursing the naked sword on his knees. On the other side crouched Blackbeard, both fists clenched, brow twisted in thought. It struck McLeod then that his own trouble might not be the only one; indeed, to them, it was insignificant. Who was to succeed the old man? That was obviously the question tormenting Blackbeard and some of the others. The fat son seemed unconcerned; he took it for granted the succession would be his, beardless eunuch though he was. If the chief were to die soon, in the next hour or so, as seemed very likely, judging by his pallor and weakness, then McLeod was going to find himself embroiled in a small civil war. He didn't think it would last long, but there might be a bullet or knife in it for him.

The old man lifted the hand off the passport to beckon to McLeod to come and sit near him. McLeod did so, with his hand pressed against his breast in greeting; but that was rather too conspicuous a place for it, and he quickly let it slip down to his side.

The chief smiled. 'The Frenchmen,' he whispered, 'are gone.'

At first McLeod didn't understand.

'About three weeks ago their lorry went past.'

Now McLeod understood; he meant the archaeologists.

The frail hand stroked the passport. 'British,' murmured the low voice. From the passport his hand crept to the buttons of the tunic and to a badge, that of a British regiment.

'I killed him,' said the chief, 'with this hand. He was young, and so was I. It was a long time ago.'

McLeod noticed one of the toughest-looking men involuntarily grinning in a kind of sympathy; squint-eyed, he picked his nose, and grinned thus.

Then they all stirred and muttered. The chief had pulled out his right hand from under the cover, and was holding it up; or rather he held up what should have been his right hand. Somehow the stump was not hideous. McLeod even felt for a foolish moment that if he was to have his own hand cut off, and the stump was to look like this, it might not be so horrible after all. But, of course, the chief's, come gory and terrible from war, had grown domesticated over those thirty or forty years.

'A life for a life,' whispered the old chief.

His fat son regarded that as a sentence passed. His own hands grew itchy on the sword.

'A hand for a hand,' said the chief.

This time McLeod was sure it was not a threat to him, but rather a strange ironic comment by the dying old man on his long, revengeful life.

'The British,' muttered the chief, 'were good fighters; but they could not conquer us.' Suddenly he turned to Blackbeard and asked if McLeod had been given anything to eat and drink. When Blackbeard replied that there hadn't been time, the old man was as indignant as his weakness let him. Someone was sent to have a meal prepared. McLeod saw no reason to say he had already eaten. In eating there was safety for hands, especially here where fingers were the only cutlery. Besides, once a man had eaten their food they would be reluctant to molest him.

The fat, would-be executioner was huffed. It seemed to McLeod, though, that most of the men seated round the walls were pleased.

The chief again signed to McLeod to bend near.

'Why do you speak our language so well?' he asked.

'I lived in your country for four years.'

The chief smiled. 'Good. You will do something for me.'

'If I can, I shall be pleased to.'

'Once, long ago, I insulted your king.'

By treacherously waylaying troops? Or murdering some envoy promised a safe passage?

'I spat on his face,' said the chief. 'It was a picture, you understand. I found it in the pocket of this tunic. The man was dead. I killed him. I spat upon it. I should not have done that. It was not a thing for a chief to do. When you go back to England you will tell him that I, Abdul Raof Khan, apologise.'

'That king is dead,' said McLeod.

The old man was disappointed like a child. 'To his son then, who has taken his place.'

'His son is dead, too.'

'To his grandson then.'

'He had no grandson. It is his grand-daughter who now sits on the throne.'

'A woman?'

'Yes. The British have a queen, not a king.'

The chief seemed personally affronted; his confidence in the paradise so close now was weakened. He looked afraid.

'Go and eat,' he whispered. 'When you have finished, come back and we shall talk again.'

McLeod bowed himself out. Blackbeard went with him, and two others chosen by nods. The chief's son, like a great fat baby, played with the sword; he seemed unaware that his own death might be as close as his father's.

In an outer room a rug was spread out, and on it was set a large plate heaped with orange-flavoured pilau, rice with pieces of tender mutton and chicken imbedded in it. There were also bowls of grapes and little pots of tea. A sniffling youth attended them.

Blackbeard sat beside McLeod, but though he was a courteous and attentive host his thoughts weren't on the food at all, but rather on what might be happening in the chief's bedroom. There the succession might at any moment have to be decided. McLeod noticed that their guns were placed where they could instantly seize them. For his own sake he hoped the old man would last the night.

He decided to ask Blackbeard about Kemp.

'I believe,' he said, 'some months ago an Englishman and his wife were travelling in these parts.'

Blackbeard made no sign he had heard.

McLeod perservered. 'According to the authorities in the capital,' he said, 'they were killed, murdered, by the people of a village not so very far from here.'

'Far enough,' said Blackbeard contemptuously.

'You know the village then?'

'As I know the dung in the fields. They are not our people.'

'I know that.'

'They are worthless creatures who scrape in the dirt like hens. If they are attacked, they do not fight like men; they hide or lie down to be flogged like sick curs. They own no horses. Even their headman rides on a donkey, with his feet in the dust. But in truth there is no headman. As in your own country, it is a woman who rules them. She is the headman's mother: she is very old, with only one eye; but she is the only one with any guts.'

'It is true then they killed this English couple? They don't sound as if they would have the courage even to do that.'

'In the snow,' said Blackbeard impatiently, 'they become desperate like wolves. A man and his wife asleep, they might attack in the dark; the whole village together, with the old woman urging them on.'

'Yes, that's how it might have happened. But did it actually happen? It is not so far from here. You would have heard the truth. Did they really kill this man and woman?'

Blackbeard was about to answer when a clamour suddenly broke out, and into the room rushed a man, with bubbles of blood at his mouth, gasping that the chief was dead and he himself had been killed by a supporter of the fat son. When he collapsed on his knees, in an attitude of prayer, the hilt of a knife was seen protruding from his back; the point was in his lungs.

Blackbeard was on his feet roaring to his men. Tramping pilau all over the carpet, and kicking cups about, they snatched up their guns with greasy hands and dashed out.

The man remained on his knees. Prayer in that country, though often performed in public with dozens of people close enough to tickle your upturned soles, was nevertheless a strictly private affair. Here now was the most grotesque example of that respected privacy.

McLeod had himself to keep alive. If he tried to flee, he would be sure to get lost and be savaged by some domestic hound or wild leopard; but if he remained there, and the fat son prevailed, he would be killed by inches. The blood that dripped from the kneeling man's mouth and vanished into the blood-red carpet might have been his own, so sharply painful did his neck and wrists become at the thought of that long sword in the big melon-like fists.

He crouched in a nook beside the fire. From inside the house came yells, screams, wails, and shots; from outside the neighing of horses, more wailing, and the braying of a donkey, perhaps the one with its nose against the wall. He saw it with the face of the frustrated Major at Mazarat. He heard, too, in his imagination that class in the school at Kalak reciting with relish: 'The fat son of the chief. He has no hand. The carpet is red. The dead man prays. The old man enters paradise.'

About half an hour later Blackbeard, accompanied by some of his men, came swaggering in. There was no sign of blood on them; it might have been washed off, for their beards glistened with wet. Blackbeard was solemn enough, but his followers were so jubilant they insisted on shaking hands with McLeod.

'If you are ready,' said Blackbeard, 'you will be taken back to your car.'

'I am ready.'

'These two men will go with you.'

'Thank you,' said McLeod. 'May I have my passport back? I'll need it.'

They looked at one another.

'You cannot have it,' said Blackbeard.

'But I am a traveller. I need my passport.'

'We need no passports.'

'If you were to cross the border into another country, you would need them.'

Blackbeard grinned at his men who grinned back. One of them slipped away. Others meantime had carried out the man who had died on his knees.

As they waited, McLeod wondered what had happened to the fat son. Likely he had found very few to support him. Blackbeard for weeks must have been preparing this coup.

The passport suggested what might have happened to the legal heir. It was sodden with blood. An effort had been made to dry and clean it, but it was still sticky and moist, and between some of the pages the blood was still fresh enough to run. McLeod held it by a corner with distaste. It made little difference whose blood it was; what mattered was that it wasn't his own. He dropped the passport into the fire and rubbed his hands on his trousers.

The others laughed, Blackbeard among them. They went outside with him to watch him in the moonlight climb on to the horse and, with his two escorts, ride away. Other horsemen rode in the gate as they rode out; these shouted what McLeod took to be allegiance to Blackbeard. The whole village was roused, and the other villages through which they passed on the way to the car.

His guards were silent, but when they reached the Land-Rover and their two comrades there they became gleefully communicative. With his own sword, they shouted to the stars, the chief's son's head had been cut off by Blackbeard. It had fallen like a child's ball on to the old man's breast, where the feringhee's passport had been lying.

When they had gone McLeod was glad to creep down to the river and plunge his hands into it. But the sight and feel and even the smell of all that blood could not so easily be washed away. As he crouched there by the river, in his mind the blood was spurting not from the headless trunk of the eunuch, but from the bodies of Kemp and Margaret Duncan. It wasn't necessary for him to go to that village now, he was at last convinced.

Eleven

That night he slept badly and had another terrifying dream. In it the small Minister stood in the middle of a vast desert, smiling, and pulling the petals off yellow roses to let them drift down upon the faces of the young mother and her dead baby. In it, too, the fat eunuch's head kept falling from the head of the great Buddha at Kalak, falling, but never reaching the ground where McLeod, passport in hand, waited in a rain of blood with the teacher, the headmaster, and the Governor's secretary.

Next day he remained by the river to rest and prepare for the long journey back, but found he could not rest, in body or mind. He wandered along the river-bank and into the poplar woods, gazing for half an hour at a time at the water or the green leaves, and not knowing what, if anything, he hoped to see. When he thought of Kemp and Margaret Duncan they were as little weight in his mind as the leaves that he broke off the thin, silver-barked trees were in his hand.

Next morning early when he suddenly began, in a frenzy he could not control, to strike camp he did not know until the last moment that when he drove off it would not be back towards the capital but onwards to the village.

For four hours he drove across that bleak, steppe-like country where there were no roads, no trees, no thorn-bushes, no flowers, no insects even. Yet there were times when he felt the high, shimmering yellow plateau was thronged, as if an army was marching across it. So strong was that illusion sometimes that he had to stop the car, in a kind of paralysis, until those thousands of men became again dust and rock and shadow and emptiness. There were other hazards and obstacles which usually he would have faced with stoicism; but now these bogs of soft, tawny dust three feet deep, these ripples of hard sand, and these great humps of rock like gigantic clots of blood, had in them a conscious malevolence that again and again unnerved him.

The silence, too, was hostile: the noise of the engine and the crunch of the wheels were its attendants merely; they added to rather than broke it. To break it he shouted; gibberish it must have been, for he could not remember it afterwards. Once he fired his revolver. And once he stopped the car, jumped out eagerly, and began trudging through the ankle-deep dust. He was almost a hundred yards from the car before he stopped, sobbing, and found he had no purpose at all. There as he stood, sweating and panting, he saw quite close a small heap of bones, and could hardly convince himself they were not his.

When, in the heat of the afternoon, he arrived at the small valley where the village was situated, he found it even more barren than he had expected. It was a mystery why any people should have chosen to settle there. No stream could be seen, and the small fields must be watered by hand from a deep well. In the lee of the high red cliff was the village, a cluster of mud hovels; and at the foot of the cliff were the dark holes of caves. In one of those Kemp and Margaret Duncan had been murdered.

As he sat in the car, listening to birds that sang with an inexplicable insistent joy, he watched the village lead its life. Some dots of red and blue were women and girls working in the fields. Men carried on their shoulders skins of water from a well in the centre of the community, and emptied them into canals that ramified through the fields. In the distance he thought he could make out a small herd of sheep and goats.

On a hillside near by children tended some bony cattle. One played a pipe. Its music, amidst the happiness of the birds, was happy, too. The others, though aware of the car, laughed and gabbled shrilly; then three of them, boys about ten or twelve, came cautiously towards it. Their friends screamed advice and warning. The boldest of the three, the one who kept in front, unlike his two companions had no loin cloth, only a dirty white shirt. As he waited for them, impatient at their slowness, he kept scratching at his privates.

McLeod stared at them in disgust and aversion. With their shaven heads, dark faces, and clawing hands, they were more like a species of monkey than human children. To prove it, when they were about thirty yards away, they began to grub in the earth, for stones to throw at the car, McLeod was sure. He got out his gun ready to fire it above their heads and scare them off. They raced and leapt about in their search, picking up stones, examining them, and dropping them again. Now and then one pleased them and they kept it. Did they think, thought McLeod, that stones of some particular colour or shape had a magical power to shatter glass and metal?

In about ten minutes they came together and began a laughing argument, with glances at McLeod. At last the one naked from the navel took all the stones they had selected and walked shyly towards the car. He kept grinning. Behind him his two friends leapt up and down, their fists clenched. On the hillside a cow lowed sourly, and the child went on piping.

Suddenly, when he was about fifteen yards from the car, the boy raced forward, with his skinny arm outstretched. Lying in the palm of his hand were three pebbles, as smooth and oval as birds' eggs, and as delicately coloured. He waited outside the car for half a minute; then, when McLeod made no move to accept the gifts, he placed them on the bonnet, which was so hot from the sun he snatched away his hand and grinned up at McLeod, who could not grin back.

This child, he thought, this kind of monkey that knew how to offer gifts, also knew treachery and murder. The gaunt head, noticeable ribs, and swollen penis, were so hideous to him at that moment that he could have shot the boy without any compunction. Did he not look so like Jamil, the confessed murderer, that he was probably his son? But then, every child in this village was a murderer's.

Starting the car, McLeod drove slowly down the track among the fields and houses. The women in their red and blue rags stood close together and hid their faces. The men had stopped their work, too, and were staring towards the car, with expressions of fear. One who had been relieving himself behind a boulder stood up. Some children, alarmed by the adults' stillness, ran excitedly about, looking for parents.

When he stopped in an open space beside the well, McLeod noticed that one of the stones placed on the bonnet by the boy was still there. Close to the well was a shrine, the usual jumble of stones, sticks, and rags. Behind it, on the slope up to the caves, were many sharp stones that indicated graves.

Slowly they gathered, and approached. If ever he had been doubtful about their guilt, their cringing meekness, their expectation of punishment, would have ended it. Amidst all the signs of poverty, malnutrition, and disease, were others: bruises, useless arms, limping legs, bodies uncomfortable with pain. A few, the boldest, tried to smile a ghastly welcome. Three young girls even tried to ogle him from behind their filthy hoods. They seemed to McLeod as sexually repellent as female baboons. If these had been raped by the police, for whom had been the punishment?

He sat there, leaning on the driving-wheel, wondering why he had come, and wishing he hadn't. Once he felt for his revolver in his pocket, but it was obvious that as long as he left before darkness he was safe enough from these human jackals. The only danger from them in sunlight was that they might transmit a loathsome disease. He saw one man half of whose face was shrivelled away.

The headman was there, a long, skinny, glaikit, grey-haired fellow whose loin swathings trailed behind him like a tail. He knew it was his duty to go forward and speak to the stranger, but he lacked the courage. Imbecilely sniggering, he stood with his right hand pressed against his breast; or rather with half his hand, because three fingers were missing; a bayonet could have sliced them off.

McLeod decided to come out of the car. As he did so, they all cried out and crept back; but one little girl of about seven, with her bare-bottomed brother of three clinging froglike to her back, came boldly forward and stood gazing up at him. He ignored her and knocked the pebble off the bonnet of the car. She followed him.

'Hallo,' she said, without a smile. 'Hallo. Hallo.'

He frowned down at her. The infant on her back, frightened, began to wail.

'Hallo,' the child repeated, still as dourly.

She must surely have learned the word from Donald and Margaret. Children in the capital used it often enough, to help them in their begging; but then, they encountered many foreigners in the streets. Here English-speaking travellers might pass once in a lifetime. The last such travellers had been Kemp and Margaret Duncan.

'Hallo.' It was now a challenge.

Still he could not bring himself to respond.

An old woman, assisted by another not just as old, was standing beside the headman. She must have been telling him what to do, for soon he came shuffling and sniggering towards McLeod. On his left cheek was a large sore, probably syphilitic, but it could also have been a wound gone bad; a blow with the butt of a gun could have caused it. At first he couldn't speak, his mouth was so parched with fear. When he did manage to make sounds, to McLeod they were unintelligible, so that he wondered if these people spoke a dialect he wouldn't be able to understand. Yet he had understood Jamil in prison well enough. Gap-toothed and big-tongued, the headman kept trying.

The old woman screeched from the background: 'Welcome to our village, sahib.'

The rest muttered among themselves and looked at her in terrified reproach. She was certainly not speaking for them. No stranger would ever be welcome in their village again.

She screamed furiously at them: 'Are you beasts or people? We shall give the stranger tea, and then he will go.'

McLeod addressed the headman. The little girl, with her weeping brother on her back, kept staring as if she had a loaded gun directed at his heart, and in a moment would fire it.

'I do not want tea,' said McLeod harshly. 'I shall tell you why I have come.' He raised his voice so that all of them could hear him. 'Four months ago two friends of mine, an Englishman and his wife, came here to this village, just as I have come today. Perhaps you offered them tea, too. But in the night, when the snow was falling, you killed them. In the prison in the city I have spoken to the two men from your village who used the knives; but all of you were guilty, and I have come to see what kind of people you are who welcome strangers and afterwards murder them in the dark.'

While the rest whimpered and turned their faces away, the old woman in a rage hobbled up to him; her attendant, afraid, held back. She pulled her cotton hood aside. One of her eyes was white and sightless, but the other glittered with a far-sighted determination. Her skin was so tight and transparent the shape of her skull was seen before the features of her face.

'You have spoken to Jamil?' she asked.

'Yes.'

'He is my son.'

'Old woman, he was your son.'

Sharp to see his meaning, she smiled. 'He is dead?'

'Yes, he is dead.'

She kept smiling. It was a smile he was never afterwards to forget. By it she accepted and forgave, and then passed beyond acceptance and forgiveness.

'God's will be done,' she said. 'And Sarwar, too?'

'Yes.' Then he surprised himself, but apparently not her, by demanding to see the families of the two murderers.

'You have looked at us, sahib,' she said. 'You have seen that we are very poor and miserable. It has pleased you. But surely there has been enough punishment?'

'Can there ever be enough punishment for such a crime?'

She put her hand on the little girl's head. 'This is Jamil's daughter,' she said. 'The boy is his son. They are my grandchildren.'

The little girl still stared up. She had shot him dead a dozen times, and she wished him dead again.

'Which one is their mother?' he asked.

'She is not here. She is in her house, sick. If you have a child in your belly, it is not good if men with heavy boots kick you, whether the kicks be just or not.'

The last thing he had expected was irony, if it was irony.

'Just enough,' he muttered; but, he thought, nothing in the world could make them just.

'So she is sick. When I tell her her husband is dead, perhaps she will get well again. It is bad to be afraid that a thing is going to happen; but after it has happened, when nothing can be done to prevent it, when God has decided, you are able to live again.'

Her other son, the headman, feeling it was time he earned his eminence, approached again.

'Sahib,' he whined, 'my people beg you not to bring the policemen back.'

The whole village then burst into a monkey-like lamentation.

The old woman listened in scorn. McLeod felt sure that the Colonel and his men had not dared to harm her; she had the spiritual force that Mrs. Bryson had seen in Donald Kemp. Yet, being their brain and heart, had not the evil to propose the murders and the courage to carry them out originated in her? It might well have been that most of them, from sheer pusilla-nimousness, had not been willing, but had been forced into it by her. He could imagine her making each one handle the knives before, and touch the blood after.

But how to show hatred to an old woman half-blind and smelling of disease? He knew he should get into his car and drive away from this place; but he could not; here, awake, he was having his most hideous dream.

'If you show me the place where it happened,' he cried, 'I shall go. The police will not come back.'

If he had asked for a dozen of them to be shot before his eyes, there couldn't have been greater consternation. The headman covered his face with his hands and wept. Others did the same. Everywhere McLeod looked men and women were covering their faces and weeping. Except in one place: in front of him the old woman and her grand-daughter were dry-eyed and scornful. Because of them, he thought the contrition and terror of the others must be genuine.

'You will show me,' he said to the old woman. He turned and looked up with a shudder at the caves in the foot of the cliff.

'Yes, I shall show you,' she replied, and lifting her head she cried to the rest not to follow but to go back to their work. She would show the sahib what he wanted to see, and then he would go away.

Then she told her grand-daughter to put the infant down, and help her to climb the path. The child at once obeyed, and let her brother slip down to the ground, where he sat bawling. Ignoring him, she placed her grandmother's hand on her shoulders and both of them set out slowly towards the path that led up to the caves.

McLeod let them get about fifty yards ahead before he followed them, keeping the same distance away. The path passed boulders which were the village latrines; behind every one were sun-dried excrements. It passed, too, a corner of the graveyard with tombstones sharp as slates, without inscriptions.

Some of the caves were inhabited. Out of one a naked child tottered to meet the old woman. She bent and patted its matted, filthy head, and then shouted to its mother who, suckling a baby, crept timidly out to seize the child and drag it howling into the hole in the rock.

No wonder, thought McLeod, murder had been done here. These people had not reached the stage of morality; baboons he had thought of, baboons he thought of again.

In front, the old woman and the little girl had stopped outside a cave. It must be the one.

He did not hurry. He halted to look back down at the village. No one was working; everyone was staring up at him. Then, outwardly calm but with his heart thumping audibly, he went on and stood at the entrance to the cave for half a minute before suddenly stooping and entering. It was more like a cell than a cave, with a stink of dung and urine. The floor was of the same red rock as the walls. There was just room for two persons to lie stretched out, if they lay close together. He imagined Donald and Margaret asleep there, their feet towards the entrance; and it was easy after that to imagine the two chosen men creep in, their movements softened by the snow, their knives ready. Well, Margaret had been spared the terror of death; she must have been killed in her sleep; and Donald too had passed straight into whatever after-world he had condescended to believe in. It would certainly not be the same as Purdie's, with angels in white nightshirts strolling amidst flowers, and blessing the sweet celestial picnickers.

Afterwards the bodies would be dragged out into the snow, where there would be more room to strip and rob them. In the morning they would be carried to the wood and left for the wolves.

As he came out of the cave he wondered where that wood was. In the last thirty miles he had seen none. It must lie beyond the cliff, on the way to the mountains. Yet why had they gone to so much trouble when ten yards away was a graveyard? Was it because they felt they would never feel at ease walking over the foreigners' bones? And stupid though they were, they would realise there was always the risk that investigators might come with spades.

Looking at the old woman, he was so startled by the expression that appeared swiftly on her face that he glanced round and put his hand into his pocket where the gun was. It was the expression of someone who, after long struggle, had taken a desperate decision; it might have been to set her baboons on him.

She came close to him, with the girl resolutely accompanying her.

'So,' he said, 'it was here?'

She shook her head. From the blind eye moisture streamed, not tears, for there were none from the other, which gazed up at him staunchly.

He frowned. 'You said it was here.'

She shook her head again, and he remembered she had said nothing, had left him to infer that this was the place.

'Where then?' he asked angrily.

She pressed still closer, so that the stench of her body, unwashed for years, nauseated him. He noticed again the traces of excrement on her skirts.

'Nowhere, sahib,' she whispered, 'nowhere.'

Some of the villagers, led by her son the headman, were coming up the path, shouting to her.

She glanced past him at them, contemptuously.

'We did not kill your friends, sahib,' she said.

The little girl, stern-faced, was shaking her head at last.

'As you can see, sahib,' whispered the old woman, 'we are very poor. Are there any people in the world poorer than we are? But we do not kill our guests. We share with them the little we have.'

Before he could, as it were, seize her distorted mind and shake the truth out of it, up panted her son and the rest. They pulled her away from McLeod, and began to blame her for – so McLeod learned as he listened – telling the truth, for not maintaining the lie.

Imperiously she screamed and struck her son and any other who tried to keep her back from McLeod.

'Your friends did not sleep in there,' she cried. 'That is for sheep. They slept in the house we keep for visitors. Sometimes in a whole year we have none, but we must keep a house ready.' She pointed to a house by itself under a few small trees, in the greenest place in the village. 'For three days they were our guests. On the fourth, after their donkeys were rested, they went on.'

'Donkeys?' He had always thought of them as on foot.

'They came on donkeys and they left on them. We do not kill, and we do not steal.'

He turned from her to the rest.

'Is this the truth?' he shouted.

At once there were screams of denial. She waited until they had died away, and were replaced by weeping.

'It is the truth, sahib,' she said.

'And where did they go, when they left?'

She pointed to a goat track that wound up the cliff about a hundred yards along. 'It leads to the lakes.'

'At Faizabad?'

'Yes. I think, sahib, that your friends are not dead.'

'Why do you say that?'

'Because two days ago a man and his son came here, on good horses. They were passing, they said, and they spent a night with us. But few people ever pass here. This is the dusty edge of the world, as you can see. These two came from the mountains, and after they had asked their questions they returned to the mountains.'

'What questions? About my friends?'

'No, sahib. About us. They came to see with their own eyes and to hear from our lips what had been done to us. I think it is well known. It is even spoken about in the city.'

'Yes, it is. But why should these two from the mountains want to know?'

'I think you know why, sahib. Was it not because your friends are in his valley now, and he is afraid? He is afraid that what was done to us might be done to his people also.'

'Why should it, if they are still alive?' But again he knew the answer.

'It is not wise to make the great ones look foolish,' she replied.

'Did this man say they were in his valley?'

'No, sahib, and we did not ask him. You forget that for us your friends are dead. Did we not kill them, and were we not rewarded for it?'

As he stood gazing at her, he heard the birds singing, with that terrifying joy. She heard them, too.

'Now he does not know what to do,' she said.

'Who does not?'

'The man who came.'

'What was he like?'

'He was tall, taller than any man here, taller than you, sahib.

And very strong. There was more hair on his face than there is ever corn in our fields; a black beard like a warrior's, with grey hairs of wisdom in it. Since he came from the mountains his eyes were blue, sahib, like yours.'

'And the boy?'

'Like his father, he was tall and strong; and he had blue eyes.'

'Had he, here, on the left side of his brow, a round scar?'

'He had. I think you know them, sahib?'

'Yes. Yes, I know them.'

They were Azim and his son Karim. When McLeod had visited the valley five years ago, Azim's father had been headman. He had been an old man; now he was probably dead and Azim had taken his place. There the succession would have been peaceful and lawful. But then, as McLeod remembered, Azim had been the most remarkable man in a remarkable community. With his courage, resource, intelligence, and above all his sweetness of mind, he could have been the successful ruler of an empire, never mind a small alpine valley. His son had been a boy of twelve at the time of McLeod's visit; he had swum in the river with McLeod, and gone hunting in the forest with him.

'Where they came from,' said the old woman, 'the ground is fertile. There are many trees and a big river. They have much to lose.'

'You said, old woman, that he does not know now what to do. What did you mean?'

'It is not my business, sahib. I should not have spoken.'

'But you did speak. What did you mean?'

She smiled, and pointed to her good eye. 'I do not see well, sahib. Sometimes I see what is not there; often I do not see what is there. This man from the mountains told me nothing of his purpose. What I know, what I think I know, I saw in his eyes. Perhaps I did not see it.'

'What do you think you saw in his eyes?'

She came close to him. 'Think, sahib,' she whispered. 'What would I see in your own eyes, if you were in his place? If your friends are found in his valley, his people will be punished.'

'Why should they be, if my friends are unharmed?'

'It is certain, sahib. So he must decide. It is very simple. I saw it in his eyes.'

'When was he here?'

'Just two days ago. He will sleep tonight at the lakes. You will find him there.'

He looked at his watch. Yes, there would be time to catch up on Azim and his son. But first there was this mystery to clear up, why had this intelligent, resolute old woman made her son, and her whole people, confess to murders they had not committed? And why even now were they all so distressed by the old woman's revealing of the truth?

She read the questions in his eyes.

'Many policemen came here,' she said. 'They came to find us guilty. No one had seen your friends after they left here. So the police were angry and we were afraid. At first we said your friends had not been. That was foolish; a little pain showed it to be a lie. They searched the village.'

'And they found a gold bangle and a photograph?'

'Yes. We told the truth then, but they would not believe us. They wanted us to say we had killed the Englishman and his wife; so in the end we said it.'

Yes. In the same circumstances he might have said it himself.

'Who was in command of the police?'

She described the Colonel. 'He told me about his own children. Perhaps he is a merciful man, but he did not think it necessary to be merciful to us.'

'I was speaking to him in Mazarat a few days ago. Since his visit here his wife and his three children have died, of smallpox.'

She did not show the slightest flicker of satisfaction. 'It is God's will,' she murmured.

'Do you think in his heart he believed you were guilty?'

'There was hatred for us in his heart; that was enough.'

'Why should he hate you, unless he believed you were guilty of these murders?'

'In his eyes we were lower even than we were in yours, sahib, when you first arrived.'

There was nothing McLeod could say to that. She had only one eye, but little escaped it.

'We were not so low in your friends' eyes,' she said. 'They were glad to be our guests, and they treated us as their hosts. The woman was very kind, though she was not well. I think she was with child, though she did not say so. The bangle she gave to my grand-daughter who was sick then. Not this one; her sister, older than she. She is dead now. The picture the sahib gave to me. It was of his mother, he said.'

'I saw it. The police showed it to me. There was blood on it.'

'Blood is easily found, sahib. There is more blood in this country than water. There was none on it when they took it from me.'

They stared at each other in silence. The birds exulted.

'Do you believe what I have told you?' she asked.

He nodded. 'Yes, I believe you. What is to be done? You are innocent and yet you have been terribly punished. Your son has been put to death. Who can compensate you?'

She smiled. 'God, if He wills it,' she said.

He hesitated. 'I can give you a little money.'

She shook her head, though her son was nudging her.

'Why not?' asked McLeod, holding out notes worth about ten pounds.

'If we go to the town with money,' she said, 'they will say we took it from the feringhees we killed.'

'If you have the blame, why should you not also have the benefit?'

'No. We cannot take your money, sahib. If you wish to help us, forget us. Tell no one you have been here.'

'But should I not go to the police and tell them you are innocent?'

'No. They would not believe you, sahib. And we do not want them to come here again, even to tell us they made a mistake.'

He saw the glint of irony in her eye.

'But if I go to the mountains,' he said, 'and find my friends, then it must become known you are innocent.'

She smiled, in such a way that he shuddered.

'What do you mean?' he asked.

'I did not speak, sahib.'

'But you were thinking.'

She smiled again, but would not speak.

He knew what she had been thinking; that if he went to the mountains, he would not find Donald and Margaret alive; that Azim for the protection of his own people must do, without retribution, what her people had been punished for doing, yet had not done. It was a situation that justified that half-blind smile.

Again he looked at his watch. He must overtake Azim before the valley.

'He was sick, too,' she murmured. 'Very sick.'

'Both were sick, then?'

'Hers was the sickness of life.'

Was she inferring Donald's had been of death?

'Were they happy together, in spite of their illness?'

'Sahib, am I, in this place, a judge of happiness?'

He could say nothing, but it was obvious that what her son had said so mildly in prison was true: Donald and Margaret, at that stage in their pilgrimage, had not been happy.

'You would not drink tea with us before,' she said. 'Will you drink it with us now?' As he hesitated she added: 'If you do this, sahib, you will compensate us. There will be time afterwards to reach the lakes. Your car is faster than horses.'

He nodded. 'I should be honoured to drink tea with you,' he said.

Proudly, with her hand on her small grand-daughter's shoulder, she led the way down to the village. Some laughing, some weeping, but all of them troubled, the rest followed.

Twelve

Those lakes at Faizabad were to McLeod more impressive than the giant Buddhas at Kalak. Here, too, was indifference to man and his attempts to scratch a brief living out of barren earth; but here it was neither ostentatious nor megalomaniac. Suddenly, in a land as arid as the moon, there they were, blue and translucent or suavely green, set in deep canyons of red cliffs. From the edge could be glimpsed, twenty fathoms down, large, tranquil fish, and on the tops of the hills round about fossils of sea-shells could be picked up, thousands of miles from the sea. Along the cliff edges the ground was so dry it would have seemed nothing could ever grow and live in it; yet hundreds of prickly plants grew in the dust, with flowers and leaves of strange shapes and colours, and myriads of grasshoppers as big as dragonflies kept leaping as high as a man's hand in a constant chirp and dance. Very different from the gentler flowers and humbler grasshoppers of the lush, West Highland sea-meadows.

Little wonder that a shrine containing the bones of a holy man had been built on the shore of the large blue lake. Every few years religious gatherings were held there, and lepers from all over the country were bathed in the water. That lake was like a gigantic cup, over whose rim of grass and flowers the water kept spilling, in a series of waterfalls. The height of the cup was increased every thousand years or so by the lime left by the water. It was possible, though hazardous, to walk along the rim, with the lake lapping at one's feet, and on the other side a sheer fall of fifty to a hundred feet into a plain of shining water. In a country of handleless cups, from which companionable tea was drunk several times a day, it was easy to see how the lake, in the native imagination, could appear as God's cup, from which He, too, often drank.

Beyond the lakes rose the high mountains. The moon was gleaming on their snowy tops as McLeod approached. Across the big lake he could see, on the shore under the shrine, a fire burning, and thought it must have been lit by Azim and his son. Wrapped in striped blankets, they would be crouched close to it, for always at night a breeze blew coldly down from the mountains. They would see his headlamps and would watch them all the way round until they disappeared at the head of the lake, to appear again only a hundred yards from their fire. They would take him for some foreign tourist come to admire the lakes, and they would be instantly hospitable in inviting him to use their fire and drink their tea. What they would do or say when they learned he intended to accompany them back to the valley, he did not know. Visitors were rare, and made all the more welcome for that, especially as their religion bade them treat strangers well, and Azim was a man who took the humane side of his religion seriously.

When McLeod arrived at the shore under the tomb, he noticed that there were three figures huddled beside the fire. The third would be the old man who kept the shrine clean, and guarded the saint's spirit from the djinns that rose out of the lake and screamed down from the hills. He was as remote as a djinn himself. Though he accepted food from travellers and sat for hours by their fires, he never spoke to them. At sunset and sunrise, on the terrace outside the chamber in the rock where the tomb was, he would wail out weird, sad prayers, more like the complaints of a bitter lifetime than homage to God. In his presence private conversations became more private; his re-collections were impossible to guess.

As McLeod walked over from the car to the fire, Azim, immensely tall in his white turban against the moon shimmers on the lake, rose to greet him.

'Salaam, stranger,' he said, his voice as deep and friendly as McLeod remembered it. Yet was there not in it a slight harshness of anxiety?

'Salaam,' said McLeod, and squatted down on a piece of rug beside the old guardian of the tomb.

Azim poured tea into a bowl and handed it across. In the firelight his face, with its black beard and glittering eyes, seemed, despite its hospitable smiling, not ruthless yet, but pledged to be.

I'm imagining it, thought McLeod; the man is just tired after a long day's dusty ride; and the boy, look, grinning out of his blanket, is as cheerful and carefree as he was five years ago when he took me swimming and hunting in the valley.

'This is my son, stranger,' said Azim.

McLeod smiled at Karim, who was now as big and brawny as his father.

'I am not a stranger,' he said. 'Do you remember, Karim, five years ago, when you were a small boy, not so tall as your gun, you took an Englishman hunting in the forest above your village?'

Karim turned to look at his father. They would remember him all right, thought McLeod. Donald would have spoken about him.

'You have grown very big,' he said to Karim. 'Do you kill the bears now with your hands?'

Laughing, Karim felt in his clothes and took out a hunting knife. It was one McLeod had given him.

McLeod turned to Azim. 'Do you remember me now?' he asked.

Azim hesitated and then shook his head. 'I do not remember you,' he said. He frowned at his son, angry with him for having produced the knife.

'I remember you, Azim,' said McLeod, 'and all the people of your valley.'

'You are a man who travels about the world,' said Azim. 'You will meet many important people. Surely you must have forgotten us.'

'No. I shall never forget you. The days I spent in the valley were very happy. Your father, the headman, is he still well?'

'My father is dead.'

'I am very sorry.'

'He was an old man. He was not unhappy to die. If the time is ripe, death is acceptable. No one can live forever.'

'No. And your wife?'

'She is well.'

'And your other sons? I think you had four others.'

'They are all well.'

'I have five brothers now,' murmured Karim, grinning.

'Congratulations,' said McLeod, laughing. 'Five boys. Did your wife hope for a daughter?'

Azim could not maintain his grimness; he had to smile and nod.

'And my host Aman?' asked McLeod. 'He was very kind to me. I hope he is still well, though he was an old man, too.'

'He still lives.'

'No man lives more,' said McLeod, remembering with affection the white-bearded, good-hearted, garrulous old busybody in whose house he had eaten.

'It is different now,' said Azim. 'He is sick and lies in his bed all day; often he is in pain.'

'I am very sorry to hear that.'

Then they spoke about others in the village, among them Fazir, another old man, so bigoted in religion that at first he and his three big, dour sons had been the only ones who refused to welcome McLeod, and who latterly had done it with condescension. If Kemp had tried to do any proselytising, the rest would have listened with politest scepticism; but Fazir and his sons would have been appalled.

'Life with us never changes,' said Azim. 'It has not changed for hundreds of years. We do not want it to change. We are too simple for the new ways of the world.'

Karim then, as if to show his disagreement, fumbled in his clothes again. This time he brought out and furtively showed one of those small toys in which three tiny pellets under glass have to be shaken or guided into three holes. In this one, though, the holes were at the nipples and pelvis of a woman completely naked. McLeod had seen similar things for sale in the bazaar, imported from India.

Karim replaced his treasure carefully. He did not heed his father's grunt of scorn.

'When they visit the town,' said Azim, 'they bring back such things.'

'Usually it is in the spring when you leave the valley,' said McLeod. 'It is unusual for you to leave it at this time.'

Azim stared at him.

'In two or three weeks' time,' went on McLeod, 'there will be snow on the pass.'

Still they waited. The old man beside him sucked at his tea.

'Today,' said McLeod, 'I came from a village called Haimir.'

Even Karim made no sign; instead, he offered to refill the old man's tea bowl. The offer was silently accepted.

'I was told,' said McLeod, smiling, 'you were there yourselves two days ago.'

Azim turned to gaze towards his horses, one of which had neighed. Then he calmly put another piece of wood on the fire. In the flames that sprang up McLeod thought he saw a flash of ferocity come and go on that bearded, Christ-like face.

'We were not at Haimir,' said Azim. 'I have heard of it, but it is not in our way.'

'The people told me you were there.'

'They do not know me.'

'They described you so well, and Karim, too, that I recognised you both.'

'Many men in this country look like us. We are ordinary men. In any case, I understand these people at Haimir are known for their lies. They have no guns, therefore they fight with lies, like women. So I have heard it said. Personally I know nothing about them.'

'You have not heard then that some months ago those people at Haimir murdered an Englishman and his wife who visited the village?'

Karim had now filled his own bowl and was concentrating on drinking; but his eyes now and then glittered across at McLeod.

'In our valley,' said Azim, 'we hear very little. Certainly we are not curious about people such as these.'

'It was a dreadful crime: to kill guests. All over the country it has been talked about. Every good man has been ashamed. The king himself has spoken of it as a great disgrace.'

'Why did they kill them?' murmured Azim. 'Was it to steal from the dead bodies?'

'So it is said. But can there ever be a noble reason for murdering guests? Surely in God's eyes no crime is more unforgivable?'

'I cannot read the mind of God,' whispered Azim, with a peculiar, quiet bitterness.

McLeod was convinced; Donald and Margaret were in the valley; and Azim was returning there, minded to put them out of the way.

'I wish to return with you to the valley,' he said.

Karim gasped as though the tea had scalded his mouth. His father smiled, and shook his head.

'This is not the time to visit us,' he said. 'You said yourself there will soon be snow on the pass. Then no one can leave. You would have to stay with us until the spring.'

'I should enjoy that. But in two weeks it is possible to enter and leave again.'

'It is a hard journey for so short a stay.'

'It would be worth it.'

Azim glanced towards the Land-Rover. 'You have no horse,' he said.

'I see you have a spare one.'

'What about your car?'

'This old man would look after it for me.'

Azim smiled at the old man. 'He looks after the moonshine on the water,' he said.

'Five years ago,' said McLeod, 'when I was leaving, you invited me to come back.'

'I am sorry. It is different now. Foreigners are not allowed to enter the valleys.'

'Who prevents them?'

'The soldiers of the government. They guard the passes, day and night, summer and winter. We must have special permission ourselves.'

Was this at any rate true? wondered McLeod. If soldiers were guarding the pass, it would be almost impossible to cross it without being stopped.

'I am sorry, my friend,' said Azim.

'Do these soldiers ever go into the valley?'

'This summer they were with us for four weeks; three hundred of them.'

'What were they doing? Searching?'

'Searching? For what would they be searching?'

McLeod didn't answer, and for a minute there was silence, broken once by a horse neighing.

'They were practising warfare,' said Azim, 'in the forest, on the river, upon the mountains.'

And all the time Donald and Margaret had been hidden from them. The whole community would have been implicated. This was another complication. No wonder Azim was desperate.

For a moment then McLeod thought of giving up, of leaving Azim and his people to decide in their own way what was to be done about Kemp and Margaret; their decision would be as just as any he could make himself.

Azim spoke quietly, but so earnestly McLeod shivered.

'You will not come to our valley,' he said. 'You must not. It would not be safe.'

'Because of the soldiers?'

'It would not be safe.'

'I have come a long way.'

'If it was ten times as long, you must go back.'

Then abruptly excusing himself he went with his son to look to their horses. They did not come back to the fire, where McLeod sat for a few minutes more, beside the silent old man. The latter, he realised, must have seen Kemp and Margaret if they had come that way, and there was no other way they could have come, bound for the valley. But his memory was far less

accessible than the valley itself, and his confidence lay beyond
the moon.

'The stars have fallen into the lake,' murmured McLeod. A
horse neighed, but the old man was silent.

'This place is holy,' went on McLeod. 'Many pilgrims come
here, and many foreigners like myself.' He felt he was speaking
to the moon and the fire's embers, but he persevered. 'About
five months ago an Englishman and his wife came to the lake,
on their way into the high hills. He was a tall man with a red
beard; she had golden hair. Do you remember them? I know it
is not easy to remember after such a time, especially when you
will have seen many visitors since. Perhaps you cannot remember now, but in the morning it will have returned to you.
If you can tell me about my friends, the Englishman and his
wife, I shall be pleased to pay God well for the information. To
God truth is precious; and to those who serve God it must be
precious, too.'

He rose up, wished the bundle of rags and blankets good
night, and went over to the car, to put up his tent. When it was
up, and he was about to creep into it, he saw the old man still
huddled by the fire.

He was awakened hours later by a harsh shrill acclamation
from the terrace above. It was the holy man saluting the sun,
and praising God; the salutation went on for a quarter of an
hour. During it McLeod crawled out, shivering in the cold, and
discovered that Azim and his son had already left. Rushing
across to where their camp had been, he saw horse dung so
fresh that it was still warm; it was pink, too, with the radiance of
the sunrise. He ran gasping up the path that climbed the cliff.
The ascent took him ten minutes. At the top, gazing into the
red hills, redder now in the dawn, he at last made out in the
distance the two horsemen, with the two pack horses. They
were heading steadily into the mountains. It seemed to him this
flight was proof that Donald and Margaret were in the valley,
and surely it was a sign that Azim wanted to waste no time in
returning to do what he had convinced himself must be done.
But, thought McLeod, Azim was a good man, with a kindly

nature; how could such a man commit cold-blooded, preme-
ditated murder, even if he thought it was to protect his own
kin? Well, in the recent war had not men of ordinary goodness
been able to kill without compunction, because it had been in
their interests to do it? They had not thought the killings
murders, and afterwards their consciences had been calm. Azim
and his people would have an even clearer, simpler vision.

When he went down to the terrace he could not see the old
man who, his prayer finished, had gone into the chamber in the
rock where the tomb was. Looking in, he saw him there,
squatted in the cold shadow beside the sacred lump of concrete.

'Salaam,' said McLeod.

Again it was hopeless; he might as well have addressed the
bones inside the tomb.

For a minute or so he hesitated there, glancing now in at the
entranced priest and now down at the bright blue lake. Then he
left, in an excitement he could not control. Like Azim he, too,
had made a decision: to go to that valley, even if he had to climb
the mountain range to reach it. Perhaps he had decided on
death also: his own; he might be carrying his bones up to the
snow which would preserve them for the rest of time.

Thirteen

It seemed to him he had at least to try. To cross a mountain range of over twenty thousand feet required a well-organised expedition. He was alone, with equipment hardly suitable for attempting Ben Lomond in winter. Nor had he much experience or intrepidity as a mountaineer. As a boy he had spent many happy days accompanying shepherds up and down West Highland hills, and once had helped to dig sheep out of twenty-foot snowdrifts. As an undergraduate he had walked or scrambled to the tops of several Scottish peaks, the highest, Ben Nevis, four thousand four hundred and six feet. Altogether, hardly a sufficient apprenticeship for an attempt on these vast, icy solitudes.

That first night he camped almost on the snow-line; the car could take him no further. Tomorrow he would leave it here, hidden among these great carbuncles of red rock, and ascend on foot. He calculated that he would have only about ten thousand feet to climb to reach the summit ridge; but what impassable ice faces, what crevasses in perpetual glaciers, what gullies, deep and wide enough to engulf the Blue Mosque at Mazarat, he might have to encounter he could only guess at, with foreboding tinged somehow with a desperate joy. He could not understand that feeling of elation; it certainly wasn't that he was looking on this attempt as a proof of his courage, or even of his devotion towards Donald and Margaret. He half expected them to be dead by the time he arrived, if ever he did arrive.

That night the moon and stars were very near, and it was fiercely cold. Once, with more relief than fear, he heard the howling of wolves; though they might tear him to pieces, yet they were living creatures and broke the vast hostile silence. When he finally fell asleep it was to dream again, this time that the leader of those wolves was Donald Kemp. The face attached to the four-legged shaggy body was clearly seen, and the expression of it was so curious, with such a peculiar kind of greed or hunger, that McLeod could not tell whether it was human or wolfish. The pack behind was shadowy, but all the time there was a probability, growing almost to a certainty, that at any moment they would change into human shape, and reveal themselves as Azim and his people. Margaret Duncan was not amongst them, either in her own shape or a wolf's. Yet it seemed to be she who sang the song that, every now and then, stopped the wolves in their howling and running. He could not say what part he himself took in the dream; he was in it somewhere, but he couldn't be seen or heard.

Next morning very early when the sun was bright but the air still icy he set off. Though he felt sure he could not succeed, he was optimistically careful in his preparations. Unless the weather turned bad, or his nerve failed, he should be able to spend at least two nights on the mountain; but with luck that should be more than enough. Tomorrow he ought to reach the summit ridge, and either glissade or pick his way by inches down some suitable slope on the other side; it would depend on his finding some such slope while he had still strength enough left to use it. It was, he thought, as he began the long upward trudge, an opportunity for prayer; but he could not think God was interested or could be persuaded to be.

For the first few hours he climbed steadily. At first the snow lay scattered here and there in heaps, like graves; but soon there was no red earth, only snow, shining so brilliantly that without dark glasses his eyes would have been in agony. It was easy snow to walk on, crisp after the night's frost, so that for a while he felt exhilarated by what seemed his astonishing progress. But, hours later, with the muscles of his legs and shoulders aching, and the back of his neck burning from the sun, he was still far from the topmost ridge; certainly he would never reach it before dark.

All day, however, the sky remained clear, as if deliberately, in serenely contemptuous contrast to the confusions that gathered in his mind. The tireder he grew the greater the confusion; and, to his dismay and shame, suffusing it all was self-pity. Sometimes, resting body and mind, gazing down the slopes of ice and snow, he tried to pretend his pity was for humanity, represented by the Colonel of Police at Mazarat, by the old woman, by the young mother with the dead baby, by the school teacher, and above all by Azim, condemned to kill. But somehow everyone of those in recollection became himself, so that in the end the pity was always self-pity. Yet there were many times when he couldn't believe it was really he who was climbing there amongst those great camels' heads of ice. He was the Colonel seeing himself in delirious dying dream; he was the old woman remembering the cool ambitions of girlhood; he was Azim's son lured here by visions of these white breasts of snow. Sometimes, it seemed, he was all these at once.

It became too dark to go on. So far there had been little danger, as long as he could see to choose a safe way; but now, with blue shadows invading every cranny of the mountain, no way was safe. With a calmness and certainty of purpose that amazed him he set about preparing to spend the night in the snow. As he worked hard and confidently building a wall round his tent, he seemed at the same time to be standing apart, admiring his own efforts. There were two of him at least, and suspicion of more; so that when he was at last lying in his sleeping-bag in the tent, drinking the soup he had heated on his Primus, he could not be sure whose gloved hands held the mug, or whose lips so cautiously sipped. At first that doubt was exciting: an identity so much more hopeful than his own might be discovered. But soon it became frightening, and for a long time, unable to sleep, he lay in terror of a stranger who occupied not just his tent but his body, too. Outside, like an unknown enemy, the cold waited.

He must have slept, for his apprehension of the brightness of dawn was sudden. Thereafter it took him long stiff minutes to gather enough will-power to pull aside the flap of the tent. The snow over all the great mountain, in its innumerable fantastic, transient shapes, was red as fire; and the sky, so close above, blazed too. Yet it was not so much the mountain and sky that were fiery; it was the solitude and cold; or rather it was the silence to which everything else, red snow, solitude, and cold, intensely contributed. In the beginning, in God's mind before decision to create formed, such silence had been; and in the end, too, after man's decision to destroy, it would be again.

It was broken, to his astonishment, by the buzzing of an insect. At first, dazzled, he couldn't see it; then he saw it was a fly. He must have carried it up with him in his pack, and it must have sheltered in the tent. But he could not, somehow, feel for it any love; rather he feared it, for its tiny noise only made the vast red lonely silence more ominous. It had concentrated in it a tremendous transmigratory terror that represented the millions of humanity dead in a universal holocaust. Thus, it implied, would the experiment of life resume.

But he did not try to kill it, although it flew about him as he made and ate breakfast, landing on his face and even his lips, as if insisting on the companionship he had rejected. Anxiety to escape from it, as much as foreboding of what the mountain still had in store, made him eager to start climbing again. After the night's frost the top of the snow was still firm, and he was able to make such good progress that, hours later, he was creeping up the last slope to the summit ridge, himself tinier than a fly on the white carcase of the mountain. His own fly climbed with him all the way.

On the top, gasping and wiping sweat from his face, he looked down, through breaks in the weird, shining cornices, at the greenness of a forest far below. Everywhere the view was magnificent and exhilarating. A man shut up in a prison cell for years might often have tormented himself with imagining such a vista: here the eyes could see as far as the imagination, and what they saw was more beautiful. All round him towered sharp peaks with veils of transparent cloud appearing and disappearing about them. Behind and below, past slopes on which he could see his own forlorn footmarks, the wide plain shimmered.

Beyond the valley were mountains lower than this on which he stood; beyond them lay Russia.

Yet it might still be that he had been lured into a trap. When he began to search for a way down, none seemed possible; there were no smooth slopes down which to glissade or crawl inch by inch, no gully littered with rocks, but only sheer precipices edged with high, brittle cornices. Even to glance down was dangerous; two or three times he started a small avalanche and almost went down with it. And all the time the ridge in front grew narrower, and at one point soared into pinnacles that he would never be able to surmount.

Then, just before the first of the great needles of ice and rock, he found what he was looking for; there, in a break in the precipice, a narrow slope, covered with unbroken snow, ran down not too steeply, until it vanished behind a ridge a long way below. Beyond that point there might be impassable difficulties not visible from the top; if there were, it was very likely he would die trying desperately to pass them. But there could be no turning back now. He could not say whether it was a good omen or bad that the fly at last had left him; the breeze on the summit had been too strong and cold for it.

There were, after all, no surprises, no heartbreaking barriers. The slope continued, never too steep for glissading so that he went down quickly; even so, it was two hours later when he reached ground where the snow lay in patches as hard as the many boulders that covered the mountainside; and the moon had begun to shine before he arrived at the first tree.

Soon afterwards he pitched his tent, wearily made himself something to eat, and crawled into his sleeping-bag, to dream again, terrifyingly. In his dream the river that surged through the valley was of blood.

Fourteen

Next morning he crept out of the tent into sunshine so bright and fragrant he could not help being reassured. Despite his premonitory dream of blood, here was an interlude of peace. The fragrance rose from the pines around him and the flowers far below. He remembered those flowers in their lush variety of scent and colour. It was a memory purged of evil, like one of infancy; but as he stood there, breathing deeply, disillusionment was drawn into his mind as inevitably as the keen sweet air into his lungs.

What awaited him in the valley was hardly an innocent situation: Margaret Duncan, pregnant, and perhaps ill, in mind as well as body; Donald Kemp, ill too, with his mind distorted into some incalculable shape; and Azim, returning with news that would compel all his fellows to share his own vow of liquidation. McLeod himself might become the third sacrifice.

Before setting off on the long tramp downhill, he made a pile of three flat stones, in the way pilgrims did to commemorate their visit to a shrine. This was to mark the place where he had descended from the ridge; perhaps he might have to ascend there, too. All the way down he would make similar heaps.

It was about an hour later, going steadily down through the forest, that he met the bear. It was seated on a grassy bank, gnawing at something bloody it held in its front paws. Its posture, its use of its paws for eating, and especially its look of astonishment and indignation at being interrupted at its breakfast, struck him as grotesquely human. Though it was huge and black, with a head like a lion's, its tawny eyes, as it kept staring at him, seemed puzzled and contemplative rather than murderous. While he stood with his revolver in his trembling hand, it rose up, growled, took a step towards him, and then went lumbering off among the trees, carrying its food to be finished where there was privacy. He saw the drops of blood, that might have been his own, glistening on the grass where they fell.

When it was gone the forest was no longer private for him, although at that moment he could see no living creature, not even a butterfly or an ant. In his imagination, however, sunlight on tree trunks and lichened boulders became leopards, wolves, and jungle cats, which he now remembered infested these northern forests. None of those would be as aloof as the bear.

Yet, despite that constant fear of wild beasts, those hours of going down through the forest were pleasant, perhaps because the pines, with their lilac-coloured branches and pearl-like scent, reminded him of home: he might have been a hiker coming down through the Rothiemurcus on a fine summer's day. Lower down, too, the azaleas and rhododendrons, in a blaze of flowers, reminded him of the gardens at Inverewe in his native Ross, where rhododendrons from the Himalayas and lilacs from China flourished side by side on the shores of the sea-loch.

Late in the afternoon, he began to smell wood smoke and hear, above the roars of falls in the river, the cries of children. These, as he saw half an hour later, through his binoculars, were playing in the green fields beside the river, dressed in vivid yellows, reds and blues, so that they were like flowers themselves. Some women were washing clothes: he could hear them slapping these against smooth stones. In the fields men and women were working, kneeling amidst the tall plants. He noticed oxen going round and round threshing what must have been the season's second harvest. Birds flew about, green, blue, golden; others sang. Pigeons moaned in the trees around him. Far behind him in the forest some animal began to snarl desperately, and went on for at least ten minutes.

This was the valley as he remembered it: sunny, fragrant, fertile, busy, happy, and if not quite carefree at any rate enduring such inevitable cares as illness, old age, and death as honourably as any people could. He could scarcely believe that their existence was now threatened, and for so fantastic a reason as the harbouring of two guests. Surely if Donald and Margaret were allowed to go, unharmed, the authorities, represented by the Minister and General Hussein, would be so pleased that the disgrace of murder was removed from the reputation of the country that they would be grateful towards Azim and his people, rather than vindictive? Yes, he thought that likely enough, especially if he, Donald, and Margaret were determined in their pleas for indulgence; but he could also see why Azim, with simpler calculation, might not think it likely. After the fuss and rejoicings were over and Donald and Margaret had returned to Britain, for more rejoicings, the authorities might decide they had been made foolish and deliberately deceived by these too independent primitives, who ought therefore to be chastised, not just for their own sakes, but as an example to similar remote communities that were in the habit of living to themselves. The chastisement need not be any more severe than that inflicted on the villagers at Haimir. Indeed, no one need be put to death, for after all no murders had been committed; it would be enough to take away a dozen or so young men, including Azim's own son, and conscript them in the army, so that when they were allowed to return to the valley they would have lost the taste for its traditional dignity of life.

He decided to camp for the night in a grassy hollow above the village. Tomorrow morning he would go boldly down, and seek out Donald and Margaret. To sneak down in the darkness, with some hope of finding and rescuing them, did occur to him, but he dismissed it as folly. If there was to be any deliverance, it must be with Azim's knowledge and help; and he felt confident that help could be won. As he lay in his tent, he remembered as a symbol the guest house where he had been lodged during his last visit. Before he had entered, it had been strewn with the petals of a white flower like meadowsweet, and sprinkled ceremonially with perfumed water. Set apart from the other houses, it stood in a garden of roses, azaleas, and rhododendrons. From its windows the views of the white peaks above the dark-green forest had been superb and exhilarating; and always, in the air as its best fragrance, had been the smell of wood smoke.

He slept longer than he had intended. At dawn the crowing of cocks had wakened him, but he had gone to sleep again. Now outside the tent he heard the bleating of sheep, and also murmurs which at first he thought were made by a stream flowing near by. Then he realised they were voices talking quietly.

Opening the flap of the tent he crept out. There, still on his knees, like a sheep, he found himself gazing into the face of a merry young lad whose pipe and staff showed him to be the shepherd. Beside him stood a brawny, red-faced, black-bearded man with a gun; and all round stood others, with guns, calf-length boots, and bandoliers of bullets, looking more like guerilla soldiers than peaceful farmers.

McLeod stood up. The morning was so splendid and invigorating, and the nearness of the human community so reassuring after the solitude of the mountain, that he would have still gazed about him in appreciation, even if his visitors had been twice as threatening as they were. Some of them looked dour enough to shoot, but before he could feel fear this pleasure of the peopled sunny morning had first to be savoured.

He noticed a group of people gathered below at the bridge across the river. There were women among them.

The leader, the burly fellow with the red farmer's cheeks, was smiling.

'Who are you, stranger,' he asked, 'and how did you come here?'

'I came over the mountain, but I am not a stranger. Five years ago I was a guest in this valley for ten days. My name is McLeod.'

'McLeod?'

Smiling, each tried to remember the other. They succeeded at the same moment. This was Rafiq, a cousin of Azim's; physical strength and cheerfulness had been his outstanding characteristics then, as they seemed to be now.

'You are Rafiq,' said McLeod, and looked round at the others to see if he remembered any of them. He thought he did, but the recognition was submerged in a surge of fear at the hostility and suspicion on every bearded face. These, he realised, must be the chosen fighting men of the valley, ready at all times now to repel intruders. If the government soldiers came here to burn and destroy as they had done at Haimir, these men would resist to the death. That the outcome might be total destruction would not deter them. This mountain toughness was a quality he had underestimated.

'Do you remember me?' asked McLeod.

Rafiq nodded.

'I met Azim your headman at the lakes at Faizabad.'

'Did he know you were coming here?'

'I asked him to let me come with him, but he refused.'

'So you came over the mountain, like an enemy? A friend enters a man's house by the door, not by a hole in the roof. If Azim said no, why did you come?'

McLeod decided to bring his purpose boldly into the sunlight. 'I shall tell you why. I have come to speak to the Englishman and his wife, who are here.'

The others had drawn nearer during this conversation. One of them let out a yell of dismay and flung a clenched fist at the sky. His companions glared at him and cried to him to be quiet. He was quiet, but looked as if at any moment he might shoot.

Not only were Kemp and Margaret there, but everyone in the valley was aware of the danger their presence represented. Before Azim had gone to see for himself what had happened at Haimir, the predicament had been much debated. The whole valley was tense with fear and expectation.

Rafiq whispered to two of them, who at once made for their horses tethered a short distance away. They mounted and rode quickly down the hillside. They were going, McLeod felt sure, to see to it that Kemp and Margaret were hidden well away.

He saw then what might happen. He would be kept captive until Azim arrived, and until the sacrificial murders had been done, hastened on by his blundering upon the scene. Perhaps they would take place that very night. If so, tomorrow he would be released, offered an apology, given liberty to investigate, and then smuggled out, either by the way he had come or through the pass. For the rest of his life he would never know the truth. If he returned to the capital he would have only suspicions to tell of, hardly credible even to himself.

He wondered if after all it would be better to capitulate and fall in with their scheme.

Rafiq came back to him. 'How long did it take you to cross the mountain?'

'Two days.'

'And all the time you were alone?'

'Yes.'

'In the mountains there are spirits that enter a man's mind and make him see what is not there, and believe what is impossible. It is a kind of madness. Surely it has affected you? You speak of an Englishman and his wife in this valley. There are no such people. It is a dream you have had.'

One of the other men cried: 'You must go back, stranger. It is not safe for you here.'

The rest shouted agreement.

'I have no food left.'

'We will give you food.'

'I am tired. It is a long, hard climb. I think it is likely I should die in the snow.'

'That is your business.'

McLeod appealed to Rafiq. 'What has happened? When I came here last time, without an invitation, I was treated so well that afterwards, everywhere I went, even across oceans, I have praised the hospitality and friendliness of this valley. Now you wish to kick me out as if I was a dog. What has happened? Why have you changed?'

'We have not changed,' said Rafiq, the smiler.

'Surely you have? The last time smiles and welcome, this time anger and guns.'

'It is our business, but I shall explain. If you had come

through the pass, you would have seen that it was guarded by soldiers. No foreigners are allowed into the valley now.'

'Why not?'

'In the next valley there are men with machines measuring the earth and making deep holes in it.'

So this was what his little Excellency's hint had meant: the Russians were prospecting in these valleys. Certainly neither they nor the government would be pleased to have foreigners, especially from the West, wandering upon the scene. Could it be possible then, that Donald and Margaret had really been taken for spies, and either shot or abducted across the border? It was not only possible, it was quite likely.

'If the soldiers found me here,' he asked, 'what would they do to me?'

Rafiq shrugged his shoulders.

'What would they do to you?' asked McLeod.

Rafiq did not reply. Instead he told McLeod to get ready, and ordered the shepherd lad to help him. The horsemen mounted and waited until the tent was struck and the rucksack packed. Then, escorting him, they walked their horses down the hillside, scattering the sheep, through the fields, to the people gathered at the bridge.

These were in contrast to the villagers at Haimir, not only because they were well fed and healthy, but also because fear sat ill on their handsome, proud faces. Some, he noticed, smiled at him in anxious sympathy.

From his horse Rafiq addressed them.

'There is no need to be afraid,' he said. 'He is a stranger who lost his way; he came over the mountains. Today he will rest; tomorrow he will return. There will be no trouble.'

A tall, thin, white-bearded old man with a peevish, pious face crept forward. McLeod recognised him as Fakir, the religious leader.

'Is it not better,' he asked Rafiq, 'for him to return at once?'

'He says he is tired and hungry.'

'Give him food. Let him rest in the forest.'

'I shall take him to my house.'

'You say he lost his way? It is a strange way that crosses the mountain.'

'Be careful what you say, Fakir. This feringhee speaks our language well.'

The old man had been staring into McLeod's face. 'I know him,' he said. 'He was here before. He was a spy then, for the English government, and he is a spy now.'

'It is possible,' agreed Rafiq.

'I am not a spy,' said McLeod. 'I have come here as a friend.'

Others pressed forward to look at him. He did not remember most of them, but they did him. They wanted very much to welcome him; the constraint that prevented them had some of the women sobbing.

'Listen,' cried Rafiq loudly, so that they could all hear. 'For two days the stranger was in the mountains alone. He is suffering from mountain madness. He says he has come here because he wishes to speak to an Englishman and his wife, who, he claims, are in the valley. I have told him this is nonsense. Azim should return today. He will decide what should be done. In the meantime, the stranger will be kept at my house. No one will try to see him. I hope everyone understands?'

They nodded, but one old woman cried from the background: 'You are to do him no harm.'

Rafiq smiled at her. 'He will not be harmed.'

'It is not only the stranger who suffers from mountain madness,' she cried. 'We all do. Look at the guns. Look at your fingers itching to shoot.'

Friends gathered round and hushed her.

Rafiq was watching McLeod. Suddenly he stooped and whispered to him. 'You are not to speak.' His voice had a brittle friendliness.

But, McLeod realised, if he allowed himself to be taken away and shut up till tomorrow morning, then any opportunity to speak to any purpose would be gone. Now only was the time.

'I have not come here to bring trouble upon you,' he cried.

Then he was reeling, falling upon his knees, clutching his head. Rafiq had thrust hard at him with the butt of his gun.

McLeod took away one of his hands; it was wet with blood. His head smarted fiercely; he felt dizzy. Rafiq, staring down, was grim.

Two women rushed forward to help, but Rafiq drove his horse at them.

'We are not playing a game of children,' he cried furiously. 'Azim returns today. He will decide what should be done. Until then, the stranger will speak to no one, and no one will speak to him. Remember, he may be a spy.'

He signalled to one of the horsemen who dismounted and with the help of others lifted McLeod into the saddle. Then the small cavalcade crossed the bridge, went through the wide meadows and woods on the other side of the river, and entered among the houses which were all half-hidden by orchards bright with fruit. Stounds of pain kept shooting through McLeod's head, but he was able to see that he was being taken by a detour so that he wouldn't pass near the guest-house.

Rafiq's house was two-storeyed. In front of it was a stretch of green grass where hens were feeding, and some lively black and white birds marauded. Two women came hurrying out. One was young, with a lovely frank face that she deliberately kept uncovered; the other, much older and wizened, half hid behind a hood of dark blue. She was Rafiq's mother; her companion was his wife.

At that moment both were more interested in McLeod than in him.

From his horse Rafiq addressed them quietly. 'It is nothing. Only a stranger who has wandered over the mountain.'

'An Englishman?' asked his wife.

'I think so.'

'Is he hurt?'

'A little.'

'How did it happen?'

He dismounted and made to take his wife's hand; she would not let him.

'Why have you brought him to our house?' she asked.

Supported by two men, McLeod waited. The old woman

had walked on to the grass and was scaring away the marauders. It was her way of making it clear that what had been done and what might still be done was not of her choosing. She had given her opinion once and for all. McLeod, listening to her cluck to her hens, loved and trusted her.

Rafiq was speaking in whispers to his wife. She was objecting to having her house used as a jail. McLeod was welcome as a guest, not as a prisoner.

With his eyes shut, listening to the bleating of the sheep on the hillsides and to the murmuring voices, McLeod felt he might have been back in Wester Ross. He kept them shut.

Rafiq's wife won the argument. She came over to McLeod. When he opened his eyes he saw her smiling at him. She had on a white blouse finely embroidered in black and gold. Though her red cotton skirts were voluminous, he noticed she was pregnant.

'You are welcome to our house, stranger,' she said.

At once the old woman came hurrying over. In a harsh, shrill, sincere voice she, too, told him he was welcome. Then she rushed in to prepare for him.

McLeod thought he didn't need the help of the two men any more; but when they removed their support he almost fell. At a signal from Rafiq they cleeked him into the house and set him down on the carpeted floor, upon cushions filled with feathers.

Rafiq knelt so close his beard touched McLeod's cheek. 'You are to say nothing to the women,' he whispered.

'About the Englishman and his wife?'

'Yes.'

'They are here then?'

'I have not said so.'

'Your women did.'

'No.'

'Listen, Rafiq, the very sheep are crying it.'

They did listen, and it seemed to McLeod that those bleatings were really saying it. He felt Rafiq shudder. Outside the house the horses stamped and their harness jingled.

'Azim went to visit the village at Haimir,' said McLeod.

Rafiq said nothing.

'I was there, too. Haimir: the village where the people were punished for murdering the Englishman and his wife.'

'So I have heard. If they were murdered, how can they be here? Do you mean their spirits are here?'

'They were not murdered at Haimir. They left it safely and came here. The people at Haimir told me.'

'Are they not wretched folk who steal and lie?'

'I believed them. So they came here, the Englishman and his wife.'

'You are mistaken.'

'You are afraid to say it, because you do not know what to do with them. You fear that what happened to the wretched folk at Haimir may happen to you. To prevent it, you would kill them, and bury their bodies so deep that neither wolves nor soldiers could ever dig them up. You forget one thing.'

'We forget nothing. But what is your one thing?'

'Their bodies will not be buried in the secrecy of the forest or far away on the mountain-side; they will be buried in your own hearts; and every day of your lives you will be forced to dig them up to look at them. If you do not, your women will.'

Rafiq sighed heavily. 'This is talk to frighten children,' he said. 'Truly, you have been so long in the mountains alone that your mind is astray. This is a dream about an Englishman and his wife. It will pass away.' Then, as his wife and mother came in, the former with a carved tray with tea-things on it and the latter with a blue bowl of warm water, he whispered what was really an appeal: 'Do not speak to them about this matter. It is not for women.'

'The Englishman's wife is a woman.'

Rafiq rose up and stood aside while the two women attended to McLeod. Later, squatted on the carpet, he drank tea with him.

'When Azim comes,' said McLeod, 'tell him there is a way. I shall show it to him.'

'What way?'

'I shall show it to Azim.'

*   *   *

It was late in the afternoon when Azim came. Beard, face, clothes were dusty from travelling. He was angry and sombre as he stood staring down at McLeod.

'Tomorrow you will be taken back,' he said.

'Over the mountain?'

'Through the pass.'

'I thought it was guarded by soldiers?'

'They can be avoided.'

'Where will I be taken to?'

'The lake.'

McLeod stood up. 'Why not let the two others go with me? Take us not to the lake but to where I left my car, on the other side of the mountain. From there I shall drive them to a place I have in mind. In summer it is a green place, like this valley. But it is far from here. There I should find them. There is no reason why this should not be done. It is simple. In the city everyone will be pleased, and no one will be blamed.'

Azim did not speak, but Rafiq asked, with incredulous hope: 'This place, are there no people there?'

'Only nomads. By this time they will be moving away. Who can ever trace nomads?'

Rafiq laughed and plucked at his beard. It was obvious he thought the scheme worth considering, but was afraid to suggest as much to his leader. At least that was how McLeod interpreted his plucks at his beard, his nervous laughter, and his quick, anxious looks at Azim.

'A person who seeks the dead,' said Azim savagely, 'is mad.'

With a chill that sank to his very bowels, McLeod saw that in Azim's mind they really *were* dead. In his imagination he had already killed and buried them. Suddenly, with a furious gesture, he turned and strode out.

Rafiq waited for a few moments. He seemed about to confide in McLeod, groaned instead, and hurried out after his chief.

McLeod went, too, but was stopped at the door by two dour, stalwart tribesmen, with knives fixed to their guns. With those weapons, that could eviscerate with a thrust and twist, pointed at his belly, he watched Azim stiffly mount and ride recklessly away. Rafiq and about a dozen others galloped after him.

Above the mountains the sky was turning red, and as McLeod watched the snow on the tops turned to blood. He could feel its iciness in his own veins.

Perhaps, he thought, I have been deluded all the time; perhaps that old woman at Haimir reserved her supreme lie for me. Donald and Margaret had been murdered in her village, and had never been near this valley. If that were true, it was easy enough to find other and equally convincing explanations for Azim's patriarchal harshness, Rafiq's perplexity, and the worried pity of all the women. Their valley might indeed be doomed, for another reason altogether. If the Russians had found what they were prospecting for in the adjacent valley, they would look for it in this one, too; and the people would be relentlessly driven out. The resolution that Azim and his people were now struggling with was whether or not to resist. He and most of the men thought yes, the women had given a wiser no. If that really was their predicament, then he and his delusions about Kemp and Margaret Duncan must be a painful strain on their patience and humanity. In those circumstances their intention to escort him safely out of the valley, at additional risk to themselves, was very generous.

These were his thoughts as, barred by the bayonets, he stood by the door and watched the blood-red snow and listened to the hoof-beats die away. A red glitter appeared on the steel itself. With a shiver, he went into the house and lay down on the cushions. There seemed nothing to do now but wait for the morning.

Fifteen

Later that evening, long after the sky had faded to dark purple, it became red again, with the reflection from a great fire burning somewhere in the village. McLeod noticed it by accident when, weary of the dim small room, he went to the window and drew back the cloth that covered it. There was no glass and the cold air rushed in, making his eyes water. Then he saw the fire, or rather its reflection in the sky, and thought it must be one of the houses blazing. As he watched he supposed such accidents must be frequent enough in houses where the wood-burning stoves and the oil-lamps were primitive. Then with a cold gush of horror it occurred to him that perhaps the fire had not been accidental, but had been chosen by Azim as the most effective way of wiping out all trace of Donald Kemp and Margaret Duncan. It would have advantages: the face-to-face recognition of murder would be avoided; blood would not have to be washed off; there would be no need of burial; the roar of the flames would drown shrieks of agony and appeals for pity; and if ever it was discovered, no investigation could prove it was not an accident.

Sick with fear, he hurried out to the door where on either side squatted the guards, wrapped in blankets.

'What is happening?' he demanded. 'What is the fire?'

Neither answered. One thrust out his gun, so that the moon sparkled on it.

'Is there a house on fire?' asked McLeod.

Again they refused to speak.

McLeod covered his face with his hands, and tried not to see in his imagination the scene inside that burning house and the scene outside. It was impossible that tomorrow the sun would shine again calmly and the children would laugh in the fields by the river.

'Go into the house,' said one of the guards. 'It is warm there.'

'It is warm, too, by the fire,' muttered his companion, with a grim chuckle.

McLeod had to fight to keep himself from rushing at them and screaming. He tried to speak calmly. 'I know what the fire is.'

'If you know, why bother us with questions? It is warmer in the house than out here. Go inside.'

'They are burning the Englishman and his wife alive,' whispered McLeod, hoarsely.

One of the guards laughed. McLeod felt he had never heard a more callous sound from a human throat. He was sure that if he made a bolt for it they would shoot; even if they missed, and he managed to find his way to the fire, what could he do there except perish in it himself?

Almost weeping, he went back into the room and lay face-down on the soft cushions; they suddenly had about them a stench of sheep-fat, at that moment unbearably nauseating. These were the cushions on which Rafiq lay with his wife; on them their child had been conceived. They hoped it would be born and live a happy life here in the valley. All over the world parents had that ambition for their children. Here the deaths of only two innocent persons were necessary as sacrifices before that natural happiness could be looked forward to; but in the civilised world millions of such deaths had to be conceded.

Behind the blanket that covered the doorway he heard the old woman. 'Sahib, I am going to bed. Do you wish me to bring you tea and food first?'

He sat up. 'Tell me, what is the reason for the fire in the village?'

'They are holding a jirgha, a council.'

'Who are?'

'All the men. It is cold outside, so they have lit fires.'

He had thought her honest; now he wondered if she was as deceitful as the rest.

'Shall I bring you tea and food, sahib?' she asked wearily.

'What is the jirgha about?'

'I think you must know that, sahib. You have not answered me: do you want tea and food before I go to my bed?'

'Yes, please.' If she brought it, he would be able to question her again.

She returned in about twenty minutes, carrying a tray. He took it from her and placed it on the carpet. Her hand, touching his, was cold. She kept sighing; it could have been in sorrow, or in mere senile breathlessness. Her face in the lamplight was as shrivelled as a witch's, and, he thought, as malevolent. Her question therefore startled him.

'Is your mother still alive, sahib?'

'Yes.'

'Is she an old woman, like me?'

'Yes; and like you she likes to look after the hens.'

'But she will be rich, with many servants?'

'No; she has no servants.'

'That is strange. I thought all feringhees were rich, with many servants.'

'No; some of them are poor. You did not tell me what the jirgha is about?'

'About the Englishman and his wife,' she said quietly. The cup rattled against his teeth; he had to put it down.

'So they are here?'

'They have been here for nearly four months.'

Now that he had the truth at last, he could not be sure whether he was pleased or not: the doubt was full of guilt, and confused him. His head throbbed afresh.

'And this council is to decide what's to be done with them?'

'There have been other councils.'

'But this is meant to be the last?'

'I understand, sahib, Azim did not like what he saw at Haimir.'

'I did not like it, either. What will they decide?'

'As you see, sahib, I am not there. My opinion is not wanted.'

'But you have given it?'

'Yes.' She spoke with contempt of all opposing opinions. 'Whatever may happen, it is not allowed to lift your hand against guests who have eaten your food and done you no harm. I was taught that at my mother's knee, and she learned it at her mother's; so it has been since the beginning. It is simply the law of God. They ask me, do I wish our valley to be turned into a graveyard? I answered them, better that than live in shame with the blood of guests on our hands. So they say I am old and will die soon in any case; but my son is not old, and my grandchild has still to be born.'

McLeod went over to look out of the window. The fires were still burning, the moon still shining. It was probable that if the council decided they would carry out their decision that very night. Azim, he thought, would himself volunteer to be the executioner: dressed in white, like a priest, with gun or knife anointed and blessed. Was it so far-fetched to remember the blessing of warship or bomber by archbishop? The principle was surely the same.

'There is nothing you can do, sahib,' said the old woman. 'They have been told to shoot you if you try to get away.'

'And would they?'

'The men they have chosen would. Perhaps they will have to shoot me now? I have told you what they were anxious you should not find out. But what could you do? You could not take them with you over the mountain. You see, sahib, the English-man is very sick.'

'Very sick?'

'Those that see him say he is dying. If we wait, they have whispered, God will take him away for us.'

'What is the matter with him? Did he have an accident?'

'No. He is sick here, in the belly.'

'And the woman, is she expecting a child?'

'Yes.'

'But she is well?'

The old woman waited before answering. 'No, sahib, she is not well, especially in her mind. You must understand he suffers much pain that confuses his mind; at times almost, so they whisper to me, he is mad. That must be the reason why he tells anyone who will listen that the child to be born is not his, and that the woman is not his wife. I have not been to their house. I mind my own business. But many have been, and these tell me the man and the woman do not sleep together. Still, I have heard it is common enough among feringhees for a man and his wife to sleep apart.'

So, thought McLeod, it had returned to this; the reconciliation represented by the names scribbled on the wall above the head of the giant idol hadn't lasted. He shuddered as he imagined the situation that might now exist between them. He could not help it, but into his mind then came a recollection of two insects that he had seen that day in the forest while he was lying on the grass resting. They had been fighting each other; if he had lifted a stone above them, they would still have gone on fighting; and if he had smashed them their pulp would have been intermingled. So, it appeared, with Azim's threat overhanging them, Donald and Margaret quarrelled.

'But why did they stay?' he asked. 'Why did they not leave, months ago?'

'I believe they wanted to stay here until the child was born.'

'I was told there were soldiers here during the summer. Is it true?'

'They were here, searching.'

'For what?'

'For the two foreigners.'

'But why didn't they find them?'

'They were hidden. Azim had them taken to a hunting hut deep in the forest.'

'Why?'

'He was afraid that if they were found here we would be in trouble. We were all afraid of that. And the two feringhees did not wish to be found. I have told you, sahib, they wished to stay here until the child was born.'

'Yes.'

It was clear enough. Donald had gone back to refusing to

accept the child as necessarily his. When it was born its colour would decide.

Again McLeod felt tempted to hope that the council's decision would be to bring that stone crashing down. If, on the other hand, the decision was to agree to his own proposal, then the responsibility of the child too, born or unborn, would become his; or at least he would become irretrievably involved.

'Well, sahib, I have told you,' said the old woman, smiling, 'what Azim and my own son ordered me not to. What are you going to do?'

'What can I do?'

'Sleep. You can try to sleep. I shall try, too. I think you wish now I had not told you?'

'No. I am grateful to you.'

'Will you return to the city and tell them there what we have done?'

He shook his head.

'They would prefer not to believe you,' she said. 'It would be trouble and disgrace for them otherwise. In any case, if the Englishman has to die, and is buried in the valley, he will laugh at us from his grave. Every night when the wind blows we shall hear him laugh. You see, sahib, the soldiers whispered to us that next spring, or the next, soon anyway, it will be the turn of our valley to be torn up, as a wolf in its hunger tears up the body of a deer. Under this earth, on which I have walked for more than seventy years, it appears there is something more precious than gold. We shall be taken to some barren place on the flat plain where we shall surely pine to death. So your friend will continue to laugh from his grave.'

'And the woman?'

'No.' The old woman was on her way to the door. 'She has a good heart. She will not be laughing; she will be weeping.' Then she disappeared behind the blanket covering the doorway.

For another half hour McLeod remained by the window, staring out at the ruddied moonlight, and trying to detect among all the usual noises of the night, such as the croaking of frogs and calling of birds, shrieks of murder.

Sixteen

Next morning it was the old woman who brought his breakfast. He could hardly bear to look at her. She was not aware of any change in herself: the aches that last night had caused her sighs were causing them again; the promise of the morning sunshine was accepted without cynicism but also without emotion; the blood in her pale, swollen veins coursed just as calmly, as she handed McLeod his food. But for him she was changed, and himself with her; both were loathsome.

While he and she had slept last night, as if it was any ordinary night, murder had been done, and they had known it would be done. The bodies had been buried in some inaccessible place, but also in their minds. Everyone in this valley, from the toddler learning to speak to old women learning to do without speech, was guilty. In spite of the sunshine and of the late-season flowers and fruit there would be in the valley, today and always, a stench of guilt. With the bread at his mouth, he suddenly thought that if he were to eat it he would in a way be eating the dead flesh of Donald Kemp and Margaret Duncan.

She noticed. 'You have no appetite this morning, sahib?'

'No.'

'The bread is good. I did not make it. My daughter-in-law made it.'

And last night, he thought, she slept with your son, after he had come creeping home from sharing in murder.

'She is very clean in her habits, sahib. Not old and forgetful like me. She washes her hands many times a day, and always before she bakes.'

He glanced up, incredulous that she could be capable of such percipient irony. It was obvious she knew the true reason for his disgust at the warm bread.

'Nothing was done last night, sahib; nothing was decided, so nothing was done.'

For a moment he saw that hope if it came must be savage; he almost wished it would not come; better this feeling of fatalism, which at least was tame and could be managed.

'When my son came home last night, sahib, I was not asleep. I called to him and made him show me his hands. There was no blood on them.'

'The river is strong, and could wash away any blood that was fresh.'

'I looked at his face, too. I do not say it will not yet be done, but it was not done last night.'

'Could the council not decide?'

She interpreted his sneer with an accuracy that shamed him. 'Did you wish in your heart it had, sahib, and the thing was over? There are many this morning who will be wishing that, but I did not think you would be among them.'

He picked up the bread and began to eat. It tasted so delicious he was dismayed, almost to tears.

She hobbled away, and a few minutes later Rafiq drew aside the curtain across the doorway and looked in. He did not enter. 'Salaam, sahib,' he said, with an eager, sheepish smile.

'Salaam.'

'This morning Azim is coming here to talk to you.' McLeod went on eating.

'It is about the plan you spoke of yesterday.'

'How can your headman wish to speak about such foolishness?'

'Foolishness, sahib?'

'Yes. My plan was to smuggle an Englishman and his wife out of the valley, but everyone, including yourself, says there is no Englishman here. How then can they be smuggled out?'

Rafiq's smile grew more sheepish, and also more eager.

'Were you lying?' asked McLeod.

'No, sahib, I was not lying. If it is necessary for a thing to be said, it is not a lie, it becomes the truth.'

'Every liar in the bazaar could justify himself in that way.'

'To protect myself I would not lie.'

Another refuge of liars, thought McLeod. 'So they are here?'

'Yes, sahib, they are here.'

'Unharmed?'

'We have not harmed them, sahib.'

'Has anyone?'

'Some say they have harmed each other. There is trouble between them.'

'What trouble?'

'I do not know, sahib. He is sick, you must understand, very sick, and she is expecting a child, like my wife.'

'Am I to be allowed to see them?'

'That is what Azim is coming to speak to you about. He should be here in half an hour.'

With Azim came Fakir, representing those who had opposed this taking of McLeod into their confidence; all during the conversation his frail fist remained clenched on his beard as if on the hilt of a bright dagger. Aman was there too, McLeod's former host, carried in on a charpoy. He was much weaker now, but just as affably garrulous, though most of what he wanted to say had to be expressed by his eyes, his throat being partly paralysed.

Rafiq, as Azim's lieutenant, made up the deputation.

Except for Aman, they sat on cushions on the floor. Azim wore the snow-white sacrificial turban he had worn in McLeod's dream of murder last night, but on his fine, proud face that expression of relentless cruelty was replaced by a curious smile of trust.

'We lied to you,' he said. 'The Englishman and his wife are here, our guests. There is no need to explain why we told you otherwise; you are not a fool, and I think you have some sympathy for us. Nor is it necessary for me to tell you why we believe their presence has become a danger to us.'

'Do you not exaggerate that danger?' asked McLeod, but even as he spoke he was remembering that the assault on

Margaret Duncan had never been disclosed. If she were to appear in the capital, the authorities would certainly be embarrassed. They might well seek private revenge.

'It may be we do,' admitted Azim. 'Others think so, too. Aman among them.'

'Yes,' croaked the old cheerful man, nodding his head. 'If a man does what is right, who can harm him? Is that not true, my friend?'

McLeod could scarcely assent. The villagers at Haimir had done what was right.

'This is a doctrine for paradise,' said Fakir.

'No, rather for men who wish to enter it,' whispered Aman.

'There is only one safe way,' muttered Fakir.

In the pause that followed Aman kept groaning.

'Now that you have told me they are here,' said McLeod, 'that way cannot be used.'

Fakir grinned at him, like a man clutching a knife.

'It is known I have come here,' said McLeod. 'If I don't return, there will be a search.'

'I have warned them, my friend,' gasped Aman.

'We think,' said Azim softly, 'that you have come here without permission. Last time you had the Governor's letter and other papers. What papers have you now?'

'No one knows you are here,' said Rafiq, 'and therefore no one will come to look for you. Why did you come over the mountain, which is dangerous? Why were you afraid of the soldiers in the pass? If you had the blessing of the government would not the soldiers have accompanied you as your escort?'

'So you believe you can kill me, too, as well as my friends, without risk?'

'Yes,' murmured Azim. 'We do believe that. We think we would be entitled to exchange three lives for many. But that may not be necessary. You have a plan. We have come to listen to it.'

'It is simple. Help us to get out of the valley to my car. I shall drive my friends to a place I know more than a hundred miles from here. In the summer it is inhabited by nomads, in the winter by no one. Soon now it will be deserted again.'

'And afterwards you would take them to the city?' asked Azim.

'I think so.'

'And you are sure everyone there would believe your story?'

'What reason would there be for doubting it?'

'You would have to lie,' said Rafiq.

'Yes.'

'We are all choked with lies,' croaked Aman. 'How can we prosper in the eyes of God?'

Fakir shook his head. 'I don't trust them,' he muttered. 'They will say we intended to kill them. They will demand that the soldiers be sent here, as they were to Haimir.'

'No,' said McLeod. 'Why should we? If we are safe and unharmed, should we not be grateful rather than revengeful? And is the woman the kind who would wish to bring disaster upon you whom she, I'm sure, regards as her friends?'

'That is very true,' gasped Aman.

Rafiq nodded, and Azim's face brightened with a smile of trust.

Even Fakir's scowl was uncertain. 'She is pregnant,' he muttered. 'Her belly is big. How can she be taken out past the soldiers?'

'She is not the difficulty,' said Azim.

'And he is dying,' cried Fakir.

'Dying?' repeated McLeod.

'He is very sick,' said Azim. 'But he could be tied to a horse.'

'You forget,' said Fakir, 'he does not wish to go.'

'No, I do not forget. Whether he wishes or not, whether he is dying or not, he must go. You will tell him that?'

'Yes, I will tell him,' said McLeod.

Rafiq was grinning, shamefaced. 'They have been our guests. We have been hospitable to them. It would be a pity . . .'

'To let them know that for weeks they have been under sentence of death?'

Rafiq turned away. 'Is it necessary for them to know?'

'It may be.'

'They know already,' said Aman hoarsely. 'She knows, I am certain of it. Perhaps she has not told him. She visits so many houses; even yours, Azim. She is not blind or deaf. She has noticed.'

'There are some who believe, Aman,' said Fakir angrily, 'that you have deliberately told her yourself.'

'No, no. I swear by God's beard that is not true. I would have plunged a knife into my own heart rather than tell her that.'

The old man was distressed and weeping.

'Never in your whole life could you keep a secret.'

'Never in my life have I had such a secret to keep.'

'Peace,' said Azim. 'It does not help for us to quarrel. Let us wait until our friend visits them, and lays his plan before them. Afterwards we can meet again and consider what is to be done.'

Seventeen

McLeod stood amidst the bushes, looking at the house and smelling the wood smoke rising from the square chimney. The house was the one he had been lodged in on his visit five years ago. He felt he was returning home after a long absence; and though he had brooded so long over the two now occupying it he expected them to be strange or even hostile.

As he waited, in no hurry, what he hoped for happened; the door opened, and Margaret Duncan – her yellow hair identified her, though she wore native clothes – came out, carrying a skin water-bag. The spring at which she intended to fill it was beside him. So she came towards him, with a resolution and courage that he did not think he was imagining. Once she stopped and turned round, listening; to what, he could not tell. He heard only birdsong and, faraway, the lowing of cattle. Perhaps, nearer to the house, she was hearing Donald call after her.

As she came on again, swinging the bag gently against her leg as brown as any native woman's, it was the tranquillity of her bronzed, thin face that struck him most; it seemed to him to have been achieved after much hardship, and not by the easy gift of religious simple-mindedness. She was pregnant, which gave her gait its peculiar pride. It was as if with every calm step, every confident contact with the green earth, she was claiming the right of proud existence, not for herself, or for Donald, but for the unborn child.

She did not notice McLeod among the bushes, so engrossed was she in her thoughts, but passed him and went on to the spring where, humming a hymn tune, she filled the water bag. Then she sat down on a mossy tree stump and began to stroke her belly, in a curious ritualistic way, still humming and smiling. She seemed to be trying to communicate to the child within her her own happiness and confidence. Thus for a minute or two she sat, dark-faced and smiling, barefooted, enjoying the unborn child's company.

Beyond her was the house, with Donald in it, ill, unable to move, apparently forgotten. Glancing from her face to its reflection in the clear water of the spring, McLeod saw there, emphasised among the tiny green water spiders, that smiling self-sufficiency. Whatever else she was thinking about, it could scarcely be Donald. A large orange butterfly fluttered about her head. She laughed at it, and when it flew off gazed happily after it; she loved it, not for itself, but because it was already living in a world into which her child would soon be born.

Surely, thought McLeod, I was wrong; this must be a kind of simple-minded obliviousness; how otherwise could she, with her lover dying, forget and relax like this?

But he had spied upon her long enough. Awkwardly he went through the bushes towards the spring. She turned, with a ready smile that did not fade though surprise and calculation came into her eyes. Unshaven and unkempt though he was, his khaki shirt and slacks must have shown her he was a foreigner like herself.

'Hello,' he said, holding out his hand. 'My name's McLeod, John McLeod.'

Seen more closely, her face did not seem so tranquil. In spite of her efforts to keep it out, distrust kept coming into her eyes.

'Hello,' she said, smiling, and taking his hand.

'You must have heard of me, from Donald. It was me, as a matter of fact, who told him about this valley.'

'Yes, I've heard of you, Mr. McLeod. But where have you dropped from?' She looked about, expecting to see his companions.

'I came across the mountain. I'm alone.'

'You're not a doctor?'

'No.'

'Azim – he's the headman – left the valley about a week ago.

He said he would try to bring back a doctor. I understand he returned yesterday.'

'Yes. But without a doctor, I'm afraid. The nearest one must be two hundred miles away. Was it for Donald? I've heard he's ill.'

'Seriously ill.'

'What's the matter?'

'I think it must be a perforated ulcer. He's been vomiting blood, and he's in great pain most of the time.'

Yet her eyes were cool, dry, and distrustful. It could be, of course, that she had already exhausted all her tears and trust. Yet five minutes ago, alone, she had been happy.

He crouched beside her on the warm grass. 'How long have you been here?'

'About three months.'

'Wasn't it possible for you to get out a message?'

'We haven't tried.'

'You must have known your people would be worried about you.'

'Yes.'

'And Donald needed medical attention.'

'Yes.'

'Did Azim refuse to take out a message?'

'He was never asked to.'

It could be, he thought, that she was practising some scheme of self-preservation, in its own way as ruthless as that abandoned by Azim.

'I'm going to have a child,' she said. 'I think we were entitled therefore to some seclusion. Don't you?'

'It's not so simple as that, surely.'

'Why isn't it? It's our business, no one else's.'

'I'm afraid it's become the business of a lot of people.'

'Why have you come here, Mr. McLeod?'

'To look for you and Donald.'

'But we were never lost.'

'Miss Duncan—'

'Margaret, please, or Mrs. Kemp. Donald and I are husband

and wife in the eyes of God. We have performed our own ceremony.'

He wondered what that had been. 'I was going to say that everybody, including your parents, think you are dead.'

After a long pause she murmured: 'Aren't millions of people dead?'

It must surely have some religious meaning, but he didn't know what it was. Her eyes were certainly far from candid, and the firmness of her mouth seemed cruel.

'There's a war on, isn't there?'

'A war?'

'Yes. And they're dropping atomic bombs on each other. Millions of people are being blown to pieces. Yet you say we should have sent out a message. We prefer to think God led us here, and wishes us to remain.'

'There's no war.'

'Why then did the soldiers come here in the summer? Why did Azim insist on hiding us? And why have the men here been going about armed ever since? And why do they keep a watch on the pass, day and night? And why are the women so upset?'

'Has it affected their attitude to you?'

'It's affected their attitude to each other.'

'Have they shown hostility to you?'

'Some have done so, from the beginning. An old man called Fakir and his sons. They're the religious leaders, or think they are; really they're stupid and bigoted. Luckily they haven't much influence.'

'What about the rest?'

'They've always been extremely kind and hospitable.'

'Even recently?'

'They've been excited, ever since the visit of the soldiers. We were sure it was because of a war. Of course I've caught them looking at me rather oddly. I've come upon them whispering. A child or two has shouted from a distance. Occasionally some-one's been rather rude. But on the whole they've been wonder-fully kind. They are delightful people.'

'I think I ought to tell you, Miss Duncan—'

'Mrs. Kemp, please.' She said it without squirm or blush.

'You've been in great danger.'

'What do you mean? Danger from whom?'

'From the people here. Last night they held a jirgha; that's a council.'

'I saw the fires.'

'It was about you and Donald.'

'I'm not surprised. They're greatly concerned about us. They know Donald's dangerously ill. They know we're far from home. I'm expecting a child. It's perfectly natural for them to be anxious about their guests.'

'They decided that you have to leave the valley at once.'

'You must have misunderstood, Mr. McLeod. Often I do myself, through not knowing the language well enough.'

'I know it pretty well. It would be difficult to misunderstand this.' He touched the lump where Rafiq had struck him with the gun.

She examined it carefully. 'Did you fall?'

'I was struck with the butt of a gun.'

'By someone here?'

'Rafiq, a kinsman of Azim's.'

'I know him. His wife's a friend of mine. He's usually very jolly and friendly. You must have provoked him.'

The complacency in her voice and smile irritated him; it considered itself invincible. This was the smugness of those who had no doubt they were God's favourites. Even misfortunes, such as the attack in the dark house at Mazarat, and even Donald's painful illness, were in reality marks of favour. Those like himself who saw God's hand in nothing could hardly be expected to see it in death and rape.

She waited, with patience and intelligence, for him to say what she had already dismissed as nonsense.

'They thought there was only one way to protect themselves.'

'From whom?' she asked, amused. 'Surely not from us.'

'From the soldiers. They thought they would have to kill you, you and Donald. Some of them still think it.'

She gave what seemed to him an imitation of Goodwood Purdie being scandalised by some awful impiety.

'What a shocking thing to say!'

'You visited a village at Haimir.'

'Did we? We visited many villages.'

'This one is before you come to the blue lake. There was an old woman, with one eye.'

'We did visit a village where there was an old woman like that; but she had two eyes; one was blind, though.'

'You remember her?'

'Very well.'

'And the village?'

'Yes. It was a very poor, desolate place. They did their best to be hospitable, poor souls. But I must admit I wasn't at ease among them.'

'Why not?'

'They were all so filthy and diseased. Syphilis mostly. I had to think of my child, and Donald was so weak and susceptible. They had no idea at all of hygiene. They defecated at their door-steps, like animals. I did what I could to train them, though the language difficulty made it almost impossible. Besides, I didn't feel well.'

'You gave a bangle to a young girl.'

'Yes. Poor thing. She took a liking to it. She was very ill.'

'She's dead now.'

'I'm not surprised. There are so many like her throughout the East; millions dying in the most dreadful misery and pain.'

'Yes. There was a photograph, too.'

'Yes, of Donald's mother. He gave it to the old woman. It fascinated her. Perhaps the poor old creature saw in it what she herself might have been, had she been given a chance. She was quite intelligent.'

'The photograph and the bangle were used as evidence to convict the whole village.'

'Of stealing? But they didn't steal them. We gave them freely.'

'Not of stealing. Of murder.'

'Murder?'

'And two of them, one the old woman's son, and the other a simpleton, were dragged off to the city, to be hanged.'

'But whom were they supposed to have murdered?'

'You and Donald. They confessed to it.'

'How could they?' she cried. 'We are still alive.'

'No one knew that. You were traced to this village. The bangle and the photograph were found; there was blood on the photograph. So they were accused, and in the end they confessed.'

'Why should they, when they knew they were innocent?'

'They were beaten into it. Haimir is now a celebrated village. Tourists will go out of their way to see it. They will peep into the cave where it is said you were sleeping when you were attacked. When Azim left here a week ago it was Haimir he went to. He wanted to see for himself what had happened to them. Now he's afraid that it might happen to his own people.'

'I find all this difficult to believe, Mr. McLeod.'

'I'm not surprised. It's true, all the same.'

'From your tone you seem to think that Donald and I are to blame.'

'I don't think you're altogether innocent. If you had got a message out of here, to let people know you were safe, it wouldn't have happened.'

She closed her eyes, and placed her clasped hands on her belly. 'Safe?' she whispered. 'You have not seen Donald yet?'

He rose. 'I'm going to.'

'He's too ill to talk to anyone.'

'I've come a long way.'

She stood up. 'I shall warn him you are here. If he agrees to see you, do not be surprised if you find him greatly changed.'

'I know he's ill.'

'I meant in his mind, in his attitude to God. All the time he suffers great pain. It confuses him. Sometimes, from the way he speaks to me, I can tell he doesn't know who I am. You mustn't excite him.'

'I'll try not to.'

She turned; after she had gone a few steps, she said, 'Mr. McLeod, we are grateful for your help; but you must allow us to decide whether or not to accept it.'

He watched her walk towards the house, leisurely in the sun. At the door she turned, looked back for almost a minute, and then waved.

So that was the beautiful, tender-souled, pious Margaret Duncan, whom Goodwood Purdie had so unctuously pitied. She was beautiful, yes; but her soul, even before this pilgrimage and the ordeal at Mazarat, must have been tough enough; a kind of stupidity and selfishness protected it. Donald and she had made love, successfully enough as her pregnancy indicated; but there could be little doubt that before it she would have gasped out some kind of grace, and after it a thanksgiving. She would have made it so pure that for Donald, his conversion still raw, it must have been intolerable.

It would be as well to keep in mind that she was – in a way too subtle for him to diagnose – mad.

Eighteen

She kept him waiting for thirty-five minutes, deliberately, he felt sure. The delay was not caused by her solicitude for Donald. No; all the time he felt she was watching him from the window, wishing with a resentment in which piety was an ingredient that he had not come. There was, of course, an obvious and pardonable reason: she could not conquer the fear that the child in her womb might not be Donald's. However resolute, pious, and self-sufficient she might be, she would find it hard to cherish a child conceived in terror on her part and criminal lust on the father's; yet she was showing great courage in facing that possibility. No one could blame her for wanting to stay here until the child was born. The bitter problem of what to do with it, if it was born dark-skinned and darker-souled, could perhaps be resolved in this remote valley of dark-skinned people; at home in Britain, or in the hospital at the British Embassy, it could never be. Yet did she not believe in a ubiquitous God who, to someone in favour like her, always intended benevolence?

McLeod tried to curb his spitefulness towards her. He could hardly judge her because he did not understand her. She and her kind were far less comprehensible to him than Azim's people. Her beliefs seemed to him almost insanely contradictory, yet to her they were so consistent that she was able, strengthened by them, to face up with remarkable courage to a situation that would have overwhelmed many a woman whose religious faith, like his own, was an intelligent postponement.

All the same, when she at last came out and walked slowly towards him, he again found it difficult to sympathise with her; his sympathies were instead with Azim. The latter at least knew humility; she had given no sign yet of knowing it. She had expressed no regret, and apparently had felt none, on hearing about the two men hanged on her account. Had she dismissed them as heathens, outside her God's concern? Hardly, for hadn't she devoted her life to nursing similar heathens?

'Donald wants to see you,' she said. 'But I think I should warn you.'

He waited.

'He has an obsession.' She kept looking at him, but he could see she was under great stress to turn away; pride, stronger than modesty, prevented her. 'He is under the delusion that the child I am expecting is not his. He will tell you that; he has told others. There are explanations. The chief one is, he thinks that love – sexual love – is shameful. Many people, whose religious faith has become uncertain, think that. You see, something happened while we were in Mazarat. I am telling you this, Mr. McLeod, but I must repeat it is our business, mine and Donald's, no one else's. Ours and God's only.'

Did God's part in it embrace the old woman's at Haimir, for instance, or her own parents'? McLeod remembered them, white-haired, respectable churchgoers, who in mild voices had blamed Kemp for their daughter's death and expected him to roast in hell for all eternity.

They walked towards the house. She led the way.

'I said something happened at Mazarat.' She did not turn round.

'I know about it.'

She swung round. 'Who told you?'

'The Colonel of the police.'

'What did he tell you? Does everyone know? They promised it would be kept secret.'

'It is secret. He told me in a delirium. He had malaria; besides, his wife and three children had died of smallpox a month or so before. His account was rather incoherent.'

'What did he tell you?'

'That you had been attacked – raped, he said.'

'Did you talk to the doctor at the hospital?'

'No, he'd been transferred.'

'You wouldn't expect to find a very skilful doctor there.'

'No.'

'And he was frightened. But surely he would be able to recognise the symptoms of pregnancy. I was already pregnant, Mr. McLeod. I asked Mr. Purdie the minister to marry us, because I knew I was pregnant. The doctor agreed. I don't enjoy talking about this. It should be forgotten. I could forget it, but Donald can't. It's part of his obsession. He'll want to tell you about it. If you can, dissuade him. In his own interests. He torments himself. He blasphemes. He humiliates me. Worst of all, he denies the child is his.'

Then from within the house a hoarse, plaintive voice called, 'Come in, Johnny,' in Gaelic.

She gripped McLeod's arm fiercely. 'What does that mean?'

'It's Gaelic for "Come in".'

'I didn't know he knew Gaelic.'

'He doesn't. Just a few phrases.'

'Talk in English, please. I want to hear everything that's said. I have a right to.'

As McLeod entered, troubled by the Gaelic words and their associations of home, he saw a leopard skin spread out on the floor, with the mouth snarling and the eyes gleaming. It gave to the sunlight in the room an atmosphere of unrest and threat that Kemp, lying on a charpoy, intensified. His grin of welcome was itself like a snarl, and his eyes glittered hungrily. But what made him look most like the dead animal was his stillness. His hands on the blue cover were as still as its claws, and his haggard, bearded face, against the orange pillows, was like John the Baptist's on a platter, in a picture McLeod had once seen. There was the same expression of sinister ecstasy.

'Well, Johnny,' he said, 'as they say in your native hills, it's a far cry from Loch Awe.'

McLeod saw that his plan was impossible. Kemp was a dying man.

'It is, Donald.'

'Come over here, and let me see you.'

McLeod went over and Kemp grinned up at him.

'Meg tells me you've been looking for us.'

'Yes.'

'Did you think we were lost, Johnny?'

'Yes.'

'We are, Johnny, so lost that neither you nor anyone else will ever find us. Is that right, Meg?'

'Don't excite yourself, Donald. You'll just bring on another attack.'

'Why shouldn't I excite myself? Here's a friend come hundreds of miles to see me.'

'He came over the mountains, Donald.'

'He looks it. Have you got the pot on, Meg? Make our guest a cup of tea. So you came over the mountains, Johnny? You'd find it cold up there, and lonely. I lie and watch them all day. Do you know what you look like Johnny? A refugee from Armageddon. Tell me, Johnny,' he went on, with a sudden eagerness in his voice, 'is it true what Meg keeps telling me? That the "war to end all humanity" has started?'

'It's you that keeps telling me, Donald.'

'The truth is, Johnny, we've been telling each other, to console ourselves.'

'There's no war, Donald.'

'You're not just saying that to spare our feelings, Johnny? You've got the wrong idea if you are. Meg's been praying there's a war. Every day she's been coming in with stories about the men carrying guns and the women being frightened. You see, she thinks the world deserves to be annihilated because of what happened to her at Mazarat. You'll have noticed she's pregnant? Do you still have your dreams, Johnny? You were always one of the astutest minions of Caesar, except that you had the kind of dreams a man of God should have. I keep telling Meg, "We're like creatures in one of Johnny McLeod's dreams." The climax was at Mazarat.'

'I've told him.'

'But your version's different from mine, Meg.'

She looked at McLeod, appealing to him to stop Donald, or at least not to believe him.

'A stinking sort of place, Mazarat. Though you were right in mentioning that the domes of the mosque are bonny in the moonlight, with the doves flying about them. In fact, it wasn't far from the mosque that Meg was attacked.'

'It was the Colonel of the police who told me about it, Donald.'

'The dapper wee chap. You could see your face in his boots. He could see his own in everything. More conceited than a rutting sparrow, but efficient at his job.'

'Since you met him his wife and three children were wiped out by smallpox.'

'Is that so now? Looks as if somebody else is efficient at his job, too. The deil, I mean, Johnny. Who else? He let loose at us a couple of the most fiendish hashish-maddened brutes out of hell. But the wee Colonel had them rounded up before you could cry "Hallelujah!" And he had them shot while you waited. And by Christ I did wait. I showed a most praiseworthy and Christian perseverance in seeing wickedness punished and virtue re-venged. The General Assembly would have been proud of me.'

Over by the stove Margaret kept her face turned away; to hide the hatred on it, McLeod felt sure.

'Those misbegotten bastards, Johnny, cheated me after all. They died with the certainty of paradise in their eyes. I saw it there myself. You don't believe in paradise, Johnny. So you're worse off than the scabbiest, skinniest, shittiest beggar in this tail-end of civilisation. I believe in it, Johnny; but I believe most of all in the deprivation of it.'

'You're killing yourself,' she cried.

'They had knives, Johnny. We were tired; we'd been travel-ling for ten hours, in a bus crammed with people. I'd been feeling sick, too.'

'What he's trying to say,' she said, 'is that he could do nothing to help me.'

'That's right, Johnny. I could do nothing. I couldn't even be killed. So poor Meg was stripped and raped.'

She covered her eyes. 'Don't talk about it,' she screamed.

'As a result, Johnny, she's pregnant. Christ, was there ever a less immaculate conception?'

She rushed over, her face wet with tears. She tried to keep her voice quiet. 'You know that isn't true. It's blasphemous and false. I was already pregnant before it happened.'

'But you never told me, Meg.'

'You know why. The doctor verified it.'

'Because I asked him to. You had to be pacified, Meg. You were going out of your mind.'

'No, Donald, you were the one going out of your mind. It was you who insisted on waiting, to gloat over their punishment.'

'Was that madness? Johnny, tell her that was the clearest-minded Christian sanity.'

'Leave Mr. McLeod out of it. Let him be a witness only. It's time I said this to you, Donald, before a witness. I think God must have sent Mr. McLeod here to be that witness.' In spite of herself, her voice kept rising, and her tears were fresh. 'I was already pregnant, Donald, because you and I had sworn, before God, that we were husband and wife.'

'An oath's not as potent as that.'

'As husband and wife we made love, Donald, not once, not twice, many times.'

'She's lying, Johnny, she's a lying bitch,' screamed Donald. 'If you hand me that Bible I'll swear upon it she's lying. I made a vow, Johnny, in India, years ago, and I've kept it. She's tried to make me break it, but I never have. Give me that Bible and I'll swear upon it. Give it to me, or I'll get up and fetch it myself. The last time I tried to get up I fainted and was unconscious for a couple of days.'

McLeod was reminded that she must attend to all Donald's needs.

The sick man was growing weaker. 'Give it to me, Johnny.'

'It's not necessary, Donald.'

'It is, I tell you.' He gasped and grimaced with pain. 'I've got to convince you she's lying.'

It was she, become calm again, who put the Bible where he could place his hand upon it. For almost a minute he lay, gasping quietly, his eyes closed, with his hand upon the Bible as another man's, in danger, might rest upon a gun. He appeared to have forgotten what he had been going to do. He began to moan, with his teeth sunk into his lip. When he opened his eyes for a moment there was no recognition in them of McLeod or Margaret, but only of pain.

She beckoned McLeod over to the window. 'I'm sorry,' she whispered. 'I had to say it in front of a witness. I don't care whether you believe me or not, Mr. McLeod. As I have said, it's our business, Donald's and mine; but I wanted to say it in front of someone. I don't know why.'

'He is very ill.'

'Yes.'

'And there's nothing can be done?'

'Nothing.'

'If he was in a hospital, could anything be done?'

'He could be given injections to lull the pain.'

'And that's all?'

'I think so.'

He noticed she was trembling, and her hands, upon her stomach, kept clasping and unclasping.

'Well, it's certainly out of the question for him to travel.'

'Yes.'

It had to be said. 'How long do you think he's got?'

'I don't know. Any day, any moment. You can see for yourself.'

'Yes.' He paused. 'And what will you do then?'

'I shall remain here.'

He thought it hardly worth while to remind her that Azim might not want her to stay.

'You mean, until the child's born?'

'Yes. After then, too, perhaps.'

If the child should turn out not to be Donald's. The doctor at Mazarat could have been mistaken, or even could have lied, as Donald said, in order to reassure her or to save himself and the authorities trouble.

Whatever was done to her, she must, for her religion's sake, see a good purpose in it. What would strike McLeod as a hellish misfortune, she was obliged to turn into a benefit. Fruit that he would have no hesitation in refusing to let ripen, or survive when ripe, she must accept and preserve and cherish. If she should need the remoteness of this valley, and the absence of fellow Christians, in order to attempt and achieve that acceptance, he would certainly never blame her.

She herself was remote. He still did not understand her, but he knew that in her there was a depth and intricacy of suffering, and also a faith that it could be profitably endured. She reminded him of the old, half-blind woman and Rafiq's mother.

Behind him he heard Kemp whisper: 'Johnny.'

He turned. Recognition, as well as pain, was now in the glittering eyes.

'I want to talk to you, Johnny.'

'Should I?'

'What difference can it make?' she answered. 'It might even help him to take his mind off the pain. Try not to let him get excited. I'll go and fetch more water.'

When she had gone out, McLeod went over to the bed and sat down on a stool there.

'I'm not going to scart a grey heid, Johnny, as they say up the Royal Mile. It's just as well. I'd never have found the vision I was looking for. Yet for years I was sure of it. I was going to get rid of all the mushmouthery. I was the height of the Buddha at Kalak. But, Johnny, I didn't know what to do with the presumptuous midgets. I wanted to squash the guts out of them. Don't ask me why, for Christ's sake. I just hated them. The Christ-tamers. That's my name for them, Johnny, the Christ-tamers. You've seen the fellows who travel about in the East with a tiny monkey dressed up to look like a man? They waylay you outside your hotel, or come knocking at your gate, to show you how clever the monkey is; they make it stand on its head, turn somersaults, hold out its paw for alms. That's them; my Christ-tamers.'

He rested for a minute or two, panting but smiling.

'Once, though, Johnny, I think I did have the god's eye view. You were with me. Do you remember, on Liatach, with Tom Forsyth?'

McLeod recalled the occasion. Liatach was a mountain in Wester Ross. With another student he and Donald had climbed it one summer's day. Seated by the cairn, Donald had caught sight through binoculars of a climber and his girl bathing naked in a lochan in a corrie below. They had afterwards romped to dry themselves, and finally had sunk down on the heather to complete their joy, first taking care to spread out some garments to lie on.

As peeping-toms Kemp and his companions had been hilarious, witty, and full of an Olympian loving-kindness towards their victims.

'I lie here, Johnny, looking out at those peaks, and I remember it. We were looking down on Eden then, and we didn't know it. That was before the Christ-tamers took command. How can you call something love that they indulge in, behind the plush curtains of their respectability, on the spring mattresses of their conceit? I did make that vow, Johnny, and I've kept it. You saw me swear it on the Bible. I called Meg a liar. That wasn't right. How can she be expected to say the child she's carrying is the seed of a drug-maddened, thigh-tormented, human rat. Yes, I've slept beside her, Johnny, close, too, for warmth and protection; but that was all, Johnny, I swear by Christ that was all.'

A whine had come into his voice, disconcerting McLeod.

'You believe me, Johnny?'

'Yes, I believe you.'

'But you're thinking I ought to lie about it, for Meg's sake. I should please her by saying the child's mine. After all, won't I be dead by the time it's born? But, Johnny, for weeks I've been lying here, dying in agony. How can I lie now? I daren't pretend. Surely you understand that, Johnny? Better in the end to keep to the truth. I've advised Meg, have the child, but when it's born, get rid of it, drop it on a stone, throw it into the river, abandon it in the forest, put an end to it in any way she can. They'd be shocked by that advice, the Christ-tamers; but wouldn't they make the poor little misbegotten bastard's life one long humiliation? If you commit murder, Johnny, and you're so ill it looks as if you're going to cheat them, they give you the best attention, show you any amount of Christian compassion, so that they can get the satisfaction of hanging you.'

His voice had grown so weak McLeod had to bend low to make out what he was saying.

'Convince her, Johnny. Go and convince her.'

McLeod rose. 'All right, Donald. You had better rest now.'

Kemp's lips kept forming the words: 'Convince her.'

Before leaving, McLeod had to go over to the stove and move the pot in which the water was boiling away.

Simpler, thought McLeod, as he walked to where Margaret seemed to be praying by the spring, to attribute every misfortune to the malice of fate, and prepare accordingly.

A few yards away, he saw that though her hands were clasped and her eyes shut, apparently in prayer, she was weeping; tears streamed down her cheeks. He halted for a moment, smitten by doubt and pity. Slowly in his mind formed the understanding that it was logical enough to believe in God's omnipotence and at the same time concede Him His right not to exert it on one's own behalf, however one pleaded, and however worthy one might think oneself. It was possible too, he realised, for a believer to accept as from God what an unbeliever like himself would regard as one of malicious fate's dirtiest blows. The former, however blindly, and with no matter how many failures of reverence, must cherish what had been given; the latter at best could only achieve a bitter dignity of acceptance.

When she looked up and saw him there watching her, she made no attempt to hide her face or even wipe the tears from it. Instead, she tried to smile at him, with a ruefulness breaking into, but by no means dispelling, the prayerful earnestness of her face. He seemed then to see in her the child she had been twenty years ago, and also the young, zealous missionary-nurse

who had left the comfort and safety of home to tend hideously
ravaged black bodies and nourish the souls within them.

'I am sorry I was angry with him,' she said.

'I don't blame you.'

'I blame myself. He is suffering great pain most of the time.
It is like torture. He says often what he does not mean. He gets
relief, I think, by saying things that outrage his true beliefs.'

'Yes.' But McLeod was by no means sure she was right. It
seemed to him Kemp had meant what he had said.

'The people in his care in India loved him, and he loved
them. He had a wonderful effect on them. If he just spoke to
them they gained confidence. It's not surprising really that he's
now lost his own. He was like a saint, Mr. McLeod.' She looked
at McLeod as she carefully chose the word. 'Yes, a saint. He
never gave the slightest thought to his own welfare. He would
have worked twenty hours a day if we had let him. You know he
gave up his career as a diplomat.'

'Yes.' McLeod remembered Minn's indignant description of
that sacrifice.

'I love him. And whatever he says, he loves me. In the eyes of
God, we are husband and wife. I'm not ashamed of what we
have done. I know he is going to die, very soon. Though I know
that death is not the end of our pilgrimage, I don't think I could
bear to go on living without him if I didn't have his child to
look forward to. It is his child, Mr. McLeod.'

He could not ask her if she was absolutely sure of that. If it
turned out not to be Donald's, what did she do then? One thing
at least was certain: he could never convince her to take
Donald's advice. He did not even want to try.

'If you did decide to remain here, as you said, what would
you want me to tell the people outside?'

'They think I am dead?'

'Yes.'

'Would it not be better to let them keep on thinking it?'

'Your own people, too?'

'Yes. If they knew, everybody would know. Do you think I
have a right to do that, Mr. McLeod?'

'Yes, I think so.'

'But I am not sure I have. This is very difficult for me to decide. There is also your part to be considered. I should be asking you to deceive people. You would have to lie. Even if you remained silent, it would be a lie.'

'Don't worry about me. As you've said yourself, it's your business.'

'I should be able to do the work I pledged myself to do. There is every opportunity here.'

'Whatever you decided, it wouldn't be irrevocable. After a year, two, three, twenty, you could go back if you wanted to. But if you do decide to stay, I'd like to know you had of your own free will made that decision. I'd also like to know what happened to Donald. Perhaps, after the baby's born, you could send a message to me, at the Embassy. I'll not be there, but it would be sent on to me. If in it you said you had decided to stay, then I go on keeping quiet; but if you said you wished to return home, then I'd be pleased to give you all the help I could.'

'Thank you. I shall think about it.'

'Azim will have to be consulted, too.'

'Yes, of course.' She rose up. 'I shall have to get back to the house. Donald may need me. Was he asleep when you left?'

'He was trying to.'

'He seldom sleeps, even at night.'

Carrying the water-bag, he walked by her side towards the house.

Nineteen

When McLeod went to see Azim he found that a holiday had been declared and a feast got ready in his honour. Near the headman's house, rising out of a level field shaded with trees, was a natural mound, as flat on the top as a table and itself ringed with trees. There the grass had been covered with many red carpets, round the edges of which the men of the valley, more than fifty of them, were already seated, waiting for him. In the field below women, dressed in their gaudy Sunday best, nursed their babies. Some boys flew kites, while others, on ponies, played a kind of buz-kashi, using a skin bag stuffed with grass as the buz.

When McLeod appeared, hesitant because he thought he might be intruding, there was an immediate clapping of hands and a cheering that astonished him with its enthusiasm and duration. When Azim, dressed in white from turban to shoes with upturned toes, came down to welcome him, the applause grew still louder until McLeod suddenly realised that in it must be an element of hysteria. This was their way of showing that the recent nightmare, in which they saw themselves murdering their guests, was at last over.

Azim's first words proved him right. The tall, bearded headman met him with outstretched arms, and a smile strange on his bearded face because of its shy, child-like joy that the necessity of distrust was past. For a moment McLeod wondered on whose face he had lately seen a smile like that; and then he remembered that it had been on Jamil's, in prison.

'Welcome, my friend,' cried Azim. 'On my own behalf, and on behalf of everyone in the valley, man, woman, and child, I make you welcome.'

Looking round, moved and surprised almost to tears, McLeod could only nod and smile. 'Thank you,' he said.

'The evil dream is past. We are awake again, and see all things clearly, as we did before. We see them as manifestations of God's goodness to us. We are grateful to you, my friend. Your coming has helped to waken us. But for you that dream might have darkened our lives forever. We hope you will come and rejoice with us.'

'I shall be greatly honoured.'

'Your friend, is he able to come? Look, Aman has been brought here on a charpoy, which his sons have carried. Many hands will be pleased to carry your friend here to join us.'

McLeod shook his head. 'I'm afraid it is not possible. He is too ill.'

'We are all sorry to hear that. Perhaps, with his wife's nursing, he will soon get well.'

'I do not think so.'

'Is he going to die?'

'I think so. Soon. Azim, afterwards when we are alone, I should like to speak to you about the woman. She tells me that if her husband dies here, and her child is born here, she herself will not wish to leave. Would she be allowed to stay?'

'We shall talk about it after we have eaten.'

Then, taking McLeod's hand, the headman led him up the steps cut in the bank to the place of honour that had strewn in front of it masses of flowers. Rafiq, dressed also in white, jumped up and helped him into his place. Two others, whom Azim introduced as his brothers, acted as hosts, too.

Old Aman was close by, propped up by two of his sons. He insisted that McLeod should come and shake his hand. 'I am very glad,' he croaked. 'Now I can look up at the mountains again, without shame.'

Seen through the branches of the pines those mountains then, in the warm sunshine with the sky blue above, were extremely beautiful. McLeod, too, found his heart lighter as he looked up at them.

At the blowing of a horn women and boys began to stream,

in single file like ants, from the houses, carrying platefuls of food which they brought and set down upon the carpets. There were huge plates of pilau, white and orange rice, with pieces of chicken and mutton embedded in it; of fruit of all kinds, including melons and grapes and juicy pears; of native bread and cakes; and of kebab, pieces of tender roasted meat on long thin skewers. There were many small teapots and bowls of sugar.

As the feast began, with his fellow guests carrying meat and rice to their mild bearded mouths with their tawny fingers, McLeod had the feeling that this might well have been an episode in the life of Christ. Almost every man there, except McLeod himself, could have been taken for one of the disciples. When he thought of that, another thought flashed irrelevantly through his mind: Judas, like Kemp, had been red-bearded.

At first the conversation among those beside McLeod was about his previous visit to the valley, and his travels since. Then they wanted to know why he wasn't yet married with half a dozen sons. When he suggested that perhaps they could provide him with a wife, they took it merrily for the joke it was, and put forward nominees. In the end they agreed that the most likely, because the most beautiful, was the sister of Rafiq's wife. According to Rafiq, eager but shy, the girl thought McLeod was very handsome.

She was seen among the women in the field below, and pointed out to him. He asked her age. Fourteen, he was told. As he laughed and protested that was far too young for him, he was wondering what might happen to Margaret Duncan if she did remain here. She must be, he thought, about thirty, perhaps a year or so younger: double the age which they preferred a bride to be here. She would be regarded as old, almost past the age when she could be expected to produce vigorous sons. No man would be willing to marry her, and yet how could she, in a primitive community of this kind, support herself as a widow with a child? Her fate might be to become some kind-hearted man's second wife, an extra bedmate and drudge for him. As a woman, too, even the consolation of prayer might be denied her. If she prayed, it would have to be in secrecy; which might be difficult, since even the relieving of nature had to be done in the open, behind some communal rock. As for her child, whether Donald's or not, it might well find life as hard here as it would among Donald's Christ-tamers.

Hours later, in the evening, the feast over, McLeod went with Azim, his two brothers, and Rafiq, to the headman's house, where they sat in a quiet room taking turns at smoking a blue hubble-bubble pipe with the stem decorated with thousands of tiny red-and-white beads. Aman, exhausted, had been carried home. Fakir had not been invited; he had stood dourly watching them go off without him. He had obviously suspected that the business of the two guests was going to be discussed, and thought he was entitled to take part. But no doubt his attitude, of prejudiced opposition, was known, and rejected. Still, if Margaret did remain, she might find him an awkward enemy.

At first they talked about McLeod's own plans. He wanted to stay for a few days, and then leave, either over the mountain again or through the pass, whichever they thought advisable. If he could be taken to where he had left his car, he would be grateful. Rafiq at once offered to escort him through the pass; it was possible to avoid the soldiers quartered there if one knew the way.

Azim agreed, and said two others would go with them, to make a strong escort.

Then it was time to speak about Kemp and Margaret.

'It is a pity my friend is too ill to travel,' said McLeod.

They murmured sympathetically, but their eyes were steady and watchful.

'He is very ill?' asked Rafiq.

'I shall be surprised if, in another week, he is still alive.'

'What is his trouble?' asked one of the brothers, Abdul, a big, dyspeptic-looking man, chronically aware that he too had organs susceptible to disease and pain.

'It is in his stomach.'

'She is like a doctor herself. Can she do nothing?'

McLeod shook his head.

'If he was in hospital, in the city, could the doctors save him?'

Yes, that was the question. 'I don't think so. It's too late. Two months ago perhaps.'

'Why did he travel then, if he was so sick?'

'I do not know.'

Abdul shook his head anxiously. He had eaten too much that afternoon, and his belly was sore. If Kemp was too far from hospital, so was he.

Azim turned to McLeod. 'I have told them, my friend, that the woman wishes to remain with us in the valley if the man dies. Like myself, they do not understand.'

'Perhaps I do not understand very clearly myself.'

'Why does she not go with you?' asked the other brother, as amiable and eupeptic as Abdul was gloomy.

'She is with child, and it is a difficult journey. Besides, she would not leave while her husband is still alive.'

'It may be winter when he dies,' muttered Abdul. 'It is the time for dying.'

'I have asked her to send me a message in the spring,' said McLeod. 'Could such a message be delivered, to the British Embassy, in the capital?'

Rafiq nodded. 'I shall deliver it myself.'

'It is a long journey.'

'If it was ten times as long, I would deliver it.'

'What would this message say?' asked Azim.

'It would tell me what she intended to do: either to come back home or remain here. If she wanted to return, I would make the arrangements.'

'It would be better,' murmured Azim. 'We could take her and the child to the Embassy, but perhaps they would not understand there.'

'Yes. But, of course, if she chose to remain, it would be up to you to decide.'

'There are difficulties,' said Azim, after a long pause, during which he puffed at the pipe. 'In the first place, she is not of our faith, and already there have been complaints that she talks too much about her own faith, which she says is superior. In the second place, it is not usual for a woman to live amongst us without some man being responsible for her. In the third place, there would be the question of the child; surely it would become one of us, it would play with our children, it would speak our tongue, and I think it would want to have our faith. There are other difficulties, my friend, but those are the greatest. You must speak to her about them.'

'I shall.'

'There is a difficulty of another kind. You will leave in a few days. Surely you will tell the people outside that you have found these two, whom everyone thinks are dead.'

'Certainly soldiers will come,' said Abdul.

'If they do,' said Azim, 'we will tell them the truth. We think now that it is possible they will believe us, and will do us no harm. But it is certain they will not allow her to remain. They will take her back with them. Tell her that also.'

'Yes, I shall tell her. But she has already asked me not to say that I have found her. She does not wish anyone to come looking for her.'

Again there was a pause. It was Abdul, the pessimist, who broke it. 'Some people here say – I do not admit I say it myself – that she and the man must have done something wrong among their own people. I know it is true that often they quarrel, as if their minds were not at peace.'

'Do you not quarrel with your own wife?' asked Azim.

'I carefully pointed out I was not expressing my own opinion, Azim. You know yourself, Fakir and his friends say they must have committed some terrible crime.'

'It is not true,' said McLeod.

'Did the woman not nurse your son when he was sick?' asked Rafiq.

'And your wife, too, Rafiq.'

'They are thought to be dead,' said Azim. 'You know that a village was punished for killing them. I have heard that two men were taken away to be hanged.'

McLeod nodded.

'Should it not now be proved to everyone that these unhappy people were innocent?'

'Perhaps it should.'

Azim smiled. 'Who can tell? You will speak to her about all these difficulties?'

McLeod promised he would.

Twenty

Margaret stood in the doorway, trying to appear as relaxed as any English housewife seeing a friend off whom she would see again in a week or two's time. But through the open door she could hear Donald's moans and grumbles of delirium, and see him almost unconscious, with his beard curiously faded and his thin fists stiffened into claws of pain on the blue coverlet.

Smiling, she watched McLeod mount his horse. By the spring his escort, Rafiq and two others, waited for him, muffled in their leather jackets and striped blankets. Their horses snorted and stamped in the keen air. The dawn was still pink on the high snows.

McLeod took a long time making himself comfortable in the saddle. She knew he was putting off looking at her to say farewell. This awkwardness in her presence had increased during his five days' stay in the valley.

'Well,' he said at last, 'I suppose I'll have to be going.'

'Yes. Goodbye, John. And thank you again.'

He frowned and shook his head. 'I've done nothing. I feel I'm going away leaving everything to be done, though God knows I don't know what it is I should do.'

'Yes, John, you are right: God does know. He knows what has already happened, and what is still to happen. It is a great comfort to me, because it means I cannot be forgotten.'

Again he was confronted by his inability to fathom the religious mind.

'I still am not sure I'm doing the right thing about Donald,' he said, unable to hide his irritation.

'You must be guided by your own conscience.'

That piety so like humbug: put your hand in God's and He will lead you into the enclosure marked: For the Saved Only.

He must be more tolerant and sympathetic; after all, this was probably the last time he would ever see her.

'I can't help thinking I ought at least to try and get help to him.'

'If you think that . . .' she whispered. 'But it would be too late.'

That was very likely. Every day Donald was weaker. Just half an hour ago McLeod, come to say goodbye, had thought him dead; then watching him begin again the painful struggle to remain alive, or at least to keep on breathing, he had almost wished him dead. Donald could not be made to understand that McLeod was going. Whimpering, and clutching Margaret's finger with the grip of a baby, he had concentrated on accommodating the agony feasting on him. Watching, McLeod had remembered Minn's contemptuous description at the cocktail party: leper-lover. And Mrs. Bryson in her bikini had called him indestructible.

'A doctor could be got here in a couple of weeks,' said McLeod. 'Don't you think it's worth trying?'

'You must do what you think is right.'

'But surely you agree with me?'

She stood smiling. He could not bear to look at that smile. It was a prophetess's, surely; by it she was mocking him for having journeyed hundreds of hard desperate miles to bring a doctor to visit a grave. Then he knew it could not be that kind of smile at all. That part of the future she was most interested in, the time of the birth of her child, was darker to her than it was to him.

'I'm afraid my mind isn't made up yet,' he said. 'I know I promised, but I shouldn't have.'

'If you were to wait for a few days longer.'

'No. I must get back.' The reason was that for him the situation in the valley had grown intolerable, because of her. 'You should be all right. Azim has given me his word.'

'I am not afraid. Please believe that. Whatever happens, I shall not be alone.'

She meant God would be with her. During those few days she had talked too much about God. It was a companionship McLeod stubbornly preferred not to take into consideration.

'In any case, you'll let me know what has happened, and what you intend to do?'

'If it is at all possible, I promise.'

'It should be possible. Rafiq has promised to deliver the message himself. He'll keep his word, too.'

'Yes. They are all very kind.'

'Well—' He stared helplessly at her. His very feelings seemed incomplete.

'May God take care of you, John, wherever you are.'

He should have returned that compliment, but he could not.

Beside the spring Rafiq waited patiently. But one of the others, a big, burly jocular man called Salamodin, had dismounted and was on his knees, busy at his morning prayers. He was in a hurry, like a man remedying an oversight. There, too, was God the companion: a different God though, in a different headquarters. Did the one cancel the other out? Again McLeod felt irritable at being left out, unable to sympathise or understand.

'I must say this, too, before I go. I promised your parents to go and see them when I got back. If I were to keep that promise, or if they were to write to me, I think I'd be forced to tell them the truth, that you were here, alive.'

She stared at him with a curious closeness, reminding him, he thought, that he had already given her his promise.

'Though what reason I should give them for your choosing to stay here—' He shook his head.

Still she stared.

'Suppose the worst does happen, suppose the child isn't what you hope it will be, you could leave it here, that could be easily arranged. Some family would adopt it, for a little recompense.' He had left some money with Azim for that purpose; all he had told Azim was that she might need it. 'You'd be able to get away and forget the whole horrible business, as you've a right to.'

She shook her head.

'Maybe you won't be able to accept Azim's conditions. Remember this is a society dominated by men.'

Then, taking him by surprise, she came running over, seized his hand and held on to it. He thought she looked suddenly old, ill, and uncertain. If ever God vanished from a human face it was then, from hers. She could not speak, and her dumbness was like some penalty, inexorably exacted; she was afraid, too, and clutched at his hand so fiercely she seemed minded to pull him headlong from the horse.

Just as abruptly she let go and hurried back to the house. She did not once look round. Inside, she closed the door.

Trembling, he sat and gazed at the house. His hand still hung down, as if maimed. Out of some green vines that covered part of the wall a bird flew, with a crest and a soft, cooing call. He watched it alight on a tree. For a moment he seemed to escape into its life, where morality did not exist.

Next moment he jerked the reins, and his horse, glad to go, went snorting to join the others.

Rafiq looked at him with sympathy. 'She will not come?'

'No.'

'I do not think she will ever leave.'

'You think not?'

'It is what my wife says. He is still very sick?'

'Yes.'

'Yet he isn't old.'

'No.'

'He was sick when he arrived here.'

The big man who had said his prayers by the spring came up to them, wiping his mouth; he had been taking a drink. He spoke in a jovial voice. 'What is pain? Or death itself, for that matter? We who are still alive and well should not forget to laugh.'

'Salamodin is always laughing,' said Rafiq.

The third man, Sofi, said drolly: 'They say he laughs when praying.'

'No, but sometimes when other men are praying. I think God must laugh in his beard, too, seeing so many rogues so busy on their knees.'

As they rode away, McLeod thought that in the house behind him Margaret was probably praying.

Two hours later, on a hillock in the forest, they stopped to rest their horses and take the last look back down at the valley. Amongst the green trees the houses shone in the sun. Through binoculars McLeod picked out Donald's and Margaret's. He saw her, or what at first he took to be her, in the garden. She was motionless, and he thought she must be gazing up at the forest, perhaps regretting in the depths of her heart that she had not gone with him. Then he began to doubt it was she he was looking at. It might have been a rock with a blue cloth spread upon it to dry. That would be like her. However despairing deep within, outwardly she would continue to show a housewife's calm, and wash, and cook, and tend her husband, and prepare for the child kicking within her. He imagined her hands, ringless, work-worn, and calm; and he wondered at the unimaginable sources of that calmness.

As they rode on again he felt that he had seen her for the last time. Indeed, he began to have a feeling that he had not seen her at all, but rather had dreamt it; and it was a dream he should start learning to forget. The people he should want to remember were those at Haimir, for instance. Had soldiers or policemen descended upon them again, to bully out of them every detail of his own visit? He thought of the old woman there, and of Rafiq's mother, and found their remembered indomitability sustaining him, as the memory of Margaret's incomprehensible devotion could never do.

So it was those old women, and the young girl with the dead baby, and the old chief with the one hand, and the teacher of English at Kalak, that he kept recalling during the long, furtive journey through dark defiles and along precipitous windy ledges, to the blue lake, and thence to the lower slopes of the mountain where his car was waiting.

Twenty-one

Through his binoculars McLeod saw that Salamodin was right: about a mile ahead, amidst the great red rocks like cinders out of hell, was his Land-Rover; and beside it stood a truck. Smoke swirled from a fire, about which men moved. Their clothes did not billow in the strong wind. Near them were two tents, about fifty yards apart.

Soldiers or police, he was sure; but had they tracked down the Land-Rover deliberately and now waited beside it for his return, or had they come upon it by accident? The former was much more likely. Even in a time of frontier uneasiness this part of the country was seldom patrolled, especially at this late season when winds thick with dust blew during the day, and at night frost was keen. Yes, they must have pursued him from Mazarat, through Haimir to the lakes, and thence to this barren wilderness under the great mountains.

'I think it would be better if you were to go no further,' he said. 'They would ask too many questions.'

Rafiq nodded. He looked sour, and kept touching the butt of the rifle across his saddle. That was a habit picked up coming through the upper pass, with soldiers not so far below.

'I can walk from here,' said McLeod.

They did not argue, though they would have thought it unmanly to walk such a distance themselves. But then the heels of their riding-boots were two inches high.

They all dismounted. Rafiq helped McLeod to strap on his rucksack.

'Will they do you harm?' he asked.

'I don't think so.'

'You have a gun?'

'Yes, but I don't think I'll need it.'

'If we hear shooting, we will come galloping.'

It was turning dark, and the wind, still blowing down from the hills, was icy. A star or two glittered.

McLeod shook hands with each of them.

'Sahib,' said Salamodin, laughing though his mouth was muffled with part of his turban cloth, 'what you say to them yonder is your business. I agree. But it could be our business, depending upon what you say. You understand?'

'Yes.'

'I mean no disrespect, sahib. But Azim told us what he saw at Haimir. You saw it yourself.'

'Yes, I saw it.'

'It is not right to count heads in such a matter, I agree, but it is still true that your friends are two, whereas there are two hundred and more in the valley.'

'What happened at Haimir would not happen to us,' said Rafiq. 'We would fight.'

'The difference would be,' said Salamodin, laughing, 'that we would all be dead, whereas at Haimir some are still alive.'

'I shall say nothing to them that will cause you any trouble,' said McLeod. 'I shall not tell them I have been to your valley.'

They were silent for almost a minute.

'Sahib,' murmured Sofi, who seldom spoke, 'will you come and visit us again in the spring?'

'I don't know. It may not be possible. In the spring I expect to be thousands of miles away.'

'There is the woman, sahib. What is to become of her?'

'I don't know that, either.'

'Does anyone know what will happen to him in the spring?' asked Rafiq harshly. 'We are all in God's hands.'

'No one can deny that,' agreed Sofi, and said no more; but it was clear that, imagining himself and his friends on a Brobdingnagian palm, he by no means felt confident.

'I shall walk a few steps with you,' said Rafiq to McLeod.

He did so, slowly, with awkward, stilted gait. Soon he halted, and gripped McLeod by the arm.

'I struck you,' he said. 'I am sorry.'

'It's all right.'

'I wish to explain. At that time we had made up our minds that we would be safe only when your friends were dead. That was the decision of the council. I agreed with it. I spoke for it. The man would soon die, in any case. Perhaps he is dead now, as we speak. So there would be only the woman.'

'I know all this.'

'Not all.' Rafiq could not keep his voice low. 'If someone has to be killed, there must be someone to do it. No one was willing.'

'I would have thought Fakir or one of his sons would have offered.'

'They could not. They are holy men. It would not be proper for them to shed blood.'

'But proper enough for them to urge that it be shed?'

'I think it will be the same with your holy men, sahib.'

'It is.'

'With all holy men. How can they intercede for us with God, if they have blood on their hands?'

'How indeed?'

'It is cold, sahib, and it will soon be dark. I shall not keep you longer. But before you go, I wish to tell you that it was I, Rafiq, who volunteered to kill the woman. Goodbye, sahib.'

He turned and stalked back to his two comrades and the horses.

McLeod called after him. 'At any rate, take care of her now.'

It was Salamodin who shouted back: 'We shall do what we can.'

McLeod felt like rushing back and demanding a stronger assurance; but he hesitated only a moment or two before hurrying away in the opposite direction, towards the fire, the police, and ultimately home. He felt he was turning his back on Margaret for the last time. She would be behind him in the darkness forever.

The hillside was littered with those great red boulders now purple with shadow, and with low thorn bushes that scratched like fierce little animals against his ankles. The wind, too, cold and dusty, held him back.

There was no guard, so that he was able to walk right up to the fire unnoticed. A sheep had just been roasted, and the policemen, wrapped in blankets, were squatted round the fire, holding pieces of hot mutton in their hands.

The smell made McLeod bold. 'Salaam,' he cried.

Though astonished, and in some cases momentarily terrified, they kept on squatting and chewing. Then a sergeant scrambled up and, like an old woman, in his blanket went hobbling fast towards the smaller of the tents.

McLeod asked if he could have a seat at the fire and a bit of mutton, as he was cold and hungry. At once room was made for him, and three knives began slicing eagerly at the carcase.

The sergeant came hurrying back. Close behind him were two officers, one a young lieutenant, and the other Major Samad of Mazarat.

'Good evening, Major,' said McLeod.

'So it is you.'

'As large as life.'

'Yes, I am glad to see that you are still alive.'

'And with a good appetite, too. Thanks for looking after my car.'

'I have questions to ask of you. Please come with me to my tent.'

'It's warm here by the fire.'

'I must insist.'

'Do you mind if I take this mutton with me?'

The Major could hardly have refused; his own mouth was still greasy. Some of the soldiers grinned.

'As you wish.' He marched back to his tent.

McLeod followed with the lieutenant who looked about eighteen.

'Tell me,' asked McLeod, 'have you come from Mazarat?'

'Yes, but I was new there.'

'Is the Colonel still there? The one whose wife and children died of smallpox?'

'There is another Colonel.'

'What happened to the other one? Did he die? He was very ill with malaria.'

'He is not there now, but I do not think he died.'

The Major was seated on a low stool. His dish of mutton lay on the ground beside him, looking like a dog's. He gave McLeod a smile that was like a snarl.

'You are talking about the Colonel?' he asked. 'You wonder what happened to him? Did you think, because he had neglected his duty in giving you a pass, that he would be degraded, or cashiered, or even imprisoned? Perhaps you have forgotten that his father is a friend of the king. He has gone home to rest, that is all. I think he is now considering taking another wife.'

McLeod squatted on the ground. 'I'm glad to hear it. He was very kind to me.'

'Too kind, Mr. McLeod.'

'Is there any tea available?'

There was a teapot, but it was empty. The Major, glaring, nodded at the lieutenant, who thrust his head out, and yelled: 'Chai.'

'Thanks,' said McLeod.

'We are at your service, sir. You would not like a bath, with hot water?'

'I'd be delighted.'

'You laugh, Mr. McLeod. Yet I assure you there are officers of no higher rank than mine who travel with such luxuries as baths. They are rich. I am poor. My father is a humble official in Hezrat.'

He paused while a soldier handed in a pot of tea.

'Help yourself, Mr. McLeod.'

McLeod was already doing so.

'Now if you please, what is the explanation?'

'What do you mean?'

'You know what I mean, Mr. McLeod. For days we have followed you, for hundreds of miles. We find you here, in this wilderness where no one lives.'

'I was climbing the mountains.'

'Why?'

'In my country it is a sport.'

'So I have heard. But, if you will pardon me, I do not believe you. You must have had another purpose.'

'What other purpose?'

'You are a bold, clever man, Mr. McLeod. Also you know the language very well. Are you not a spy?'

'What is there to spy on here? You said yourself it was a wilderness.'

'I do not know this part of the country, Mr. McLeod. I do not know what is here to spy on. What I do know is that General Hussein, Commandant of the Secret Police, himself flew to Mazarat, to order me to follow you and bring you back.'

'The General is a friend of mine.'

'So you said before in Mazarat. He was very angry.'

'Not with me, I'm sure.'

'Not with you, you think? And not with the Colonel, whose father is the king's friend. With whom then? Yes, with everyone else; and especially with poor Major Samad. He was very angry with him.' The Major's hand shot up to his cheek, where perhaps it had been slapped by Hussein's glove.

'Is he still in Mazarat?'

'No. He flew back the same day, by special plane. I believe I am grateful to you, Mr. McLeod. I have enjoyed the travelling; and since I have found you, alive and well, it is possible some credit will be given to me.'

'And now you've found me, what are you going to do with me?'

'Take you back to Mazarat first; thereafter you will be conducted back to the capital, where the General, and perhaps the Minister himself, will ask you questions.'

'I see.' McLeod contemplated the sheep-bone he had in his hand. 'In your travels, did you come through a village called Haimir?'

The Major made a noise of disgust. 'A filthy hole.' Then he brightened. 'We passed the blue lakes, too, and talked with the holy man. He told me there was much good fortune in store for me.'

No doubt in astute return for some free tea and nan.

'He is a very holy man,' said the Major. 'All year he guards the shrine, alone. In the winter the snow is higher than a camel's head. Often his only food is his dreams of God. I should think such a man's prophecies are to be respected. Do you not agree?'

'Did he tell you I had been there?'

The Major frowned. He glanced at the lieutenant, who looked at the ground.

'I see he didn't,' said McLeod. 'Well, I was there.'

'We saw the marks of the tyres,' murmured the lieutenant.

'Do not think we are so foolish, Mr. McLeod,' said the Major. 'You spoke of Haimir. I know why. It was there your friends were killed. I think you went there on a sad pilgrimage. Is that not right, Mr. McLeod?'

McLeod nodded.

'That is what General Hussein said, too. So you saw Haimir? I do not think you would enjoy seeing it.'

'No.'

The Major grinned. 'You would have approved of us, Mr. McLeod. Our visit was short, but I think they will remember it.'

McLeod closed his eyes. The bone in his hand became a human bone. The tea in his cup turned to blood.

'What did you do to them?' he whispered.

'Oh, we just kicked them about a bit. For the sake of authority. That place must become known throughout the whole country as a place of terror. As an example, you understand.'

McLeod wished he could pray. He saw the old woman's face, and the little girl's, who had so boldly confronted him, with her small brother on her back.

The Major laughed, and poured himself another cup of tea. Into it he dropped six spoonfuls of sugar. When he drank he sucked loudly.

'I see you are still sick with hatred. Perhaps you think our justice is weak; we should have put them all to death, because all were equally guilty. I am inclined to agree, because to make it a place of terror the ground ought to have been soaked with their blood so that it could be seen for years. But then, it is a good thing, too, to keep some of them alive, for further punishment.'

'I don't want to hear any more about them.'

'I understand, Mr. McLeod.'

'The old woman, with the blind eye?'

'You remember her? Yes, she's the she-wolf that leads the pack. I wouldn't be surprised if she's crawling about on all fours at this moment.'

'Why?'

Again the Major misinterpreted McLeod's difficulty of speech. 'She got in the way and showed her fangs; so somebody took his boot to her. I heard her leg was broken. At her age it won't mend in a hurry.'

McLeod shuddered.

Laughing, the Major patted him on the shoulder. 'You enjoy such talk? You and I will ride together back to Mazarat, and I shall tell you more about what we did at Haimir.'

'No.' Yet despite that snarl of denial McLeod did want to hear and hear again of every single act of cruelty perpetrated there; and he wanted, too, to rush back to the valley and yell it all to Donald before he died, and to Margaret before her child was born.

Whatever else he did, surely he must at least exonerate those people at Haimir so that persecution of them would end. If necessary, to prove their innocence he should produce Margaret alive. But though that would prove they were guiltless of her death, it would also reveal that they had helped to involve despotic authority in a folly whose consequences might be disastrous to it, both at home and abroad. Would it not be better then to think of Donald's agony in the valley, and Margaret's peculiar martyrdom, as, in some way he could not understand, acts of expiation that would be heeded? That, he thought, was how Goodwood Purdie, with a little more grace perhaps, might shuffle off responsibility.

Round their fire the policemen were chanting a melancholy song of love.

He got up. 'I'll have to put up my tent.'

'Sleep in here.'

'No, thank you. You're crowded enough.'

'Do you wish me to order some men to help you?'

'It's not necessary.'

As he was about to go out, the Major stopped him: 'Mr. McLeod, if you wish, we shall return by way of Haimir.'

McLeod was tempted.

'I think you would like to see that old woman again, Mr. McLeod?'

'I'll tell you in the morning.'

'Yes. And in the meantime dream of them. Let me tell you a strange thing for your dreams: most of the men have a disease which makes their members large.'

As McLeod crept out into the cold wind, he heard the Major keep on laughing, heartily and cruelly.

Twenty-two

It was afternoon, four days later, when the Land-Rover, tawny with dust, passed the British Embassy with the Union Jack fluttering over the white Residence.

Major Samad, still escorting him, was relieved when McLeod did not stop. 'You prefer to live at the hotel?' he asked discreetly.

'Yes.'

'I am glad, because, to tell you a secret, I was instructed not to allow you to enter your Embassy until General Hussein or the Minister himself had spoken with you. See, I have had my hand on my gun. You and I are now friends, McLeod. It would have been very unpleasant for me to ask you to do what you did not wish to do.'

McLeod's reason for not wanting to stop at the Embassy was that he still hadn't been able to decide what he should report to Minn and Gillie. By his silence he might very well be burying Margaret Duncan alive; but by speaking he might be the means of her being dragged out to face a world whose curiosity would be much more persevering than its compassion.

'You will pardon me if I must leave two of my men at the hotel,' said the Major. 'Not as guards, you understand, but as attendants.'

'When will you report?'

'At once. It is possible the General may wish to see you this evening.'

'I'll need a shave first, a bath, and a change of clothing.'

'Can you not get all those at the hotel?'

'If I'm lucky.'

'You will be lucky.'

At the hotel the Major strode in, as demanding as destiny. He roared at the timid servants in their fierce shaggy uniforms the colour of dried blood. Some scampered out to carry in McLeod's luggage, others rushed upstairs to prepare a room, and a few flocked into the manager's office to fetch that reluctant official.

He recognised McLeod. 'So they have caught you again?' he murmured in French.

'I'd like a room.'

'Impossible, Mr. McLeod. Not a single one is vacant. In any case, would you not be safer, and more comfortable, at your Embassy?'

'What does he say?' demanded the Major.

'He says there's no room vacant.'

'Tell him there must be a room. No, let us find one ourselves.' He shouted to the four policemen who had accompanied him from Mazarat. 'Go upstairs and find a room, a good room. If there is already someone in it, throw him out.'

The policemen dashed off, delighted as schoolboys.

The manager was dismayed. 'How can I run a hotel in such a country?'

McLeod refused to heed the appeal in the sad eyes.

'They may insult a Russian or an American,' sighed the manager.

The Major, tapping at his holster, was admiring a poster advertising Indian Airlines; it showed an Indian beauty, with flowers in her hair.

Outside a crowd had gathered.

From above came, in an American accent, sounds of amused indignation. Then at the top of the steps appeared a small bespectacled man, who needed a shave, a bath, and a change of clothing almost as much as McLeod himself. He seemed to have been interrupted at his afternoon nap, for he yawned and kept stuffing his flowered shirt into his khaki slacks.

'Mr. Bolton, an American writer,' whispered the manager. 'He has come to write a book about the country, but he is having a little trouble about a visa. I understand they think he asks too many impertinent questions.'

The questions the American was asking then were pertinent enough. 'Is there a revolution in progress, gentlemen? But I've been in revolutions before and never been dragged off my bed. Is it a matter of insufficient baksheesh? Or am I personally considered unworthy?'

He had come down the stairs as he spoke. He winked at McLeod. 'Is it for you, sir, that I am being asked, so rudely, to make way?'

McLeod could only scowl in shame.

'I don't know who you are, sir, though I hope to have that honour as soon as you feel inclined to tell me. My name's Josh Bolton, author, here in the way of business. I don't resent this. I find it fascinating. It will make, not a chapter, unless I pad like hell, but a section of a chapter; and the folks reading will think it quaint.'

'But, Mr. Bolton,' said the manager, in some agitation, 'I promised you the room only for three days. Those three days are up. You said you would be moving to the I.C.A. rest-house.'

'True,' agreed Bolton. 'But it has transpired that some compatriot in authority, some obstructive bastard, has made the discovery that I'm not eligible.'

McLeod could not help grinning at that gently spoken parenthesis. 'Couldn't we share the room?' he asked. 'In any case, I might not need it. Technically, I'm under arrest. I've just been brought in from Mazarat, and I'm to be held here until this monkey with the holster has reported to his superiors.'

Bolton held out his hand. 'Your name will be McLeod then?'

'Yes.'

'I've heard a lot about you, Mr. McLeod. Delighted to know you. Certainly we can share the room. There happens to be two beds; one with maybe ten less fleas than the other; but what's ten in a thousand?'

'I want a bath.'

'So do I; so does every other guest in the place. I understand a colony of rats, not all of them alive, occupies the pipes. If you're the loud-voiced aggressive type, which I'm not, you can cuss them into fetching you up hot water in jugs; but the first jugful's turned cold by the time the second arrives, so what's the use of a third?'

'I'll get a bath.'

'Show me, sir.'

A word to Major Samad started it. Feeling neglected during the conversation between McLeod and the American, he relished the chance to assert himself again. Up to the room he rushed, and roared at the servants who soon brought a large rumbling zinc bath and about a dozen jugfuls of hot water that, save for a little greasy scum on top, was reasonably clean.

'I could almost find it in my heart, sir,' said Bolton, as he watched the wonder, 'to ask you not to throw it out when you're through with it, but let me use it after you. I could pass it on in my turn.'

Then the Major ordered everyone to leave McLeod alone in the room. Bolton was pushed out by two policemen.

'Perhaps in a short time someone will telephone, Mr. McLeod,' said the Major. 'Until then you must see no one and speak to no one.'

McLeod was already undressing. By removing his trousers he also removed the Major, who fled, so embarrassed he felt obliged to push out of his way, on the stairs, an old man in a black karakul hat, who despite his age was undeniably male and so, under his greasy clothes, endowed with that virility that the Major had still to prove he possessed himself.

Outside the room, on one of the easy chairs in the corridor, Mr. Bolton smoked a cigar and scribbled notes.

Two hours later the Major returned, much subdued, to report that General Hussein intended to call at six o'clock, in half an hour.

'After he has said his prayers.'

The reason for the Major's bitterness was that he now foresaw no promotion for himself out of this business. Indeed, he smelled disaster. The fat Commandant had been in a slimming panic about his own position, in danger because of some other secret matter; it was rumoured he had displeased the Prime Minister. Certainly when he had snarled that he would go to see McLeod after he had said his prayers, he had not been jesting.

It was already dusk. Crossing to the window, McLeod counted eight men on their knees in the street. Somewhere, with creaks and groans, Hussein would be down on his. And somewhere else, with smiles and smoothness, his successor or deposer prayed, too, no froth of desperation on his lips.

So, thought McLeod, Mrs. Bryson's fat creep looks like creeping under the heavy flat stone of oblivion. He remembered him in the prison with the scented handkerchief at his nose; and he remembered, too, his wife and five children.

A policeman knocked at the door. It was to say the General was coming. The Major ran out to meet him.

Mohammed Hussein walked splay-footed on the red carpet, gazing down as if he saw his own blood under his feet. He had forgotten his gold-tipped staff, but made gestures as if it was in his hand. Two officers who accompanied him looked apprehensive and peeved; Major Samad could understand their feelings; they had to choose the right time to desert their chief, and it wouldn't be easy; moreover, there was always the possibility that Hussein might not be deposed after all; or worse, that he might be reinstated after a few days.

'Leave me alone with Mr. McLeod,' said Hussein at the door. 'See that we are not disturbed.'

His subordinates saluted. He waddled in. A policeman shut the door.

Mr. Bolton, watching from a discreet distance, now sneaked off downstairs to the telephone in the manager's room, where he rang up the British Embassy. Twice already that afternoon he had tried, but only an orderly had replied, in fluent Pushtu and inaccessible English.

Third time was lucky. After an afternoon's tennis Roger Minn had called in to take some papers home, where he could study them with the inspiration of Hilda and whisky.

'Minn speaking,' he said suspiciously, for really no one ought to have telephoned after office hours.

'Good. This is Josh Bolton. You remember me?'

'Bolton? Of course.' Though he didn't.

'Speaking from the hotel, Mr. Minn. Thought someone ought to let you know that one of your people is here, in some kind of trouble. Name's McLeod.'

'McLeod? Is he back?'

'I would say yes, wherever he's been he's back; surrounded by police; and at this moment is being put through the hoop by none other than General Hussein, who's the chief of the secret police, I understand.'

'But McLeod's a pal of his.'

'That may be, sir. I am a newcomer here, not yet invited to join in the games.'

'What games?'

'Metaphorically speaking.'

'I see.' Minn was thinking hard; something that was really nothing had to be said, yet it must sound authoritative. The trouble was this soft-voiced American seemed no fool. 'What do you suggest I do?'

'I guess that's up to you, sir.'

'You don't know McLeod? No, of course you don't.'

'But I sure would like to. He has the appearance of a man with a story to tell about this country. I understand he went off to investigate the disappearance of the two Britishers.'

'I'm afraid that's a closed case as far as we're concerned. Well, Mr. Bolton, thanks for letting me know. We'll keep an eye on McLeod.'

'Struck me as though he knew what he was about. But then, in my travels about the world, I've looked more than once on the corpses of men who when they were fizzing like the rest of us thought they knew what they were about. If you get what I mean. Trouble with speaking, you got no time to polish or retract. McLeod speaks the lingo here pretty well.'

'Yes. Well, I'm afraid I must push off. Thanks again.'

They both hung up. Bolton was sure Minn had done it first;

yet it was a buddy of Minn's who was in trouble. Bolton pictured him hurrying off to tea and muffins. At the American Embassy it would have been coffee and cookies.

Bolton went upstairs to have another look at his baggage. It was piled up in the corridor outside his room, looking pretty tattered and patient. Just like myself, he thought, as he sat down in the armchair to scribble more notes.

Meanwhile General Hussein, from under his imperious hat, was sorrowfully confiding in McLeod. He had first glanced under the two beds, and then, for an obscurer reason, taken the rusted lid off the bokkhari stove to gaze down at the ashes.

'As you know, McLeod, my friend, I am a humane, a religious man. I like to watch my children play, I like to hear birds singing, I always give baksheesh to holy men by the wayside. But I am dutiful also. My country is backward, so I devote all my energies to helping it to advance. I am told: a tight grip is necessary, leniency might provoke some adventure which would destroy the state. So I impose the tight grip, and turn my back on leniency. I am fierce, my name is detested, even my children look at me with shudders. As a humane man, given regularly to prayer, I suffer in my inside.'

McLeod sat and smoked and listened with a show of sympathy.

'Then what happens, McLeod, my friend? Policy is changed. Do not ask me why. Perhaps the Americans are considering a loan of millions of dollars. Suddenly I find myself in disfavour. Deeds for which I was praised before, in private, I am now blamed for, in public. I am made to feel the blood is on my hands alone.'

He stared at those soft pudgy hands, with their manicured nails, and then pulling out his handkerchief sniffed it avidly. McLeod recognised the scent. During the visit to the prison it had been used to make endurable the stink of mortality; now, from the tremulousness of those despairing nostrils, it appeared to have lost all efficacy.

'For instance, McLeod, I am blamed for the deaths of your two friends.'

McLeod tried not to show his interest was at last roused. 'In what way?'

'Because, if you please, I had given an example of violence. But, as you know, my friend, this has always been a violent country. It has been so for hundreds of years. Blood feuds continue.'

McLeod's own fingers felt sticky as he remembered his passport, sodden with the blood spouting from the fat man's head. He remembered, too, the marks of brutality on those patient faces at Haimir.

'And, of course, the tragedy is, McLeod, that if they do get rid of me, as is contemplated, and institute a period of leniency, it will be a sham, designed to deceive for some secret purpose. As soon as that purpose has been achieved, the tight grip will be imposed again, tighter than ever, to prevent chaos and bloodshed and rebellion. But where will I be then? I assure you I do not know. I am on the razor's edge. Conversations are taking place at this very moment.'

'What's likely to happen?' asked McLeod. Inwardly he added: 'You should know; you've made it happen to others.'

The fat shoulders hunched, the thick underlip pushed out, and from the sad, self-pitying brown eyes a couple of tears crept out, to trickle down the plump jowls.

'I am thinking of my children, McLeod.'

There are children at Haimir, thought McLeod. Outwardly he murmured: 'I'm sorry.'

A hand glittering with two gold rings stroked his knee. 'Thank you for your sympathy, McLeod. If you can help, I should be grateful.'

'How can I help?'

'The Minister is well-disposed towards you.'

'Not now surely?'

'Yes. He does not blame you for your escape. No, he blames me. But there are a thousand things besides. You will be going home now?'

'Yes. As soon as I can arrange it.'

'By car?'

McLeod wondered if he was going to be asked to do some

smuggling out. 'No. I'm flying. I'm going to sell the car. I've had enough of it.'

'I understand.' The General shook his head. 'I wish you every happiness, McLeod, my friend. Before I leave you, possibly for the last time, is there anything I can do to help you? Perhaps I can give you some advice.'

'You didn't tell me that my friends were attacked at Mazarat.'

'No. That was to be kept a secret. Who told you?'

'Never mind that. It doesn't matter now.'

'Since they are dead, what matters now to them? Nothing, nothing at all.'

'But what actually happened?'

'It was a simple case of assault. Perhaps the intention was also rape. Two were caught and put to death at once. It really does not matter whether they were the guilty ones or not. It is the example that counts.'

'Was there any doubt?'

'Yes, I believe so. But the man in charge was much too efficient to sit for weeks until he was sure.'

'It wasn't rape?'

'McLeod, the poor woman's dead. Why dig her up out of her grave?'

'I'd like to know exactly what happened.'

'It would need God Himself to tell you that. Our brains, our tongues, our memories, confuse everything.'

'Was she raped?'

'According to the doctor who examined her, no. According to her husband, Mr. Kemp, yes. He made a great fuss, I believe. He watched the two men being shot. I understand that pacified him. I do not blame him. In the circumstances, it might also have pacified me.'

'The doctor had left Mazarat. I believe he's here now.'

'Yes.'

'I'd like to have a talk with him.'

'McLeod, now you are asking me to dig my own grave.'

'I'd be discreet about it.'

'I am not a fool, McLeod. If you hear in a day or two that

your fat friend General Mohammed Hussein, who used to drink your whisky, has disappeared, you will shed no tears. I shall tell you this doctor's name. It is Dr. Mohammed Aslam. Tell him I gave it to you. You will find his number in the telephone directory. This is the new policy, you see, McLeod: leniency and forgiveness and lack of fear.'

While the General was enjoying, at some cost, that pout of irony, there was a hearty knock on the door.

'Who is it?' he bellowed, pretending authoritative rage; at the same time he winked sadly. 'Did I not say I was not to be disturbed?'

'I'm afraid it's me, General,' called out Roger Minn. 'Mr. Gillie's with me, and Colonel Rodgers. We heard McLeod was back, so we've come to pay him a visit and carry him off with us. I hope we're not disturbing anything of vital importance.' Nevertheless, in spite of that hope, he laughed, with the rather high-pitched, Britannic assurance which proclaimed that were he disturbing the routine of God he should be awfully sorry, but it just couldn't be helped, could it?

As Hussein listened, he laughed, too, trying to put into it his country's proud history of resistance to imperialists; but it was only a sad little squeal he managed.

He waddled to the door and opened it.

The three Englishmen had flowers in their button-holes. They were dressed as for a party.

'Enter in, gentlemen,' he said, in English. 'I am leaving. You will find I have not shot our friend McLeod. Goodbye, McLeod. I wish you happiness.'

Minn and the two others, the Consul and the Military Attaché, watched in astonishment as he went so docilely, taking all his minions with him, including Major Samad.

'So it was as easy as that?' said Minn. 'We thought we'd better come in force.'

You laughed, McLeod almost said.

They were, it turned out, going to a party. It was being held at the Colonel's.

'For no particular reason, old boy,' said the host. 'Just my turn to kill the fatted calf. Return of the prodigal makes it more appropriate, don't you think? Besides, you may have seen one or two things on your recent travels that I might find professionally interesting.'

'Well, for God's sake,' cried Minn, 'let's get out of this hellish place. McLeod, Hilda insists, with my fullest support, that you now accept the hospitality you so precipitately fled from last time.'

'I'm sorry about that.'

'Say no more. Get a few bods to carry your stuff down, old man, and we'll be on our way.'

Outside, the corridor was thronged with servants and hotel guests. Among the latter was Mr. Bolton, smoking a cigar. He pushed through to McLeod. 'I'd sure be obliged, Mr. McLeod, if you'd let me have a chat with you some time.'

Minn hustled McLeod along. 'I'm afraid Mr. McLeod's going to be pretty busy,' he called back. He added, in a whisper: 'I hope you don't mind? I had to protect you from that fellow. A writer. Poking his nose in. Investigating the position of women, among other things.'

'Why not?'

'Well, I'm inclined to believe that if they want to treat their women like medieval chattels, and the women like it, then we've got no bloody right to interfere.'

When McLeod's bags were stowed into his Land-Rover, Gillie said he'd ride with him to keep him company.

'Good idea,' said Minn. 'Bruce will come with me.'

McLeod knew Gillie's reason; this was to pump him about Donald and Margaret. It would be done officially, too, with grunts of complacency.

'I'm afraid you'll find it pretty dusty,' he said.

'That's all right,' said Gillie, though he sounded anxious. Big and brusque, with a red, unhandsome face, he still was very fastidious about his clothes, which were expensive. When he saw how dusty the Land-Rover was, he changed his mind. 'Maybe you're right. Thanks for the warning. What about yourself? You'll get filthy, too.'

'Can't be helped. I'll follow behind.'

'Right, old man,' said Minn.

'By the way, I suppose it'll be all right if I stop for a minute or two at the Chancery to use the telephone?'

Minn looked frankly doubtful. 'Somebody you want to tell you're back? Ten to one that somebody will be at Bruce's tonight. Mrs. Bryson, for instance.'

McLeod shook his head, climbed into his car, and waited for Minn to drive off. He noticed Bolton on the steps of the hotel, and gave him a wave.

As he drove along the tree-lined road towards the Embassy, he realised he had still not made up his mind about the statement he would make about Kemp and Miss Duncan. It might be this telephone call would help him to decide.

The Chancery, like the dwelling-houses, was within the great compound, known among the junior staff as 'the ghetto'. Minn drew up outside it and waited for McLeod.

'You won't need us, I suppose?' he asked.

'No, thanks.'

'Of course you know your own business, old man, but after all this is the Embassy telephone. Do I have your assurance no trouble's likely to arise?'

'I don't see why it should.'

'Some people might think you're a bit myopic in that respect, old man. We'll see you at Bruce's?'

'You know where the old homestead is, of course?' asked the Colonel.

'Yes, thanks.'

McLeod watched the car drive off, then he hurried into the building with its white-washed corridors. The orderly conducted him to the small room where the telephone was.

'Is there a directory?'

'Yes, sahib. But not English.'

McLeod took it and quickly found the name he was looking for. He dialled the number. As he waited he noticed that the moon was rising above the hill called Legation Hill.

A woman's voice answered. 'Who is it? This is Dr. Aslam's house.'

'Thank you. I'd like to speak to the doctor. Is he at home.'

'Yes, he is at home. Who are you, please?'

'That doesn't matter. I just want to ask him something.'

'You are a foreigner?'

'Yes.'

'I shall tell him. Perhaps he will speak to you.'

In a short time the doctor's voice was heard, soft with reluctance. 'Dr. Aslam here. I understand you wish to speak to me.'

'Yes, doctor. I'm sorry for disturbing you.'

'You have not disturbed me yet.'

'A few months ago you were in charge of the hospital at Mazarat.'

There was a pause. McLeod could hear the doctor conferring anxiously with his wife. At last the doctor replied: 'That is so. I have come from Mazarat.'

'While you were there an Englishwoman was brought to you for examination. She had been attacked.'

'I must ask you to tell me who you are.'

'All right. My name's McLeod. I'm telephoning from the British Embassy.'

'You are a British diplomat?'

'Yes.'

'I understood this affair was to be kept a secret. Has the government informed you officially?'

'No. I found it out myself. I have just returned from Mazarat.'

'I see. Of course you will know that after she left Mazarat the woman was killed, along with her husband?'

'Yes, I know that.'

'What difference does it make then what happened at Mazarat?'

'What I want to know is this: was there any possibility of her becoming pregnant as a result of that attack?'

'No.'

'Are you sure, doctor?'

'Certainly I am sure. In the first place, she was not raped; and in the second place, she was already pregnant.'

'You are certain of that?'

'In the circumstances I could make only a superficial examination, but I was satisfied.'

'She was pregnant?'

'Yes. It is a common enough condition. I advised her against continuing her journey.'

'Was she ill?'

'Not ill; exhausted, especially in mind. She knew she was pregnant. She had been a nurse, I believe. She seemed to be of the opinion that her professional knowledge was greater than mine. She struck me as a woman very likely to provoke fate. I was not surprised to hear afterwards that she had been killed.'

McLeod heard the doctor's wife whispering, no doubt again warning him.

'What about the woman's husband, doctor?'

'I know nothing about him. Was he her husband? There seemed to be some doubt. I wanted to see him, to reassure him about her, and also to advise him, but he refused. Yet he waited to see the two young men shot.'

'Young men?'

'They were both under twenty. But, sir, my wife advises me I should say no more. She thinks I have already said too much. Good evening.'

His wife took the telephone. 'You will not cause my husband any harm?'

'No.'

'Thank you.' She put down the receiver.

McLeod put down his. He took out his packet of cigarettes. Outside a motor-horn tooted jocularly.

The orderly looked in. 'All right, sahib?'

'Yes.'

'Car, sahib.'

'What? Oh, yes.' His car was blocking the way. Some early reveller for the party couldn't get past.

He went outside. The car obstructed was a long white Chevrolet shining in the moonlight.

'No especial hurry,' an American voice drawled pleasantly.

'Sorry.'

'Say, pardon the impertinence, but is your name McLeod? Are you the bold spirit that gave them all the slip about a couple of weeks or so back?'

'Yes.'

'Mrs. Bryson's a friend of ours. Are you heading for Bruce Rodgers's party?'

'Yes.'

'Has he roped you in to thrill us all with an account of your adventures?'

A woman's voice murmured: 'Dean, don't be so forward. You must forgive him, Mr. McLeod. He still looks at cowboy comics.'

That was the second time within a few minutes that a woman had been beside her husband, advising and protecting him. McLeod vividly remembered Margaret Duncan weeping by the spring, and Donald in the house lying on the bed with the blue cover.

Climbing into the Land-Rover he drove along the avenue, past the Colonel's house in which every light blazed. The car behind tooted in a friendly way to tell him he had gone past. But he felt he wasn't ready just yet for the social smile, the amiable triviality, and the whisky-and-water thrust into his hand. He had first to try and reconcile what the doctor had told him with what he remembered Margaret and Donald saying. It was obvious both of them had lied to him, just as they had lied to each other. Could there be any conceivable reason for those lies?

It was nearly an hour later when he drove back to the house. All round it, even on the lawn, cars were parked. The party was already as animated as the Colonel and his wife, diligently stirring, could make it. Every guest had a glass in his or her hand. Most had chosen whisky, and with its encouragement could listen brightly to conversations that palled, smile at people disliked, laugh at flat jokes, and show glistening eyes of expectancy during silences imposed by vacuity.

In the dining-room the tables, some borrowed from neighbouring houses, were crowded with insignia'd plates, on which were heaped curried stew, sliced turkey, mutton in rice, boiled ham, vegetables, trifle, and cake. Servants, also borrowed, waited in readiness, wearing red cummerbunds and tall, white turbans.

His host met him at the door. 'Where have you been, old man? Colonel Wallace, the American Air Attaché, told me you'd driven past. We thought you'd gone off again. What's it to be? I have no doubt the beverage of your beloved motherland.' As he handed McLeod the glass he winked, and lowered his voice: 'H.E.'s here. Roger suggests best not to talk, until we've had his verdict.'

'I'm afraid I've got nothing to talk about.'

'Exactly. That's what I've been telling them. What could you have to talk about unless you'd found both of them alive; which, of course, is absurd even to mention.'

'Yes.'

'Maybe, though, you noticed troop movements?'

'Not even that.'

Minn came hurrying up. 'There you are, McLeod, old man. H.E. would like to have a word with you. You don't mind?'

McLeod shook his head. If he had minded, would Minn have clubbed him with the nearest whisky bottle and dragged his carcase at least to the ambassadorial feet?

The Ambassador was waiting in another room, standing in front of the fire with a glass of whisky in his hand.

'McLeod, sir,' announced Minn, urgently.

'So I see, Roger. Had a good trip, McLeod?'

'Yes, sir.'

'Not very eventful, I should think. I mean, considering half the army were alerted to stop you.'

They all laughed, Minn loudest.

'Did you manage to reach this place, where it happened?'

'Yes, sir.'

'Jolly good. I mean, it must have taken some persistence, and, of course, the roads are damnable. You look as though you could do with a rest. But was the trip worth it? Did you find out anything? They're dead, aren't they?'

'Yes, sir.'

He thought the Ambassador glanced curiously at him. Minn, however, was beaming with relief.

'Rum fellow, Kemp, from what I heard,' murmured the Ambassador. 'But he was a friend of yours, McLeod.'

'Not really, sir. An acquaintance. We were students together. I didn't know him very well.'

'Did anyone? Roger here called him a leper-lover.'

'What I mean, sir, was that he wanted above all to show how much he despised normality. What was wrong with marrying the girl and settling down like ordinary people? Yet that was a prospect worse than death to him; or so he claimed.'

'It would seem,' said the Ambassador quietly, 'that, whatever else he did, he justified that claim.'

'But what about the girl, sir? She had normal desires and ambitions.'

'Really, Roger? How many normal girls undertake to spend their lives nursing the black-skinned heathen? Not to mention making so extraordinary a journey with a companion like Kemp. It seems to me they were well-matched. Do you agree, McLeod?'

'I think so, sir.'

'Well, they're both gone now.'

All three took a sip of whisky. It seemed the only appropriate gesture.

'You're a man of mysterious contacts, I understand, McLeod,' said the Ambassador. 'Heard anything about the present subterranean rumbles?'

'A little, sir. From General Husscin.'

'The secret police man?'

'Yes, sir.'

'What did he tell you?'

'Principally that his own position seems to be very shaky. A new era of tolerance is going to be announced. He thinks he'll be the chief scapegoat.'

'Does it mean they're thinking of coming down on our side, after all? Or should I say, on the American side.'

'He thinks so, sir; but he also thinks it will only be temporary.'

'I see. You'd be a useful man here, McLeod. Ever think of coming back?'

'I have thought of it, sir.'

Minn was piqued. 'I understand, McLeod, you actually contemplated marrying one of the women here, a native, I mean?'

'I'd rather not talk about that.'

Minn laughed. 'Sorry. I didn't think you'd still be touchy. It was five years ago.'

The Ambassador smiled. 'Well, Roger, I wonder if you'd be so good as to lead me back to my fair spouse. I'll see you again, McLeod, before you go.'

'Yes, sir.'

As the Ambassador left the room with Minn, he said: 'You weren't very tactful there, Roger.'

'You mean, sir, mentioning his ex-girlfriend?'

'Yes, though I should have chosen a rather more romantic term.'

'But, sir, I understood it was just some kind of escapade on McLeod's part. We've seen how headstrong he is. After all, who in his senses would ever think of marrying one of these women?'

'I think our Scottish friend was in his senses all right. It might have come off, too. From what I've heard' – he paused, to emphasise that he had sources of information unknown to his First Secretary – 'she was an extremely beautiful, emancipated girl. She's married now, and has a child. The marriage was, of course, arranged. I believe she has not forgotten our young friend; and you and I, Roger, have just seen that he has certainly not forgotten her.'

'By Jove, sir, I had no idea.'

The Ambassador smiled: it meant that all the things about which his subordinate had no idea would fill both the Gobi and the Kalahari Deserts. He chose wildernesses far apart to symbolise the gaps even in Minn's ignorance. Yet, despite it, Roger would probably one day become an ambassador like himself, who was also vastly ignorant, if not quite so triumphantly.

When McLeod rejoined the party, Mrs. Bryson came hurrying to introduce her husband, Sam, a big, smiling, fair-haired man, whose thoughts went at an easy, charitable pace.

'I was sorry I missed you when you called, Mr. McLeod,' he said.

'Did you get the snags unravelled?'

'Well, you know how it is. Snags breed snags. But they don't bother me much. What about yourself, Mr. McLeod? You've had a few difficulties yourself recently to overcome.'

'Sam doesn't know it,' said his wife, quickly, 'but what he's got is faith. He's always sure everything's going to come out all right in the end.'

'It's just got to be all right, Jean; that's all.'

'See what I mean, Mr. McLeod? Sam's the old original smiler over the spilt milk. Gee!' And then to McLeod's surprise, if not to her husband's, she shed some tears. Was it too much whisky? wondered McLeod. Certainly she looked flushed and excited. Whatever her husband thought he did it fondly, and gave her his handkerchief.

'I just remembered that poor girl,' she said.

McLeod's hand trembled.

'I guess I'll never forget her.'

'Best to try all the same, Jean.'

'You know I lie and think about her.'

'Sure, I know that.'

'She was so young and beautiful. She could have been a film star.'

'I understood she had talents and ambitions above that, Jean.'

'I guess so. But what I mean is, she seemed to be acting in

some film; she wasn't real, somehow. Don't expect sense from me; I'm all confused. But that film I saw her in, her letting our kids comb her hair, her singing hymns to them, and then her going off as cool as you like on that journey, with a madman like Kemp, it just couldn't have had a happy ending. I mean,' she glanced round at the other guests, 'she just would never have fitted in here.'

'There are other places to fit in, Jean. You'd never see Goodwood P. here.'

'No, I guess not. But I can't think of any place where she and Kemp would fit in, except, God forgive me, that place where they were both killed, side by side, in the snow. I know I never saw it, but it's in my imagination, and it sure terrifies me.' She tried to laugh. 'What's making me so talkative all of a sudden? It must be the Scotch.'

She smiled at McLeod, and for a moment he was tempted to say: 'She's not dead, Mrs. Bryson. He probably is, by this time. But she's alive, and is going to have a child. Why did she not come back with me? I don't know, I don't really know.'

Mrs. Bryson still smiled, in a rather silly, tipsy way. She held up her glass. 'To the living, Mr. McLeod.' As she drank, she shivered.

'But here's Dr. Spinker, Mr. McLeod. I understand he's got a bone to pick with you.'

Dr. Spinker was tall, thin, silvery-haired. As he shook hands with McLeod, he put on a severe magisterial frown.

'Dr. Spinker's an educationist,' explained Mrs. Bryson. 'He's the head of a team here.'

'And one of my staff, Mr. McLeod, is a gentleman known to you.'

McLeod smiled and shook his head. It couldn't be the man he'd met in the hotel bathroom.

'Henry Shoopbaum,' cried the doctor, and went off into a rage of laughter.

McLeod remembered.

'Yes, sir, Henry came back shocked to the depths. I doubt if he's recovered even yet. Lacks a sense of humour, poor man. I nearly killed myself laughing when he told me about it.'

McLeod couldn't help grinning. Shoopbaum's account would have been funny.

'But why did you do it, Mr. McLeod? For a gag?'

McLeod explained.

'What happened to the young fellow, the teacher?' he asked. 'I hope he wasn't sacked?'

'Not on your life. He's been promoted. Yes, sir, they've made him a principal, so that he no longer teaches. We trained him for two years just so he can sit at a desk and make up time-tables.'

'I hope his salary's better.'

'It's a fair raise, by their standards.'

McLeod heard that sad but determined voice: 'The salary is not much, but I need it.' He heard, too, the whole class bellowing: 'We think he's a very good teacher.'

'My wife,' Dr. Spinker was saying, 'thinks it's a damn silly book anyway. She's not here tonight, because yesterday she ate lettuce, which was a damn silly thing, too. But I'm sure she'd be delighted to hear your account of it, Mr. McLeod. What about honouring us with your presence at dinner, any night that suits you? Our good friends Jean and Sam will come, too.'

'Will Mr. Shoopbaum be there?'

'Why not? It would be lovely watching Henry listen to your explanation.'

McLeod promised he would try to attend.

Twenty-Three

After weeks of hesitation McLeod wrote from Rome, his new post, to Margaret's parents: 'I'm sorry I wasn't able to keep my promise to visit you and let you know how I got on in my search. Perhaps it was just as well I couldn't, for the meeting would have been painful to us all. I reached the place where it is said to have happened, and saw the people who are said to have done it. They are now, I can assure you, sufficiently miserable and penitent; and, of course, the two alleged chief culprits, one an idiot, were properly executed, according to the law of the country. Everyone, from the Minister of the Interior, whom I saw, to the British Ambassador, was satisfied that everything had been done which could be done. It is true that no traces were found, except for the bangle (now returned to you, I understand) and the photograph; and you may feel that this continues to give excuse for hope. If so, it is certainly not for me to extinguish it; but, then, no one could ever do that for you, who have the good fortune to believe in God, as your daughter certainly did.

'Everyone who had met Margaret spoke very highly of her. She will certainly not be forgotten there for a long time.

'I am sorry if this letter sounds, as I feel it does, too callous, as if in some way my sympathies were exhausted. This is not so. It may be that I am still there, in imagination, carrying on that search, visiting those villages in the desert and the valleys in the mountains, and all the time hoping for what my reason tells me is impossible. I have no faith such as you have, and hope for me must exist on earth if it is to exist at all. This is confused, I know; and I must ask you to excuse me. If you feel that I have disappointed you, or let you down, I am most humbly sorry.'

He was far from pleased with it, but after half a dozen rewritings it still remained false, cold-hearted, and cruel. Yet it was the best he could do.

The truth itself, indeed, would have been as difficult to write, and, for her parents, even more difficult to accept. For having met them he felt they would prefer to remember their daughter as the innocent victim of brutal, ungrateful heathens, than as a woman who, professing sincerity of faith, had unchastely travelled with, and slept with, a man they looked upon as insane and evil, so that not only had she become pregnant but also so distorted and ashamed in mind that she had chosen to spend the rest of her life in an insignificant valley in an outlandish country where the people did not speak English or acknowledge Christ. They would certainly insist that she be brought home to their suburban bungalow, to be daily re-proached – or pitied. As for her child, to thwart the dead man, they would do their best to have it discreetly received into some institution for illegitimates.

Yet it was not a desire to protect her that kept him from trying to explain truthfully what had happened to her; nor was it loyalty to the promise he had half-given her; nor considera-tion for Azim's people. Rather it was a kind of paralysis of his moral judgment; it prevented him from ever seeing the situa-tion clearly and dispassionately; and the more he tried the worse it got, until in the end he almost believed there never had been a situation to be judged. It had been a dream, where the ordinary rules of morality did not apply; and his daily expecta-tion of a message was surely part of the dream.

In June, though, it arrived, along with a letter from Minn, which he read first.

'Dear McLeod,
    'The accompanying most mysterious missive was handed in yesterday at the gate, for "Sahib McLeod". According to the orderly the character who handed it in was a primitive hill-man from the north, his beard hoary with dust. He had a couple of friends with him, just as

wild-looking. They wouldn't wait or give their names, but galloped off as if afraid they might be arrested. It was brought to me, and I think I ought to admit that, after considerable reflection, I considered it a matter to go up to H.E. himself. You remember, McLeod, at Bruce's party you more or less confessed you still had an interest in the woman you once contemplated marrying. I know I blundered in trying to make a joke of it then, but you had a look in your eyes which made me wonder. Then you will recall that at the airport, with an air of casualness that didn't in the least deceive me, you mentioned there might be a message of some sort for you which you would like to be sent on to you as quickly as possible. I felt rather suspicious at the time.

'Now, McLeod, old man, what all this amounts to is: H.E. and I are apprehensive that you may be about to attempt another of your foolhardy – you must pardon the word, in my opinion justified – expeditions to this country, this time on a mission that would certainly have far more serious repercussions than your last. The woman, McLeod, is married, with a child. That she may not be happy does not really concern us. I think you know both her father and her husband are wealthy men, with considerable influence among members of the Government. If you are harbouring any mad hope of coming here and snatching her away, for God's sake, drop it. If you managed to stay alive, which I doubt, at least your career would be more disastrously ended than your pal Kemp's was.

'Of course this letter may not be from her at all. You have many acquaintances here, some too unsavoury for me, I must say. But I thought, with H.E.'s concurrence, that you ought to be most solemnly warned, even at the risk of a certain amount of impertinence on my part. It was, of course, out of the question our opening the envelope. That sort of thing just can't be done among friends.

'Various people here send their regards, among them Mr. and Mrs. Bryson, and General Hussein, who weathered the crisis and struts as obnoxiously as ever. I never see him but he talks about you. You remember Bolton, the American writer, whom you rather encouraged? Well, he's been giving us some trouble lately; in fact, largely because of him we've got an awkward little problem on our hands. It appears an English girl intends coming here shortly to marry some official of the Ministry of Works. He met her while he was on a course in England. No doubt he filled her with lies about his wealth and position here. You know as well as I do the kind of life foreign women are forced to lead here if they marry men of the country. A Frenchwoman once committed suicide, didn't she? But really how can the Embassy officially interfere? Bolton thinks we should, or rather a pal of his does, a fellow called Moffat who teaches English at the University. He's been here for two years and speaks the language pretty well, almost as well as yourself. He knows any number of natives, too, and maintains openly that he does more for the British cause here than the whole Embassy combined. Some like his brand of humour; I don't. Anyway, he's making a damned nuisance of himself over this Englishwoman. I don't know yet just what we're going to do about it. You're well out of it all, McLeod, in so civilised a city as Rome.

'We had a terrific amount of snow last winter. It was possible to ski on Legation Hill, just outside the gate; usually, as you know, we've to travel about five miles. Hilda hurt her leg. She's an intrepid skier, unlike myself who, in this kind of descent anyway, am reasonably cautious. I'm glad to say she's recovered now, and is bounding about the tennis court like a giddy impala. She sends her warmest regards. A woman like Hilda, McLeod, really, she's a wonderful asset to a man in a career like ours. However, enough said.

'If, as a consequence of this intriguing missive, there's something you want done here, I'll only be too glad to oblige, provided, of course, it involves nothing prejudicial to our national interests.'

McLeod read that letter slowly, yet, during the first reading anyway, with little attention. The other envelope, which he recognised as one he had given Margaret for that purpose, was all the time in his thoughts. For a long time he put off opening it.

His name was written on it, and the address was care of the British Embassy. The word 'Personal' appeared twice. Yet, in spite of those precautions, how near to discovery her secret had been. Another Head of Chancery might have risked opening it, on the grounds that the message it contained was likely to be not prejudicial, but unimportant. Minn's staff joked about the little Union Jacks he had fluttering at the side of his head, instead of his ample ears; this was on account of his comical and often bizarre scrupulosity, which he himself interpreted as the British way of life.

At last McLeod opened the envelope. There were two sheets of notepaper, neatly folded, and covered with small, careful writing.

'Dear John McLeod,

'You will be sorry to hear that, only two days after you left, Donald passed away. I did my best to give him a Christian burial, and these kind people assisted me in every way they could. My baby is now nearly six months old, and, I thank God, continues to be bonny and healthy. I have called him Donald, after his father. He does not look, to me at any rate, illegitimate.

'I find I have no wish to return to what is called the world. It may be that when Donald grows up, and I tell him about his father, he will want to leave; but at the moment I hope not. I have discovered that the attachment of these people to their Moslem faith is not nearly as strong as I supposed. What is strong is their love of God, and their determination to lead godly lives. It would seem to me that, if I show patience and, above all, a good example, I may succeed in interesting some of them in Christ. One or two – I shall mention no names – are already almost converts. This is a great comfort and encouragement to me.

'You will not be so foolish as to be sorry for me. I am happy here, especially in the knowledge that my son and I will be able to achieve a relationship akin to that between another mother and her son, in a place as primitive as this, almost two thousand years ago. I am referring to a simplicity and fullness of love which would not be possible in a society where one stigma would be attached to him, despite his innocence, and another to me.

'I am in your debt for your faithfulness in keeping my secret. It may be you sometimes feel that you are wrong to remain silent and so perpetuate in people's minds what you feel to be a lie. You will not have the guidance or comfort of prayer; but I nightly pray for us both, and I am confident that at the Judgment Day the help you have given me and my child and my dead husband will not be held against you.

'There is a spot above the house like a natural garden. In spring and summer hundreds of different kinds of flowers, and many shrubs, bloom. The colour and fragrance are almost divine. They are blooming round me now as I write. In their midst is Donald's grave. I cannot say that before he died he had found peace again; his pain was too great; but assuredly he has found it now. A carpenter, a son of old Aman, who by the way died during the winter, fashioned a simple cross for me. I am aware that this might rouse the curiosity of any travellers who might venture here, but that risk must be taken. It would be unthinkable to have no cross, or else to have it and pull it up from time to time to deceive intruders. In any case, Azim assures me no travellers will

now be allowed into the valley. On the other hand, he
fears there is still a possibility that the valley may have to
be evacuated if the mining operations now proceeding in
adjacent valleys spread to it. This, too, I constantly pray
to avert. Nevertheless, if it were to happen, and we were
all transplanted, it would have one advantage at least:
then you would be able truthfully to say you did not know
where I was.

'I do not think I shall ever write to you again, or to
anyone else. There is really no more to be said. God bless
you.'

She signed herself M.K.

POLYGON is an imprint of Birlinn Limited. Our list includes titles by Alexander McCall Smith, Liz Lochhead, Kenneth White, Robin Jenkins and other critically acclaimed authors. Should you wish to be put on our catalogue mailing list contact:

Catalogue Request
Polygon
West Newington House
10 Newington Road
Edinburgh EH9 1QS
Scotland, UK

Tel: +44 (0) 131 668 4371
Fax: +44 (0) 131 668 4466
e-mail: info@birlinn.co.uk

Postage and packing is free within the UK. For overseas orders, postage and packing (airmail) will be charged at 30% of the total order value.

Our complete list can be viewed on our website. Go to www.birlinn.co.uk and click on the Polygon logo at the top of the home page.